MENDING FENCES

Visit us at www.boldstrokesbooks.com

MENDING FENCES

by

Angie Williams

2020

MENDING FENCES

ISBN 13: 978-1-63555-708-4

This Trade Paperback Original Is Published By
Bold Strokes Books, Inc.
P.O. Box 249
Valley Falls, NY 12185

First Edition: April 2020

Credits
Editor: Cindy Cresap
Production Design: Susan Ramundo
Cover Design By Ty Justice

Acknowledgments

First of all, thank you to BSB for giving me this opportunity. A big thank you to Cindy Cresap for helping me become a better author, and for not giving up on me.

Thanks to Ty Justice for the awesome cover.

Thanks to my friends, family, and high school English teacher, Cheryl Carter, for always believing in me and pushing me to put myself out there.

Thank you to our son, Ryan, for being self-sufficient and an awesome kid so two of his moms can carve out time to write.

Thanks to my parents and our co-parents for their unwavering love and support.

Last but not least, thank you to the love of my life, Meghan. You are my absolute everything. You make me a better person, and I couldn't ask for a better wife and life partner. I love you.

Dedication

To Meghan, for mending my heart.

CHAPTER ONE

The dust and heat of the day tested Bobbie Del Ray's typically unwavering good humor as she rode the fence line of her family's four-hundred-acre ranch. She'd been responsible for this chore since she was thirteen and knew every inch by heart. Bobbie regretted the extra hour she'd spent fixing an old tractor that pushed her ride around the property later than she liked. The security and care of her herd had been the lifeblood of her family's livelihood for three generations, and now that her father was gone, the responsibility sat squarely on her shoulders.

Bobbie wiped the sweat from her face when it trickled down her temple and tickled her cheek. She calculated how much daylight she had left. She would be cutting it close if she wanted to finish before the light was gone, and the storm clouds she noticed quickly moving her direction would only make it worse.

"Trot." She nudged her horse to move faster. The years she'd spent checking the fence taught her it never paid to rush and miss something that could potentially cost her money in the long run, but she knew she would need to move faster if she didn't want to end up getting rained on in the dark.

At times like these she couldn't blame her brother for not wanting to stay on the family ranch, instead choosing a life in the big city without fences and dirt and endless chores. Bobbie's older brother, Wyatt, had always been her father's favorite, but as soon as Bobbie was old enough to take over, he had simply left a note on the kitchen table informing them he didn't want to spend his life on horseback, tending to cattle and struggling to make it from one season to the next. It had taken her a couple of years to forgive him for leaving her with the care of the ranch, her ailing mother, and their younger brother. She knew deep down Wyatt would have only made things more difficult if he had stayed where he wasn't happy so she'd moved on and did her duty to her family the best she could.

Her horse picked up his pace when the final stretch of fence lay out before them. "Almost done, Frankie." She patted his neck as the first drops of rain bounced off her cowboy hat with a dull thud.

When Bobbie crested the last hill, she noticed movement in the distance. She pulled Frankie to a stop and retrieved a small pair of binoculars she kept in her saddlebag so she could get a better look. The rain that dripped down the lens made it difficult to tell for sure, but she thought she could see a tiny gray animal caught in the middle of what used to be her barbed wire fence.

"Let's go, Frankie." She sat back in the saddle and nudged the horse forward, cautiously approaching the pile of broken wire. When she was close enough to see it was a small dog she slid from her saddle to get a closer look. She pulled her rain jacket and a pair of sturdy gloves from her saddlebag moments before the skies opened up and the rain began to pour.

Bobbie strained against the strengthening winds to reach what she could now see was a small dog.

"There now, little one, what have you gotten yourself into?" The pup tried to lift its head when she approached, but the movement was restricted by the tangle of wire surrounding it. Bobbie realized the poor animal could be in shock so she removed her heavy canvas jacket and placed it over the injured pup to protect it from the ever increasing rain.

"How in the world did you get yourself into this mess?"

Sharp metal from the barbs cut into Bobbie's skin sending drops of blood down her arms. "Dammit, this isn't going to work." She pulled her hat off and brushed rain soaked bangs from her forehead before jogging back to retrieve a pair of wire snips from the saddlebag.

"I don't think there's any way to salvage this bit of fence. Not in this weather at least. We've got to get you to the doc, my friend."

Bobbie worked fast to cut the pup from the jagged claws of the barbs while the rain pelted her back, soaking her from head to toe.

"This storm came out of nowhere, didn't it?" The lack of response to her voice worried her, but she knew she couldn't waste any time working the animal free.

"There we go. I've got you," she said as she cut the last wire and pulled the limp little ball of fur safely into her arms.

Bobbie wrapped the puppy up tight in her jacket. She jumped when lightning struck a tree only a couple of miles from where she stood. On instinct, she grabbed Frankie's reins where they dangled on the ground only a moment before he reared at the deafening crack of thunder that almost immediately followed.

"Whoa, boy, whoa there." She slung the reins over his neck and pulled herself into the saddle with one hand while she cradled the exhausted pup with the other. "Let's go, Frankie," she said. She held tight when the horse darted forward, running for the safety of the barn.

As the weathered building came into view, she could make out the outline of her ranch hand, Cotton, waiting just inside the barn. By the time she slid from her saddle, he was there to take Frankie from her.

"I found a pup tangled in some wire in the east pasture. Looks like she's been out there for a bit and isn't in good shape. I'm going to rush her down to the clinic to see if there's anything Doc Randolph can do for her."

Cotton pulled a restless Frankie toward the barn. "Roger that, boss. I'll get Frankie put away."

"Thanks, Cotton," Bobbie said before securing the puppy in the passenger seat of her truck. "If this rain lets up, can you go out and check the fence? I left a big gap when I cut her free."

"Will do. You be careful in this storm."

"You, too. Let my mom know where I'm headin'." Bobbie's tires threw up a spray of mud as she sped down the bumpy ranch road toward the asphalt that would lead them to town. She glanced at the furry bundle in the seat next to her and hoped the clinic was open and willing to take a late emergency visit. "Hang in there, little girl, we're on our way to get help."

CHAPTER TWO

D r. Grace Hammond tidied up the exam room after her last patient of the day. The Great Dane puppy had peed no less than twice in the room while waiting for his appointment. With her vet tech out of town, it was up to her to clean up the lakes of pee he left behind.

Once everything was tidy, she walked from room to room turning off equipment and lights. The whirring of electricity was replaced by the raging storm outside her door. The wind whipped the shutters against the building, and she wondered if she should try to secure them somehow.

She peeked out the window while turning off the entryway lights and noticed a truck slide to a stop in front of the clinic. A chill ran through her as she saw a tall figure in a cowboy hat exit the vehicle and run toward the door cradling a bundle in their arms. She grabbed her keys from behind the counter and opened the door when the stranger reached the first step. She moved out of the way to allow the late customer entry and noticed a puppy nose poking out through an opening in the blanket.

"Come in. You're soaking wet. What seems to be the problem?"

The stranger turned to speak, and Grace gasped when she recognized the handsome woman standing in front of her. "Bobbie?"

It had been twenty years since she'd last seen her first love, but Grace recognized her immediately. The years apart did nothing to stop her heart from skipping a beat when she looked into the bright blue eyes she had thought she would drown in so many years ago.

Bobbie's soaking wet hair and clothes dripped onto the clinic floor as she stood silently holding the bundle tightly against her body.

"Grace?" she finally asked in disbelief. "What are you doing here?"

"I work here. I'm a vet now. I…let's take care of you and your little friend here, and then we'll catch up. Explain to me what happened while I grab you some clean scrubs from the back. Doc Randolph has a stack in the closet that I think will fit you fine. You both look like you've been drug behind a boat."

Now that the initial shock of seeing her had passed, she realized Bobbie was covered in scratches and there was blood on her shirt. "Are you hurt?" Grace pulled her sleeve back to inspect her arm.

"I got a little scratched up while I was trying to get her out of the barbed wire, but I'll be fine. Let's get her fixed up first. I think the bleeding has stopped. It looks more dramatic than it is." Bobbie was obviously not comfortable being the focus of concern.

Grace wasn't completely satisfied but knew she was right; the puppy was the bigger emergency. She handed Bobbie the dry scrubs before gently taking it from her arms. She held the quivering animal close to her body as she carried it to the back room. Bobbie was right on her heels explaining what brought them to the clinic in the middle of a storm.

"I was out checking the fence when I saw this little girl tangled up in a mess of barbed wire. She must've been there for a while because she hardly made a sound when she saw me ride up. I cut her loose, wrapped her in the blanket, and got here as fast as I could. Is she going to be okay?"

The concerned look on Bobbie's face tugged at Grace's heart. She was an animal lover herself so she understood, but for some reason seeing Bobbie so unguarded about her feelings made Grace swoon a bit.

"We're going to take good care of her," Grace said. She carefully unwrapped the blanket. "There's an exam room right there if you want to change. You'll find a dry towel in the bottom left cabinet behind me."

Bobbie seemed to hesitate but finally walked away to dry off and get changed. Grace tried to focus on her patient and not the urge to help Bobbie out of her wet clothes. Get it together, Grace, she admonished herself as she began her examination of the injured pup.

A couple of minutes later, Bobbie was back by her side looking better than anyone had a right to in the usually unflattering scrubs.

"What's her name?" Grace asked. She saw Bobbie watching her closely as she ran her fingers through the dog's fur checking for foreign objects that could still be stuck in her skin.

Bobbie thought for a minute. "Riley. She looks like a Riley to me."

"Okay, Riley, you're being a very brave little girl." Grace spoke gently trying to keep her calm while she assessed her injuries. "She must have been trapped in the wire for a long time because the bleeding seems to have mostly stopped, but these gashes look angry and painful."

Grace knew she needed to warm her patient up and get her heart rate down as soon as possible, but the myriad of cuts and tears to her coat made it difficult to see if she still had something stuck in her fur.

"Bobbie, I'd like to get these cuts cleaned up a little so we can make sure she doesn't still have a barb or some other foreign object still embedded in her skin. Once we're sure, I would like to get her wrapped up and start her on an IV of antibiotics and fluids. Does that sound like a plan?"

"Absolutely, whatever it takes," Bobbie said.

"It's just you and me tonight so do you mind playing the part of the vet tech? I've been told I'm a pretty good boss," Grace said. She carried Riley to the big sink in the back of her clinic to bathe her.

Bobbie smiled, obviously thankful for a little levity at that moment. "I haven't been bossed around by you in years, but I remember it being fun at the time."

She gently washed the mud and blood from Riley's fur and tried to wrap her brain around the fact that she was standing next to Bobbie Del Ray. She vividly recalled the day her parents sent her off to boarding school only hours after discovering she was in a relationship with a girl. Grace's heart had broken that day, and if she were honest with herself, had never truly recovered.

"Here we go." Grace picked up tweezers from a table and gently pulled a barb from Riley's skin. The puppy gave a weak yelp when it was removed. "There's a good girl, Riley. Poor girl. You're going to be okay." Grace ran her fingers through her fur once more and decided that was the best she could do for now. Nothing large was poking her so she would do a more thorough search once she was stable.

"I think that will do for now. Let's wrap her up and get some fluids in her. She was obviously in the sun for a long time."

Grace turned off the water and asked Bobbie to hand her a towel from the shelf. The warm water and massage from the bath had helped bring a little focus back into Riley's eyes, and she gently gave Grace a timid lick on the cheek as she dried her off. "I think someone is finally starting to come around. Do you need to go, Bobbie, or can you give me a little more time?"

"I'm all yours for as long as you need me."

Grace knew she was only answering her question, but something in the way she said it told her she meant more than just that night.

CHAPTER THREE

Bobbie took Riley from Grace, still trying to sort through her feelings about their unexpected reunion. The closeness they felt as kids came rushing back, but Bobbie knew it would be inappropriate to allow herself to treat this near stranger with the familiarity they once shared.

She cradled Riley in a clean blanket as Grace led them to her office where there was a comfortable couch against one wall.

"Go ahead and keep her wrapped up for now. I'm going to get some supplies and I'll be back," Grace said.

When she was finally alone, Bobbie felt her muscles relax for the first time since she'd arrived at the clinic. She couldn't remember the last time she'd been so nervous around another woman. She knew Grace wasn't just any woman, but still, Bobbie liked to think she was usually capable of controlling the fifteen-year-old in her brain that was sometimes in charge of her hormones.

As Grace walked into the hall outside her office, there was a violent crack of thunder followed by darkness. "You okay, Gracie?" Bobbie yelled, the nickname slipping from her as if they'd never been apart.

"I'm okay. I'll get candles. How is our little friend?"

"Startled but fine."

Bobbie held Riley close as she shook at the sounds raging outside. "You're okay, pretty girl. Grace is going to get you all fixed up and you'll be good as new." The pup nuzzled into Bobbie's arms even closer. "She's so nice isn't she?" Bobbie glanced at the doorway to make sure they were still alone. "And so beautiful," she said softly to the dog, careful not to be overheard.

Bobbie closed her eyes and pictured the young, bright-eyed girl she had been in love with so many years ago. She remembered feeling at the time that Grace was the most beautiful girl in the world, and seeing her now, she agreed with her teenage assessment.

She smiled when she thought about the woman her childhood love had grown to be. Grace had the same strawberry blond hair and sea green eyes, but she had blossomed into a breathtaking woman.

"Did you fall asleep?" Grace quietly asked.

Bobbie opened her eyes and scooted over so Grace could sit next to them on the couch. "Nope. Here, have a seat."

Grace lit two candles and set them on the table in front of them. She reached into her pocket and pulled out the supplies she needed. "You looked so peaceful I almost hated to disturb you." She scruffed the fur on Riley's neck and inserted a needle to administer the fluids.

Bobbie ran a finger across Grace's knuckles where they rested between them on Riley's back. "I was just closing my eyes and thinking about a beautiful young girl I used to know."

Grace blushed and pulled her hand away.

"I'm sorry if I embarrassed you," Bobbie said.

"You didn't embarrass me. You've done nothing wrong. I...it's difficult to explain. That girl had an idealistic view of love and the world. It turns out reality isn't nearly as romantic."

"You don't think love and happiness are real?" Bobbie asked.

"They're real, but I think the reality of love and happiness isn't as much rainbows and unicorns as it is hard work and sacrifice."

The idea of Grace being so jaded about love made Bobbie almost as sad as the fact that she was robbed of the chance to show her how good love and happiness could be.

"Are you still out on the ranch?" Grace asked.

Bobbie knew she was changing the subject and wanted to press for more but didn't think this was the time. "I am. I'll probably be on that ranch until the day I die, which, on days like today with the stifling heat, feels like it will be sooner than later."

Grace laughed. "I can't believe how hot it was. I don't remember it ever being that hot when we were kids."

"It's not like global warming is real or anything," Bobbie joked. She winked at Grace to make sure she knew she was being sarcastic. "So, you became a vet just like you always said you would."

"It never occurred to me to do anything else. It hasn't always been what I dreamt it would be, but I don't regret it one bit."

Bobbie couldn't help but smile thinking back to a teenaged Grace going on and on about becoming a vet and helping Bobbie on the ranch when they were older. They both knew where their lives were going to end up; they just thought it would be together. That thought made her heart ache.

"It looks like our patient is feeling better," Grace said. Bobbie laughed as Riley lifted her head to lick her hand.

Grace carefully removed the needle before checking her heart and gums once again. "How in the world did she get all the way out there and pull the fence down? She's not big enough to cause that kind of damage."

Bobbie snuggled Riley closer and kissed the top of her scruffy head. "I have no idea although I suspect the neighbor's son was involved. He's a little asshole. He thinks it's funny to tear down my fence and drive his ATV across my land to visit his girlfriend at the Duncans' ranch on the other side of me. I've contacted Sheriff Buck, but unless I can get proof it was him, there's not much she can do. I know they have a couple of cattle dogs so my guess is Riley is a puppy that followed her mother who was probably with Jason on the ATV. I'll talk to his dad and tell him I won't call the sheriff on this incident if he lets me keep her. I don't want that little bastard anywhere near her so it's just easier to repair the fence myself. This little thing doesn't weigh more than a sack of flour so she definitely didn't pull the fence down herself, did you, my perfect little girl?"

Riley wagged her tail in approval as Grace laughed. "I can already tell who's going to be in charge in this relationship."

Grace leaned over to kiss the top of Riley's head. "You don't take advantage of this big, tough cowgirl's tender heart, little one." Bobbie blushed when Grace gave her a wink.

Bobbie knew she needed to get Riley home but hated to leave Grace so soon after seeing her again. "Hey, would you be interested in having coffee with me this week?" Bobbie held her breath as a million emotions swam in Grace's green eyes.

"I would love to catch up," she finally answered. "What day is good for you? I'm at the clinic every day except Sunday until around seven, is that too late for coffee?"

"That's perfect. Can I pick you up here around seven on Tuesday? We can decide then if we want coffee or maybe something more substantial."

Grace hesitated a moment before answering as if she wanted to say more but finally agreed. "That sounds great. We've got a lot to catch up on."

"I can't wait," Bobbie said. She stood with Riley still cradled in her arms and followed Grace to the front lobby. She wasn't sure how she was going to find the strength to get in her truck and drive away. She'd dreamt of seeing Grace for so long, the thought of leaving seemed impossible.

Grace picked up Bobbie's wet clothes from a bench where they'd been left, neatly folded them and handed them to her. "Don't forget these."

"Thanks." Bobbie could smell the sweet scent of Grace's shampoo as they stood next to each other in the near dark. She was sure Grace could hear her heart beating above the sound of the raging storm outside as her eyes were drawn to plump, pink lips. "Grace, I—" Bobbie jumped as the power came back on and light filled the room, breaking whatever spell they were under.

"Well…" Bobbie started as she stepped back to put some space between them. "What do I owe you, Doc?"

"Oh, yeah." Grace walked around the counter and booted up the reception PC. "I'm sure I'm totally doing this wrong and will hear about it from my office manager later." She quickly entered information into the computer. "Okay, you are officially a patient, Riley Del Ray. Can I have Amy figure out all the billing stuff later? I have no idea what I'm doing with this. I do know how to make you a return appointment, though. Let's say in two weeks?"

"Works for us. Riley and I thank you for the hospitality and your gentle hands. I mean Riley thanks you for the gentle hands. I didn't feel your gentle hands. Not that I should have felt your gentle hands..." Bobbie felt her face flush as Grace laughed.

"I get your point." Grace reached out and touched Bobbie's cheek with the tips of her fingers. "If you are ever in need of a gentle touch, I'm here for you as well." A look of panic flashed across Grace's face as if she hadn't meant to say those words out loud.

"Thanks, Doc." Bobbie bent to give Grace a gentle kiss on the cheek. "I'll see you Tuesday."

CHAPTER FOUR

2002

Bobbie stretched her long legs, body aching from being crammed into an awkward position as she slept. She smiled when she heard a groan from beneath the pile of blankets next to her in bed.

"Gracie?"

The lump in the blankets moved but the person hidden below them remained completely covered. "What did we do to ourselves, Bobbie? I'm never drinking again."

Bobbie chuckled and pulled the blanket down so she could see Grace's face.

"No," Grace yelped. "I don't want you to see me like this. I look like death."

"How do you know you look like death? You haven't even seen yourself yet."

Grace scooted back, pressing her body against Bobbie's as she pulled the blanket over her head. "I know because I feel like death, so it only makes sense that I would look like it, too."

"Touché"

"Don't be mean."

Bobbie laughed and wrapped her arm around the blanketed bundle that held Grace. The party at Gavin Parker's house the night before had been insane, and Bobbie only remembered bits and pieces.

They hadn't planned to have more than a beer each, but Gavin had found the key to his parents' liquor cabinet and the next thing Bobbie knew they were trying creative concoctions she was now regretting.

"What time do you need me to drop you off at Kelly's?" Bobbie asked. Grace had told her parents she was spending the night with her friend Kelly Barnes. Kelly's parents were out of town so the lie allowed Grace to sneak away to Bobbie's since Kelly would be staying at her boyfriend Gavin's house. The plan worked out nicely, but she'd need a ride back to Kelly's house so Kelly could take her home.

"I told her I'd be there at ten this morning. Is that okay?"

Bobbie pulled the blanket up and crawled under it with Grace. "I don't want you to go."

Grace turned over to face Bobbie. She brushed Bobbie's bangs from her face and softly kissed her lips. "I don't want to go, either. I can't wait until we can wake up like this every morning and never have to be apart."

Bobbie loved to hear Grace talk about their future. They'd known each other since her family had moved to Preston when they were in the second grade. She'd been drawn to her from the first moment they met, and those feelings had only grown the older they got.

They'd been best friends for what seemed like their entire lives, and once they were old enough to understand the feelings they had for each other, they'd become girlfriends. Only a couple of people knew the truth since the town and especially their parents wouldn't be pleased to know they were lesbians, but they'd been able to keep it mostly a secret.

They were both two weeks from starting their senior year of high school and knew once they graduated things would become more difficult with Grace wanting to go to Stanford and Bobbie wanting to stay closer to home. Even so, Bobbie knew they'd figure it out when the time came.

"Bobbie?"

"Hmm?"

"Let's run away together."

Bobbie pulled back to look into Grace's eyes. "What?"

"Let's just go. We'll figure something out. We're both almost eighteen. We can find jobs and I'm sure your aunt Cathy would let us live with her in Dallas. She loves me."

Bobbie rubbed the sleep from her eyes and tried to wrap her mind around what Grace was saying. "We can't run away, sweetheart. You're going to be valedictorian. You're going to Stanford University for Christ's sake. You can't just throw that all away to live in my aunt's spare room in Dallas. That's insanity."

Grace sat up and threw her legs over the side of the bed. Bobbie immediately regretted her bluntness. "I'm sorry. Come on, sweetheart. Come here and let me hold you. Let's talk."

"I don't want to go to Stanford, Bobbie. I'm so sick of hiding my love for you, and I don't want to struggle to have time together this year only to move hours away after we graduate. I don't want to do it. It's not fair."

The same thoughts had plagued Bobbie. "I don't want to be away from you either, baby, but Stanford is what you've worked so hard for. I can't let you throw that opportunity away for me. I couldn't live with myself. Even though you'll be at Stanford, things will be easier because you won't be living under your parents' roof."

"Will they?" Grace walked into the bathroom and poured herself a glass of water. They'd spent the night in the spare room at Bobbie's brother Wyatt's house. He was only a couple of years older and was one of the few people who knew of their relationship. He'd always been supportive and allowed them to stay in his spare room when they were able to find a way to be together. "Do you think once I graduate that my parents are just going to allow me to be with you, Bobbie? Do you honestly think they won't do everything in their power to keep us apart?"

"We won't let them."

"How do you propose we do that? They'll cut me off and won't pay for Stanford or vet school or anything else."

Bobbie was silent. She knew Grace was right, but there had to be something they could do to stay together but still allow her the education she'd worked so hard to secure. "Come back to bed, baby."

Grace set the water glass on the sink and crawled into Bobbie's arms. Bobbie wiped the tears that had spilled onto her cheeks and kissed the corners of her eyes. "I love you, sweetheart. We'll figure this out."

Bobbie pulled Grace as tight against her as she could. They needed to get up so they could drop Grace off at Emily's, but she wasn't ready to leave their nest just yet. She'd rest her eyes for a few minutes and let Grace sleep a little more.

"Bobbie, get up right now."

Bobbie's eyes shot open as her brother shook her vigorously. "What the fuck, Wyatt?"

"Wyatt?" Grace pulled the blanket closer to her body to make sure she was fully covered.

"You've got to get up. Mom called and said Grace's parents are looking for her and are on their way over here right now."

Bobbie bolted out of bed and pulled on jeans. Thankfully she'd been wearing a shirt and boxers when she'd fallen asleep. Grace still had the blanket wrapped around herself and was frantically searching for her clothes.

"Get out so we can get dressed, Wyatt," Bobbie said. "Here, baby." Bobbie tossed Grace her shirt and pants from the night before. They could hear a car pull up in front of the house followed by banging on the front door.

"Answer the door right now, Del Ray. We know our daughter's in there."

Bobbie heard Wyatt's voice but couldn't make out what he was saying. Bobbie's heart sank when her own father barked at Wyatt to move out of the way. She knew if both sets of parents were there, the shit had hit the fan.

"Roberta Del Ray, you get your scrawny ass out here right this minute," Bobbie's dad boomed from the other room.

Grace's eyes went wide and Bobbie knew in that moment that things for them were about to change forever. "Bobbie?" Grace seemed so fragile that Bobbie wanted nothing more than to pull her into her arms and shelter her from what was about to happen.

"It'll be okay, baby." In that moment the door was thrown open and Bobbie held Grace to her as Mr. Hammond stormed into the room.

"Let's go, Grace." The fury in his eyes made Bobbie hold Grace even tighter.

"Please don't do this, Daddy," Grace begged.

Without another word, her father picked her up and carried her from the room. Bobbie was completely helpless as they got into their car and drove the person she loved more than anything, out of her life.

CHAPTER FIVE

W hat's next, Amy?" Grace asked her office manager as she tossed the previous patient's chart on the completed pile. "What's gotten into you, Doc? You're not usually grumpy in the mornings, but you're never this chipper. You didn't find a unicorn last night or something did you?" Amy pushed a file folder across the counter to her.

Grace laughed. "I love that the first possibility you go to for happiness is finding a unicorn. I completely agree of course, but unfortunately no, I just had a nice evening."

"Uh-huh," Amy said. "This isn't going to help your mood." Grace opened the folder and realized it was a résumé and not another patient.

"Did you get laid last night?" Amy asked.

Grace looked up from the document, a little shocked by the question. "No. Why?"

"Because you have the 'I had an orgasm' look. At first I thought you saw a unicorn, but now I'm thinking orgasm. They're very similar looks."

Grace rolled her eyes. "You're crazy. It's been so long I barely remember what sex is like, but I can assure you, I didn't have it last night. What is this résumé for, by the way?"

"You have an interview with a potential new vet for the clinic. Be nice, we need help," Amy said.

Grace frowned. She hated doing interviews, which was part of the reason she'd never opened her own clinic. "Doc Randolph can't do this? It's technically his employee."

"Doc Randolph is busy taking care of his very sick wife. Come on, I know it's not the most fun thing to do, but we desperately need help. Don't you want to be able to have more than one day off a week?"

Grace sighed and opened the folder again to scan the résumé. "Okay, I'm sorry. I'm going to make this quick so I can get back to the doctoring part I love so much."

"You're a dork." Amy rolled her eyes before answering the phone.

Grace sighed then removed her white lab coat and walked into her office to greet the potential new employee. She recognized the young woman waiting for her immediately. It had been several years since she last saw her, but she would recognize the beautiful long blond hair and piercing blue eyes anywhere. "Lena?"

"Hey, Grace. I mean, Dr. Hammond." Lena stood up and awkwardly started to hug Grace but stopped short as if remembering she was in a job interview.

Grace wrapped her arms around her and squeezed before holding her at arm's length so she could get a good look at her. "None of this Dr. Hammond stuff, call me Grace. Look at you. I can't believe you're all grown up. How long has it been?"

Grace sat on the couch and motioned for Lena to join her. She tried to push away the vision of Bobbie sitting on the same couch the night before. She'd been trying to push that vision from her mind since the moment Bobbie drove off into the rain.

"Well, you babysat me when I was about eight, and I'm twenty-nine now so it must be about twenty-one years." Lena seemed intelligent, well spoken, and everything Grace imagined she would grow into when she was that precocious eight-year-old.

"I can't believe you're a vet now," Lena said.

"You, too. And it looks like you've been on the fast track. Did you just finish your residency?"

"I did and now I'm out looking for a permanent home as close to my parents as possible. I'm living with them for the time being, but my plan is to eventually buy a home near them. They're getting older and I want to spend time with them while I still can, but I also want to have my own space."

Grace smiled. "That's great, Lena. Your parents were always great people, and you were obviously the light of their lives."

Lena blushed at the compliment. "My mom had a stroke a couple of years ago and hasn't been the same since. I want to be close in case something else happens and to be there for my dad if he needs me."

"You're a good daughter."

"What about you, when did you move back to town?"

Grace closed the folder with Lena's paperwork and sat back against the couch cushions. "That's a long and complicated story for another day, but the short answer is, I'm not sure I've exactly moved back. I'm filling in for Doc Randolph while he's taking care of his wife, Carol. I have commitments in Seattle that are still a bit up in the air at the moment."

Lena reached out and took Grace's hand, giving it a gentle squeeze. "It sounds like you're in transition. I completely understand what that's like. If you ever need to talk, just let me know."

Grace smiled at Lena and nodded her head. "Thanks. Okay, I've looked over your résumé and the glowing recommendation from your previous employer. We would love to have you on board here. This clinic is the only one in town now that East River Emergency closed two months ago, and with Doc Randolph out I'm the only veterinarian for twenty miles. Needless to say, I've been pretty busy so if you're willing to hit the ground running you can start tomorrow. Speak to Amy on your way out and she will give you an offer letter. Feel free to look it over and shoot me an email if you have questions or concerns. If it all looks good, sign it and bring it with you tomorrow morning."

Lena looked like she would burst with excitement. "Thank you so much, Grace. I can't wait to get started and to work with you."

She gave Lena one more hug before she opened the door and told Amy to please type up an offer letter. Amy gave her a thumbs-up and sat down at her computer.

Lena turned back to Grace before walking away. "Hey, have you seen Bobbie Del Ray? My mom said she's still living out on her family ranch. I had the biggest crush on her when I was a kid and loved it when she would stop by to see you when you were babysitting me. You guys were pretty tight back in the day. Did you stay in touch?"

Grace tried her best to suppress a grin with no success. "I actually just saw her last night. She found a puppy on her ranch that was caught in a barbed wire fence. The poor girl was pretty banged up when Bobbie arrived, but we were able to get her fixed up. I think she'll be fine. They'll be in for a checkup in a couple of weeks. I'll let you know so you can say hello. Hopefully, we'll see you tomorrow morning, Lena. Welcome aboard."

Lena waved and headed over to Amy for her offer letter. Everything in Grace's work life was starting to fall into place. Now she needed to get her personal life together and she would be back on track. Unfortunately, that was going to be a much more difficult task.

Chapter Six

B obbie carefully placed Riley on her new bed in the corner of the living room the following day. She had come in from her chores to check on the pup and needed to get back out before it was too dark to get the fence repaired from the night before, but she couldn't resist snuggling her new pup one more time.

"Who's my good girl?" Riley's tail wagged at the question, but with the pain medication she had in her that was all the effort she could muster. Bobbie lay on the floor next to her and stroked her fur as she thought about the events of the evening before.

"Can you believe we saw Grace? I wonder what the story is with her. She seemed so sad, don't you think?" Riley answered the question with a wag of her tail. "You don't give advice, but you're a good listener and I appreciate that."

"You're going to love being a Del Ray, buddy. We have tons of land to run around on and chase small creatures. We get to go on trail rides into the mountains and through redwoods and sleep under the stars. You'll love it." Riley scooted forward on her tummy and gave Bobbie a lick on the lips. "Easy, girl, I like to get to know someone a little better first."

Bobbie heard laughter from the doorway and turned to find her mom gazing lovingly at them. "Looks like you have a new friend," she said. Bobbie's mom was tall, dark, and beautiful. Years of living on the ranch had taken a toll on her physically, but at seventy-three, she was still mentally quick as a whip.

"Hey, Mama, this is Riley. I found her stuck in a bunch of broken fence by that old oak on the east side of the property."

Her mom sat on the floor next to Riley's pillow and carefully stroked her as she examined her injuries. "Looks like the poor thing has been through a war. Where did you take her? Doc Randolph is out while Carol is sick, isn't he?"

"They have a new vet up there now. You remember Grace Hammond, don't you?"

The look that briefly shadowed her mom's face told Bobbie she remembered her all too well. "That mess wasn't Grace's fault. Her parents didn't give her a choice when they sent her away. Her heart was broken just as much as mine."

"I'm aware of that, Roberta, but her heart wasn't my concern."

Bobbie hated when her mom called her by her proper name. "Well, she's a vet now and she's working over at Doc Randolph's clinic. She's been back a couple of weeks, but she's still getting settled."

"Just be careful, Peanut. I don't want you getting your heart hurt by that girl again," her mom said. "She's been gone a long time, and you have no idea who she is now. Don't get your hopes up until you know her better."

"Why have you always been so hard on Grace? I used to think it was because you suspected we were together and didn't approve, but I openly dated other girls after Grace and you never blinked an eye. Grace was a good kid who kept me out of trouble more times than I should admit to my own mother." Bobbie's wink brought a smile to her mom's face, but her concern was still evident.

"You're my baby and she broke your heart. That's as good a reason as any. Come up to the house this evening for dinner if you don't have plans, and bring my new grandpup. I'll make burgers and potato salad." Bobbie knew her mom was trying to change the subject and decided to let it pass for now.

"Can I bring anything?" Bobbie asked.

"Just you and this little bundle. I need to head into town to make a grocery run. Do you have a list?"

Bobbie got up and pulled the grocery list from under the magnet on the fridge. She handed it to her mother before helping her to her feet. She slipped her arm through Bobbie's as they walked out the front door. "You know I love you, don't you?"

"With all your heart, Mama, and I love you just as much." Bobbie kissed her mom's cheek and walked toward the barn to saddle her horse for the ride out to fix the fence.

Bobbie knew her mother was just being overly cautious because she was a protective mother, but it was difficult to feel like she had to defend Grace when she hadn't done anything wrong.

CHAPTER SEVEN

Grace dropped her bag in the guest room she was using at her mother's house and walked downstairs to find something to eat. Her mother was at a bird club meeting and wouldn't be home until late that evening so Grace had the house to herself.

She heated up a bowl of soup leftover from the night before and sat at the giant dining room table that was typically reserved for special occasions. The small act of rebellion made her smile. Growing up, she'd always been expected to adhere to a restrictive set of rules. Sit up straight, Grace. Don't get your clothes dirty, Grace. Act more like a lady, Grace. Sometimes she'd related to the birds her mother kept locked in cages. Only there for her to control, never allowed to stretch their wings.

When she finished her meal, she washed and dried the dishes and took a book into the sunroom where her mother kept her birds. She'd never been allowed to come near the room as a child, and even now she was paranoid she'd be caught in there and suffer the wrath of her mother.

June 1992

Grace squealed with delight when her friend Bobbie caught the frog they'd been chasing in the creek. The amphibian had eluded them for hours, but they'd devised a plan to have Grace use her dress to create a barrier from escaping on one side while Bobbie scooped it into a basket on the other. The plan worked and they were now the proud owners of a frog.

"What are we going to name him?" Bobbie asked.

Grace shrugged and tried to brush as much mud from her dress as she could. She knew her mother would be upset, but the frog had left them no choice. "How do you know it's a boy?"

Bobbie studied the frog closer and scratched her head. "I guess I don't know. We could ask Wyatt. He might know."

Bobbie's brother was a couple of years older and knew a lot more about stuff like that than they did. "Good idea." Grace took one last look at their new pet. "I have to get home for dinner."

"Sure."

Grace always loved it when Bobbie would ride her bike into town so they could play. Grace's mom would never let her ride her bike that far.

"If he's a boy, can we name him Greg?" Bobbie asked.

Grace laughed. "Greg is a funny name for a frog."

Bobbie shrugged. "I think he looks like a Greg."

"If she's a girl, can we name her Susan?"

"Isn't that your maid's name?"

Grace thought Susan would think it was neat to have a frog named after her. "Yep."

"I'm cool with it. I'll talk to Wyatt and let you know at school on Monday if we have a Greg or a Susan."

"See ya Monday." Grace skipped toward her house. She was usually only able to get as far as Mr. Sanders's before having to walk, but she'd been practicing and it had paid off. She was able to get half a block farther than ever before. She was beaming by the time she reached her house.

She came in through the side door that led straight into the kitchen so she could tell Susan what they'd caught.

"Susan, guess what?" Grace kicked off her shoes at the door and ran to where she stood at the stove.

"Grace, don't run," Susan said. Grace saw her eyes go wide the moment she felt her feet slip out from under her as she went crashing to the floor.

Grace was stunned into silence for a moment before the pain from landing on the hard floor registered in her brain. Susan rushed to her side as Grace began to cry.

"Oh, sweetheart. You can't run on these slick floors in your tights. Why are you soaking wet?"

Susan was checking Grace for injuries when her mother came storming through the door. "What's happening in here?" she asked.

"Grace slipped and fell, Mrs. Hammond. Nothing seems to be broken, but she hit pretty hard so I wouldn't be surprised if she woke up with a few bruises."

Her mother stood over her and took in the scene. "What has happened to your dress, Grace Hammond?"

"Bobbie and I caught a frog at the park, and I named it Susan, and I came to tell her about it, and I fell." She did her best to control her tears, knowing it would only upset her mother even more.

"Go to your room and get cleaned up. Wait there and when your father gets home, we'll be in to discuss your behavior."

Susan helped Grace get to her feet. She should be used to the lack of concern from her mother, but it never stopped bothering her that she showed more love for her precious birds than she ever did for her own daughter.

Grace climbed the stairs, careful not to brush against the railing, and sullenly walked into her room. She knew her troubles had only just begun. Her father was the enforcer of her mother's rules. She couldn't even be bothered to do it herself.

Once she was clean and dressed in dry clothes, she waited patiently on her bed. When her father didn't come, Grace peeked into the hallway outside her door. Silence. Sometimes he had to work late so she thought this might be one of those times. She knew her mother would be in the study since it was Saturday and she always took care of her bird club business on Saturdays. Grace looked left and right to make sure the coast was clear before she quietly snuck down the stairs and slipped into the room where her mother kept her birds. As she crept closer to the cages, she noticed a beautiful rainbow bird huddled in the corner of its cage.

"Are you okay?" she asked quietly. The bird tilted its head as if it was trying to understand what she was asking. "Hi." Grace poked a little finger through the bars and laughed when the bird bowed so she could scratch the back of its neck. "You're a sweet little guy, aren't you?"

The bird made a noise that Grace was sure meant it understood what she was saying. "My name is Grace." The bird tilted its head in the other direction, never taking its eye off of her. "Do you want to be my friend?" Grace gasped when the bird jumped on the finger she'd been petting it with and rubbed its head against the bars. This was surely a sign the bird understood. She no longer had any doubt.

"I'm sorry she keeps you in there." Grace glanced toward the door to make sure her mother wasn't there. She knew what it was like to feel trapped and pitied her new friend for being locked in the cage.

Grace watched the bird as it rubbed itself against the bars and couldn't stand to see it be sad. After checking the door one more time, she quietly pulled the latch up and turned it so the gate could be opened. She would hold him to comfort him and then put him back in the cage without her mother ever knowing a thing. Maybe this could be a new thing she could do to make the birds happier.

Her mother never allowed her to have a pet of her own because it might upset her birds so it only made sense that one of the birds would become hers. She could never tell her mother, of course. She'd asked for a bird of her own before and her mother had said she wasn't responsible enough to care for one. Maybe if she came in to cuddle this one occasionally, it would like her and her mother would see that they were friends. "I think you look like a Josh. There's a boy in my class named Josh and he's very sweet like you."

"Come on, Josh." Grace held out her hand and the bird jumped on so she could lift it out of the cage. Josh stretched his wings and shook once he was free of the cage. "See, doesn't that feel better?"

"Grace Hammond, what do you think you're doing?" Grace's father boomed from the door. The sound of the loud voice startled Josh and he flew off Grace's hand and up toward the top of the vaulted ceiling.

"Josh!" Grace called. She had to get him back in his cage before something terrible happened to him. "Please come down."

Just then, Grace's mother came into the room and found Grace standing next to a cage with its door wide open. "What have you done? Where is my sun conure?"

Grace pointed to the ceiling where Josh was flying around, trying to get away from the loud humans. Her mother screeched and, as if in slow motion, Josh flew down from the ceiling and through the open window in the back of the room.

"Noooo..." She heard her mother scream, as she ran to the window like she had any hope of catching the bird before it flew off into the darkness.

Grace burst into tears. Her new friend was gone and she knew there was no way her mother would ever let her have a pet now.

The sound of the front door opening startled Grace, and she quietly slipped from the bird room and up to the safety of her own space. Once she was alone, she tossed her book on the bed and sat on the bench by the open window. They'd never found Josh and her mother had never forgiven her for his escape. She wished she could go back to the little girl she was, wrap her in a hug, and reassure her that everything would be okay.

Grace sighed and shut the window. Nothing brought down her mood like being in her mother's house. If she was going to stay in Preston much longer, she knew she'd need to find another place to stay.

CHAPTER EIGHT

Grace heard Bobbie's truck pull into the parking lot just as she was slipping on her shoes. She had changed into something a little nicer than her scrubs even though they'd only planned to have coffee.

The thought of seeing Bobbie again had distracted her all day, and now that the time had arrived to be picked up, the butterflies in her stomach were working overtime. With one final glance at the clinic to ensure everything looked secure, she walked out the door.

Bobbie jogged around her truck and pulled open the passenger door so Grace could climb in. "Wow, you look beautiful."

Grace flushed at the compliment. "You clean up nice yourself."

"Have you eaten yet? I know we'd only talked about having coffee, but I haven't had a chance to eat since eleven this morning and I'm starving. I thought maybe we could turn this into a dinner instead of just coffee if you're up for it." Bobbie's question was a surprise, and Grace hesitated a moment before answering.

"Dinner would be great. I'm a vegetarian, but I can find something almost anywhere so please feel free to go anywhere you want."

"Would it be forward of me to make you dinner at my house? Riley would love to see her favorite doc." Bobbie looked at Grace for an answer. When she gave a slight nod, she pulled onto the street and headed north. "I have some leftover homemade pasta sauce from last night, and I know a vegetarian dish I can make that I think you'll like. There's wine!"

"That sounds great. I had no idea you were a chef."

Bobbie laughed. "Well, I don't want to get your hopes up or anything, but I think you'll like this dish. It has veggies, pasta, cheese, and sauce. How can you go wrong with that?"

"Especially with the promise of wine." Grace winked and folded her hands in her lap as she fought the urge to reach out and touch Bobbie's hand where it rested on the gearshift.

As they pulled up to what Grace remembered as Wyatt's house, memories came rushing back like a flood. She bit her lip in an attempt to hold back the tears and keep her emotions in check. They were so young and so in love. The last time Grace had seen the house was the morning after she and Bobbie had made love for the first time. The last time she saw her before she walked into the clinic that night and back into her life.

As Bobbie opened her door and held out a hand to help her down from the truck, Grace did her best to hide the emotions she was sure were written all over her face. The concerned look from Bobbie told her she hadn't succeeded.

"Shit, are you okay, Gracie? I shouldn't have brought you here. I'm such an idiot. I wasn't thinking. I've lived here so long, it doesn't remind me of that morning anymore, but I can see from the look on your face that it's still difficult for you. I'm so sorry." Bobbie looked like she was about to cry herself.

"I had no idea it would hit me like this. It's not your fault. I'm fine. The memories just took me by surprise. Let's go inside." Grace took Bobbie's offered hand as they walked into the house.

"I'm really sorry, Grace. Why don't I take you somewhere else for dinner? It didn't occur to me this place might bring back bad memories for you." Bobbie didn't take her farther into the house, obviously waiting for Grace to decide if they should leave or not.

"Don't be silly. I'll be just fine. I have bad memories of this house, but I have some of my favorite memories as well." An image of a naked Bobbie lying next to her flashed through her mind and sent goose bumps up her arms.

"I moved in after I graduated and Wyatt moved to the city. He did basic maintenance while he was here but no upgrades so I've spent the last few years trying to bring it into this century."

"I want a tour, but I'm so hungry it will have to wait until after you feed me." As if on cue, Grace's stomach grumbled loudly proving her point.

When they walked into the main part of the house, Grace heard little paws clatter against the tile floor as Riley came scrambling down the hall to greet them. "Hey, kiddo," she said. Grace and Bobbie both laughed when Riley excitedly flopped onto her back to expose her belly for scratches.

"You have no shame, my furry friend," Bobbie said.

Grace sat on the floor next to her and pulled Riley's lips up to look at her gums. "How has she been feeling? She looks much better to me, but dogs have a way of putting on a brave face." Grace checked her cuts to make sure they didn't look infected.

Bobbie sat on the floor next to them to join in on the belly rub club. "I think she's been fine," she said. "She has a checkup in a couple of days so you'll be able to get a good look at her then."

Grace looked around the front area of the house as she got back to her feet. Bobbie had changed everything from the time it was Wyatt's from the flooring to the paint. She admired the rustic, homey feel Bobbie had created. "I love what you've done with the house." Bobbie smiled at the compliment as Grace reached down to help her up.

"Thanks. It's been a pain in the ass but pretty fun." Bobbie led Grace into the kitchen. "Would you like a glass of wine?"

"Please, red if you have it." Grace sat on a stool at the kitchen counter so she could talk to Bobbie as she poured her a healthy glass of her favorite social lubricant.

"Are you trying to get me drunk?" Grace asked. Bobbie winked at her as she pulled a Star Wars apron over her head and tied the string around her waist. "Princess Leia?" Grace laughed. "Not at all who I would have expected you to choose."

"Hey, General Leia was a kick-ass rebel and totally kept the others in line. Why she chose that stuck up, half-witted, scruffy-looking nerf herder Han, I'll never understand."

Grace giggled, already starting to feel the warmth of the wine loosen the tension she hadn't realized she was carrying. "How is

Wyatt? You said he moved to the city?" She pulled over a bag of chips from the counter to snack on. "Do you mind?"

"Not at all. This will take a bit to get ready. Wyatt moved out after I graduated from high school. Dad passed halfway through my senior year and Wyatt took over care of the ranch. He was good at it, but it made him miserable. He never was happy out here away from the action of the big city. Evan was just a little kid, and Wyatt wasn't ready for the responsibilities Dad left him. Mom did her best, but her health has never been good after the accident."

"Oh, that's right. She was in a car accident, right?" Grace remembered going to the hospital with Bobbie when they were kids to visit Mrs. Del Ray while she recovered. The matriarch of the Del Ray clan was a strong woman, and when she was injured it was hard on the whole family.

"She was. Her leg still bothers her sometimes but not like it did back then. She was told she would never walk again when the accident happened, but she's too stubborn to listen. She's able to do things around the house just fine, but ranch work was over for her. It was up to us kids to help Dad, and when he was gone, it was just too much for Wyatt. I was angry with him for a bit, but after a while I just let it be. My anger wasn't going to change anything, and it wasn't doing anyone any good. Wyatt was never interested in being a rancher no matter how much Dad wanted him to be."

"How is Evan?" Grace asked.

"He's great." Bobbie's face lit up at the mention of her little brother. "He got into UC Davis with a full academic scholarship and graduated with honors. He's down in Texas now getting his master's in ranch management. He plans to come back here when he's done to help me try to keep this place afloat. I'm happy doing most things around here, but I can't stand doing paperwork, and Mom's ready to hand that part over to him so she can enjoy the rest of her life without the stress."

"Sounds like you did a good job raising him." Grace loved to hear Bobbie talk about her family. They might not have been as wealthy as her family, but they were far richer in love, and Grace valued that more than money any day.

Bobbie blushed at the compliment. "Well, Mom and I did what we could. Evan was always a great kid, and we had no doubt he would grow up to be something special."

"He had an incredible sister to impress; it's no surprise he's turned out so well." Grace walked around the counter to pour herself another glass of wine as Bobbie put their dinner in the oven. "Would you like another glass?"

"Now, Grace, are you trying to get me drunk?" Bobbie gave Grace the heart-stopping smile that had always made her swoon.

Grace laughed and poured them both more wine. Bobbie picked hers up from the counter and waved Grace toward the living area. "Let's sit in here where it'll be more comfortable to talk. Dinner will be ready in forty-five minutes. Sorry it'll be so late."

"No worries, the way it smells I'm sure it will be well worth the wait." Grace sat on a couch in the den while Bobbie sat across from her. As she sank into the big comfortable cushions, she let out a sigh. "I don't think I've been this relaxed in years."

Bobbie smiled at her admission. "So, tell me what you've been up to since we last saw each other."

Grace swirled the deep red liquid in her glass and took a sip. She wanted to talk to Bobbie about so many things, but she knew once she did, things between them would change and she wasn't ready for that to happen just yet.

"Sorry to say, I'm pretty boring."

"I don't believe that. Do you have any pets?" Bobbie asked.

"Nope."

"Okay, a veterinarian who doesn't have pets. Seems strange but okay."

Grace laughed. "I don't have time for pets and I travel so much it wouldn't be fair."

"You get a pass, then."

"Thanks, I think?"

A timer went off in the kitchen and Bobbie set her glass down and stood to check on it. "Can I get you more wine while I'm up?"

"No, thanks. I need to take it easy."

She watched as Bobbie placed a loaf of buttered bread on a sheet pan and stuck it in the oven. "About fifteen more minutes and it should be ready."

She sat across from Grace again and picked up her glass. "Back to you telling me something interesting about grown-up Grace. I know you're not boring so don't even try. It doesn't have to be earth-shattering. Where did you live before you moved back to Preston?"

Grace took another sip of wine before looking at Bobbie. "I'm...I haven't actually, technically moved back to Preston. I live in Seattle."

"Oh," Bobbie said. "I guess I just assumed you'd moved back."

Grace cleared her throat. "When my dad died I thought I would come home to stay with my mom for a bit to help her take care of my dad's affairs. His death wasn't exactly expected since he was only in his sixties and seemingly healthy. My mom would have just hired someone to go through his stuff, and I thought it would be better for me to do it myself."

"I was sorry to hear about your dad's passing. He was a respected man in the community and we were all shocked."

"Yeah, well, he certainly gave the impression that he was a real stand-up guy."

Bobbie checked her watch and walked back into the kitchen. "I take it your relationship with them never improved?"

Grace chuckled. "We stopped screaming at each other a few years ago and just pretended like the other one didn't exist. I guess that could be considered an improvement."

"What about your mom?"

"My mom is my mom. You know how she is. She keeps up with her social engagements. She dines at the club three nights a week."

Grace knew Bobbie had always despised her mom. "I'm sorry she wasn't a better mother to you."

Grace smiled. "It's fine. What doesn't kill us and all that business. Let's talk about something happier."

"Good idea. How do you like working at the clinic again? Does it bring back happy memories from when you worked there as a kid?"

Grace perked up at the mention of the clinic. Doc Randolph had always been very kind to them both and a sort of mentor to Grace when they were young. "It's great. Most of his employees retired fairly recently so when he left to take care of Carol, I had to hire a new vet. His office manager, Amy, and I have become good friends."

"It's always nice when you work with good people."

"Does Jenson still work at the Ranch?" Grace asked.

Bobbie nodded. "He'll never leave. He's more like family than anything else."

"Do you remember Lena Thompson?"

"That little girl you used to babysit?"

Grace stood when she heard the timer go off again. "That's the one. She's a vet now and I just hired her to work at the clinic."

"You're kidding." Bobbie followed Grace into the kitchen and pulled the food from the oven while Grace found plates. "How can she be old enough to be a vet?"

"Well, she's sharp as a whip for one thing, but also, she's all grown up. I couldn't believe it when she came in for an interview. She's moved back to town to be closer to her parents. I think one of them isn't doing well."

"I'm sorry to hear that. The Thompsons were always really nice people." Bobbie dished them each a portion of pasta and waved for Grace to follow her to the small table in the breakfast nook.

"Yeah. Lena seems to be doing well though. I'm so happy to get to know her as an adult."

"Tell her I said, hello."

"I will." Grace took a bite of her pasta and moaned. "This is amazing, Bobbie."

Bobbie smiled at the compliment. "Thanks."

"So—"

"There's—"

"Sorry, you go," Grace said.

"There's supposed to be a full moon this evening. Can I talk you into taking a walk with me out by the pond?"

Grace stared at her plate for a few seconds before looking at Bobbie. "Sure."

"Great."

When they were both finished with their food, Bobbie placed their plates in the sink. "I'll clean up later. Let's go take that walk."

Grace thought again that it was probably the time she should talk to Bobbie about her life in Seattle, but she decided it could wait until after their walk.

"It's a full moon tonight so I hope you aren't afraid of werewolves."

"I'd like to see the werewolf that thinks it can take you on," Grace said.

"Werewolves aren't super smart. Everyone knows that."

"Dork." Grace laughed.

The night was perfectly warm with a light breeze. Grace could see the full moon reflecting off the pond as they walked toward the beach.

"Doesn't it look like the moon is inside the lake?" Bobbie asked. "Wouldn't that be a crazy story where the moon is still there, but all of its reflected light is caught in some body of water like the ocean or something and the earth is cloaked in complete darkness at night until they figure out how to release the light?" Bobbie stared at the water like she was trying to figure out exactly how they would do it.

Grace laughed. "Still reading science fiction? I remember you were really into it when we were kids."

Bobbie smiled as she led them toward the lake. "One does not simply stop reading science fiction."

"You are such a dork. It's one of my favorite things about you," Grace said.

Bobbie reached over and took Grace's hand, threading their fingers together perfectly as if they were a set. Grace squeezed her hand and gently pulled it away.

"Let's sit and watch the water," Bobbie said. She unfolded the blanket and spread it out on the ground. "Have a seat." She held out her hand to help Grace get seated before settling next to her.

"You're so chivalrous," Grace said.

Bobbie stretched out on her side, leaning on an elbow with her ankles crossed. Grace sat beside her leaning back on her hands with her eyes closed and head tilted toward the sky.

Grace never wanted the night to end. Bobbie made her feel so safe, so special. She knew she couldn't keep the charade going on much longer, but she couldn't resist enjoying the warmth of her hand as she caressed Grace's arm…wait…Grace opened her eyes as she realized Bobbie had scooted closer and was looking at her in a way that Grace knew would lead to more than she could handle at that moment. She pulled her arm away. "Bobbie—"

"Sorry." Bobbie sat up and Grace felt terrible for hurting her feelings.

"Bobbie—"

"If you don't mind, I'm going to take a dip in the lake to cool off a bit." Without waiting for a response, Bobbie pulled her boots and socks off and stripped down to her boxer briefs and undershirt before running down the dock and diving into the cool water.

Grace shook her head. Some things about Bobbie would never change. She stood, kicked off her shoes, and walked down the dock toward where Bobbie was splashing around. She swam over to hold on to the side of the dock as Grace sat on the edge and stuck her feet in the water.

"You okay?" Grace asked. She knew from past experience that when Bobbie had emotions she wasn't sure how to deal with she tended to do something rash to shock her system, like jump into the lake. Her theory had always been that it would help her focus. Grace had no idea if it actually did anything for her, but she'd always found it amusing.

"Honestly?" Bobbie asked.

"Always and above all else."

"I have no idea," Bobbie said. "I have a difficult time being around you and not wanting to touch you. I know we haven't seen each other in years, but the moment I saw you in the clinic, it felt like just yesterday and no time had passed. Ever since you've come back into my life, I've thought about you every waking moment. I'm trying to figure out what to do with myself, with my hands, with my heart. I want nothing more than to lay you on that blanket and make love to you until you pass out, completely sated and without a stress in the world. I want to take you back to the house, to my bed and do it again.

I want to wake up with you safely in my arms, but it's clear you're holding back. I don't want to push you to do anything you don't want or aren't ready for. I just wanted to let you know how I felt."

Without saying a word, Grace stood and held out her hand to help Bobbie up onto the dock. She was soaking wet and Grace's cheeks flushed at the sight of her shirt clinging to her muscular body and small, firm breasts.

Bobbie walked over and collapsed onto the blanket, staring up at the stars.

When Grace reached the blanket she stretched out next to her, resting her head on Bobbie's shoulder and her arm across her middle.

"I'm really sorry," Bobbie said.

Grace squeezed her tighter but didn't say a word. They lay like that for several minutes before Grace sat up leaning on her elbow and looked down at Bobbie. Her heart ached for something she couldn't have. She reached down and gave Bobbie a gentle kiss on the lips. "No matter what has happened in my past, Bobbie Del Ray, my heart was always yours."

Grace stood and reached down to help Bobbie up. "Get your clothes on, goofball, I need to get home so I'm not falling asleep at work tomorrow."

Bobbie grabbed her clothes and the blanket as they walked back to the truck side by side. Grace knew nothing about her life would ever be the same. She just wasn't sure if it would be better or worse. At that moment, with the taste of Bobbie still on her lips, she didn't really care.

CHAPTER NINE

G race placed the last patient of the day's file on top of the pile on Amy's desk. Amy flipped the file open and began to update the patient's account in the computer. It didn't take long for Grace to realize Amy was the grease that made the clinic run so smoothly. She made sure everyone was where they needed to be, when they needed to be there, and took care of all the necessary stuff that helped everything work without bogging things down. Grace knew she was very lucky to have her and never wanted to take her for granted. "Thanks for taking such good care of everything," Grace said.

Amy stopped typing and looked at Grace. "What's wrong?"

"What do you mean, what's wrong?"

"You've been moping around here all day. What gives?"

Grace sighed and covered her face with her hands. "I have this thing and I don't really want to talk about it, but I need to talk about it, but I really want to just pretend like it isn't a thing because I feel like a total and complete asshole on so many levels."

"Okay…"

"Never mind that. How did Lena do today?"

Grace looked around to see if she could find their newest addition to ask her. "Maybe I should check on her to make sure she's okay." As if on cue, Lena walked into the main clinic looking exhausted. "How was it, new girl?"

Lena laughed and laid her head on the counter with a thud.

"Poor baby, we're already working her to death," Grace said.

"Wait a minute." Amy put her hand up to stop the conversation. "What in the world are you talking about, Grace? What are you pretending isn't a thing?"

"What's she talking about?" Lena looked from Grace to Amy, and Grace knew she needed to just pull the Band-Aid off and get this part over.

"I can't do this without ice cream. Would you guys be interested in going out for a scoop?" Grace asked.

"I'm in." Amy moved the stack of files to a cart and turned off her computer. "I'll drive."

"Before dinner? How reckless. I'm in," Lena joked.

"Doctor's orders. Let's lock up and I'll tell you my whole sordid tale." Grace removed her lab coat and grabbed her purse as she headed for the door. "Ice cream is on me."

The other two grabbed their bags and followed Grace out the door. "You're the best," Lena said.

Amy drove them all to the nearest ice cream shop and Grace bought them each a sundae. The air was still warm from the heat of the day so they found a table outside where they could enjoy the light breeze.

"So, Lena, what's your love situation like?" Grace asked before trying to catch a runaway drop of vanilla with her tongue as it dripped down her finger.

"Nope," Amy interrupted before Lena could answer. "What's going on, Grace? You've been acting like you're in line for the firing squad all day. You promised us ice cream and an answer."

Grace swirled her spoon in her ice cream trying to think of where to start. She'd put off this conversation since she arrived, and that fact alone left her feeling shame. "I'm...married."

"You're what?" Amy asked.

"I'm married. To a man. To a lovely man. A man I'm not in love with, and if I'm honest with myself, never have been in love with."

"Whoa." Lena set down her ice cream spoon and stared at Grace. "I thought you went out for coffee with Bobbie last night?"

"I did. It was actually dinner. We were just catching up." Grace felt sick to her stomach. She'd spent the entire time she was with Bobbie trying to think of the best way to tell her about Jake. How do you tell someone you have very intense feelings for that you are unhappily married to man?

"So Bobbie has no idea you're married to…who are you married to?" Lena asked.

"Jake."

"Bobbie has no idea about Jake, but you spent the evening having dinner with her?"

"Yes, I know. I'm a complete asshole."

Amy squeezed Grace's forearm. "You're not an asshole, sweetie. Tell us what's going on. If you're married to Jake, why are you here?"

Grace took a deep breath and pushed her ice cream dish away. "Jake and I met the summer before college. My parents had always been emotionally distant, and when they found out Bobbie and I were together, they shipped me off to boarding school so they wouldn't have to deal with me. I had a few good friends but never really let anyone close until Jake. He was the older brother of my best friend, Margaret. She and her family invited me to spend the summer with them at their lake house, and since my parents didn't want me near Bobbie and didn't want me to come home, I took them up on their offer. It was one of the best summers of my life. Margaret and I spent all of our time together at first, but then she started dating this boy and I quickly became a third wheel. Jake was a year older so we started hanging out. He was sweet and handsome, and I desperately needed someone to love me. I had been adrift since Bobbie and I were separated, and Jake was my port in a storm. By the time school started, we were dating. My parents were thrilled because he comes from money, lots of money, and my mom loves nothing more than to brag about her daughter being married to a senator's son."

"Wow," Lena said. "Sorry, go ahead."

"Jake asked me to marry him the summer before I started vet school. By that time we'd been together for several years, and even though I'd never really felt a spark for him, I did love him. I knew I could do a lot worse, so I said yes. It was the ridiculously large and extravagant wedding my mother had always dreamed of. The woman had been cold to me my entire life, but those few months we spent planning the wedding, she actually seemed proud of me. It was intoxicating for a girl who'd only ever wanted her acceptance."

Amy rubbed Grace's arm. "I'm so sorry, Grace."

"It's okay. She got over it once the wedding was over." Grace smiled and wiped a tear from her cheek. "Jake eventually got a job in Seattle. We moved there and have been there ever since. He's not a bad guy. We get along okay and I certainly could have done worse, but it's obvious that we're just phoning it in. We've tried romantic vacations, therapy, everything we can think of, and it just isn't there. The last couple of years we've barely seen each other. He works late and I'll be out with my friends, and the next thing we know, our only communication with each other is Post-it Notes left on the fridge. We had a big fight a couple of months ago and decided maybe we should take a break. Three days later, I got the call that my dad had died, and as the executor of his will, I decided to come here to get his affairs in order."

"So you guys are separated?" Amy asked.

"I think so?" Grace wasn't sure how to answer that question since things were so vague when she left Seattle. "We decided to take a break, but we hadn't really worked out exactly what that meant before I left. I hadn't planned to stay here so long, but when Doc Randolph asked me to take care of the clinic so he could be with Carol, I couldn't say no. They were like family to me when I was a kid, and it's the least I can do to pay them back for their kindness. And then Bobbie Del Ray walked into my clinic, tall, dark, and soaking wet."

"I hear that," Lena said.

"Bobbie makes me feel the things I'm supposed to feel for my husband, and I have no idea what to do. I spent years getting on with my life, convincing myself she'd moved on, and now I'm here and she's the same old Bobbie. Sexy, funny, adorable Bobbie. Tell me what I should do. I am so capable in other parts of my life, but with this, with my heart, I have no idea what the fuck I'm doing."

"How honest do you want us to be?" Amy asked.

"What do you mean? Don't be a jerk or anything, but I'm seriously asking for your advice so give me your honest opinion."

Lena took Grace's hand and looked her straight in the eyes. "You need to start by talking to Bobbie."

"I know." Grace wiped tears from her face. "I desperately wanted to tell her at dinner, but I just couldn't think of the best way to do it. It's going to break her heart. It breaks my heart and I'm the one that got myself into this mess."

"Oh, sweetie." Amy wrapped her arms around Grace. "You were young and alone, and it sounds like you could have done much worse than marrying a man who is kind to you, even if there isn't a spark. That being said, you have too much love to give to be stuck in a loveless marriage. You need to figure what you want and start figuring out how to make that happen. Whether you decide to try to fix your marriage or you want to get a divorce, Lena and I will be there for you without judgment. Right, Lena?"

"Absolutely." Lena wrapped her arms around Grace from the other side.

"I love you guys so much." Grace leaned back as they all wiped their eyes. "I can't thank you enough for letting me get that off my chest."

"We're honored to be your friends, but next time big talks like this need to include alcohol," Amy said.

"Hear, hear," Lena said. "I'm sorry you've been dealing with this on your own. Please don't ever feel like you can't talk to us, Grace. We're your friends and that's what we're for."

"Thanks." Grace felt lighter than she had in months.

CHAPTER TEN

Grace woke the next morning with a plan. She knew Bobbie would bring Riley in for her checkup that day, and she was both relieved and completely freaked out at the thought of talking to her about Jake. She knew Bobbie would be upset when she found out Grace was married, but she hoped she would understand her situation.

Grace felt terrible it had taken so long to mention Jake, but she'd been so caught up in the excitement of seeing Bobbie she didn't want to burst the bubble. She owed Bobbie the truth and had decided she would ask her to lunch after her appointment so they could talk.

As the morning wore on, Grace kept checking the clock. She knew Bobbie's appointment was at ten so when she finished her nine thirty, she popped into her office to check her makeup and hair. "God, I'm such a dork," she admonished herself as she hurried to peek through the tiny window in the employee only door with a good view of the clinic's entrance.

At ten on the dot, she saw them walk in. "Watcha' looking at?" Lena startled Grace as she squeezed next to her at the little window. "You look like you're staring at a chocolate cake. That's my chocolate cake look at least."

"Nothing, just looking to see how many people are in the waiting room."

"Uh-huh." Lena pushed Grace aside to get a better look. "Holy crap. Is that Bobbie Del Ray? She grew up all studly."

Grace playfully shoved Lena away from the window so she could look again.

"Have you talked to her yet?" Lena asked.

Grace sighed. "No. I'm going to ask her to lunch after her appointment. I'm so scared."

Lena wrapped her arm around her shoulders and gave her a kiss on the cheek. "You're doing the right thing. It might get messy, but it'll work out in the end."

"I know. I have to talk to her, but the thought of her being upset with me has my stomach in knots."

"Why would she be upset with you? She might be upset with the situation. She might be upset that you're just getting around to telling her, but she's not going to be upset with you for being married. That has nothing to do with her. Bobbie is good people, Grace. Give her a little credit."

"You're completely right. I know you're right. I'm just scared."

"I know, sweetie. If you need to talk just let us know. Amy and I are happy to be your shoulders if you need a good cry."

"Thanks, Lena."

"You got this."

Grace gave her a quick hug as she pulled the chart from the door outside Bobbie and Riley's room. After a quick glance to remind herself what she'd already done, she took a deep breath and ran her fingers through her hair one last time to make sure everything was in place before entering the room.

Bobbie was sitting on the bench with Riley lazily draped over her lap. "How is our little patient?" Grace asked.

"She seems tip-top, Doc. She's drinking water and pooping like a champ, and she eats enough for a dog three times her size."

"I can see that, my chubby little friend." Grace lifted Riley to place her on the table for her exam.

"Her chart says she's about twenty-four pounds and she should be closer to twenty-one or twenty-two at the most. You may want to limit her food a bit more to take off that extra weight."

Bobbie stuck out her lower lip in a pout.

"Aww, what seems to be the issue?" Grace put her hand on Bobbie's shoulder in mock comfort.

"We have a couple of problems. Well, Riley has one on her own, and then we share one," Bobbie admitted.

"Let's hear them." Grace feigned seriousness.

"First, Riley has a real issue with kitty food. I'm working on securing it where short stack here can't reach it, but thus far she has foiled my every attempt. I think I've worked something out now, but not in time for her to get to her fighting weight before this appointment. She'll be better next time, Doc."

Grace laughed and kissed Riley on the nose. "What's the other problem? The one you both share."

"Well…" Bobbie looked down at the exam table as if she didn't want to admit what she was going to say. "We have a bit of a goldfish problem."

"Goldfish problem?" Grace laughed. "I'm not exactly sure what that even means."

"Goldfish cracker addiction is more accurate," Bobbie explained. "We like to eat them when we watch our shows on TV before bed. It was Riley's idea, and I just didn't have the heart to tell her no. You remember she was trapped in wire and injured, right? She's had a really hard life so far." Bobbie was trying her best to garner as much sympathy for the both of them, but Grace wasn't buying it.

"I appreciate your predicament, but maybe Riley should cut back to only one or two goldfish a night." Grace couldn't stop herself from giving Bobbie an appraising glance. "They don't seem to be affecting Riley's mom negatively at all so I won't put the same restriction on you."

Bobbie smiled at the comment as Grace blushed.

"Well, Doc, I hate to make her feel bad, so we'll both cut back on the goldfish. Maybe sometime soon you can come over and have some with us and watch a show. We're just about to start a new series on Netflix and there's plenty of room on the couch." Bobbie's arm touched Grace's as they stood next to each other. The unexpected contact sent Grace's heart rate into overdrive, which caused her to feel a little unsteady on her feet.

"You okay?" Bobbie looked concerned as she put her hand on Grace's arm to steady her.

Laughing, Grace placed her hand on Bobbie's where it touched her arm. "I'm okay, I just lost my balance for a minute."

"You take care of yourself, Doc. Riley is going on a diet and she wants you to be around to see her slim down." Bobbie joked, but Grace could hear real concern in her voice.

Grace swallowed around the lump in her throat. She felt like she was walking to the gallows. "Bobbie, do you have plans for lunch?"

Bobbie's face brightened at the invitation. "Nope. Riley and I need to go to the feed store before we head home, but we have plenty of time to have lunch with a beautiful lady. As a rule we try to keep our calendar open for just such invitations."

"Great." Grace could hear the apprehension in her own voice.

"Everything okay?" Bobbie asked.

"Sure, yeah, I just have some things I need to talk to you about. That's all."

"Sounds good. Should we hang around until you're ready or did you want to meet somewhere?"

Grace checked her watch. "I think I can actually get Lena to take my next appointment if you're ready now. I just need to go to my office to throw on real clothes instead of scrubs and I'll be ready. Want to get checked out with Amy and I'll meet you up front?"

"Perfect. See you in a minute." Grace watched as Bobbie walked out the door and headed to the front desk. She tucked Riley's file under her arm, closed her eyes, and took a deep breath, letting it out slowly in an effort to calm her nerves.

"It's now or never, Grace," she said before heading toward her office.

CHAPTER ELEVEN

Bobbie left the exam room with a smile. She wondered if the people in the waiting room would think she was smiling from the awesome service, which made her smile even bigger. Who needed good Yelp reviews when you saw people come out of the exam room looking like they just had Christmas and a birthday during a fifteen-minute visit with the vet. Even Riley looked happy. Bobbie was pretty sure they should be on the advertisements for the clinic.

As she approached the counter, she noticed a handsome man speaking to a very startled looking Amy. Amy looked from the man to Bobbie and back to the man before quickly walking toward the back of the clinic.

While Bobbie and Riley stood at the counter waiting for Amy to return, the stranger pulled out his phone and scrolled through a couple of texts before dropping it back in his pocket.

"Do you like this vet?" the man asked Bobbie.

"Pardon?"

"Did you have a good appointment? Do you like this vet?" the man asked again. "My wife works at this clinic, and I was just wondering if it was a good place."

Bobbie knew of only three women working at the clinic, and as far as she had heard, Lena wasn't married and Amy was married to John Miller. The man hadn't introduced himself so Bobbie stuck out her hand. "I'm Bobbie Del Ray."

The man returned her handshake. "Jake Barrington, it's a pleasure to meet you."

"Good to meet you Jake. Do you mind if I ask who your wife is?"

Bobbie watched as the man's face lit up. "Dr. Grace Hammond. Do you know her?"

The world seemed to stop as Bobbie tried to force herself to breathe. She stared at the man, trying to process the words that had just come out of the stranger's mouth. Grace was his wife? What did he mean by that? Bobbie wracked her brain to try to interpret what he was saying because there was no way he actually meant that he and Grace were married, like husband and wife married. That made no sense. Why wouldn't Grace have told her?

"Are you okay, Bobbie?" Jake placed a hand on her arm as she felt her world spin out of control. "Hey, Bobbie, let's find a place for you to sit."

Jake led Bobbie toward the waiting area as Grace and Amy burst through the door. "What happened?" Grace jogged toward them and took Bobbie's other arm. "What are you doing here, Jake? What's wrong with Bobbie?"

"I have no idea. We were just chatting at the counter and I asked her if she knew you and the next thing I knew she turned white and looked like she was going to pass out."

"I got her, Jake." Amy slipped under Bobbie's arm and led her to the back of the clinic. Bobbie vaguely registered Grace talking to Jake before the door closed and she was left alone with Amy.

"You doing okay, Bobbie?" Amy guided Bobbie onto the couch in Grace's office and encouraged her to lie back with her feet up on the armrest.

"I'm okay. I don't know what happened. Where's Riley?"

"It's going to be okay. Riley's with Lena right now. I'm going to get you a glass of water and Grace will be back in just a minute so you guys can talk."

"That man said he was her husband. Is that for real?"

Amy handed Bobbie a glass of water and brushed the bangs from her forehead. "I think you need to talk to Grace. Give her a chance to explain. I'm sorry it all happened like this, Bobbie."

"I'm the one who owes her an apology." Grace stood in the doorway with tears in her eyes. "Thanks, Amy, would you mind giving us a minute to talk?"

"Sure." Amy gave Grace a hug before leaving and shutting the door closed behind her.

Grace walked into the bathroom attached to her office and came back with a wet washcloth. She pulled a chair next to the couch and gently placed the folded cloth on Bobbie's head.

"Are you married?" Bobbie held her breath, somehow hoping the answer would be anything other than what she knew it would be.

Grace leaned forward and covered her face with her hands. "Yes," she said with a sob.

"Why, Grace? Why am I just hearing about this now?"

Grace looked at her with red rimmed eyes and what looked like the weight of the world on her shoulders. "I wanted to tell you. I almost told you a thousand times, but I didn't want things to change between us. I didn't want you to look at me like you're looking at me now."

Bobbie sat up and leaned her head back on the couch. She stared at the ceiling and thought about what she should do next. The nice thing would be for her to tell Grace she understood and it was no big deal, but it was a big deal. Not only was Bobbie dealing with the disappointment of knowing that the relationship she thought was blossoming between them was obviously only one-sided but Grace had lied to her. It was more of a lie by omission, but at that moment it felt like a lie, nonetheless.

"I know it's cold comfort, but I had planned to tell you at lunch today. I had no idea Jake was going to come here. He decided to surprise me by showing up in Preston. It's no excuse and I don't expect you to understand, but I just want you to know that I never meant to hurt you."

"You never do, Grace." Bobbie stood and tossed the washcloth on the couch. "I'll see you around."

Bobbie's heart broke in two as she walked out the door. The sound of Grace sobbing almost caused her to turn back around and wrap her in her arms, but she knew that would be a mistake. It was Jake's job to comfort his wife, not Bobbie's. It would never be Bobbie's. She felt like some essential part of her soul had cracked and she wasn't sure if the world would ever be right again.

"Thanks for watching Riley for me," Bobbie said as she approached the desk and retrieved her very excited pup from Amy.

"No problem. Are you okay, Bobbie?" Amy walked around the desk and wrapped her in a hug. "Please don't be too upset with her. I know it doesn't seem like it right now, but everything's going to be okay."

Bobbie patted Amy's back and took a step back. "Would you mind billing me? I have some errands I need to run and really need to get those started."

"Sure," Amy said. "You don't be a stranger."

"See ya, Amy. Thanks for everything." Bobbie walked out of the clinic and out of Grace Hammond's life.

CHAPTER TWELVE

Riley whined from the passenger seat as the truck bumped down the long road to the ranch. Bobbie wondered if the dog could sense her sadness or if she just wanted the bumping to stop.

"It's okay, girl. We'll be okay," she said, wiping tears from her eyes.

Bobbie slid to a stop in front of the barn and jerked her vehicle into park. She slammed the door behind her as she stormed toward the barn. Halfway there, she realized she'd left Riley in her harness in the passenger seat, probably scared to death from all the noise. She doubled back and released her from the harness as she was showered in doggy kisses.

"God, I'm such an asshole."

The soft tongue on her cheek began to pull Bobbie back from her anger. "I'm so sorry, sweetie." She cradled the shaggy mutt in her arms. "Sometimes Mom gets mad and takes it out on her vehicle, but it's no excuse to freak you out."

"Riley isn't the only one you freaked out."

Bobbie turned to find her mom walking toward her with a concerned look.

"I'm sorry, Mama. I'll control my frustration better." Bobbie hugged her mom as she gave Riley a kiss on top of her head.

"Been a rough day, Peanut?"

"You could say that. Nothing I can't handle though. How about you? How are you feeling?" Bobbie doubted it would work, but she had to attempt to change the subject.

"Nice try, kiddo. What's going on? Anything I can help you with?" The concern in her eyes made any thought Bobbie had of not being honest with her all-knowing mother out of the question.

"It's a bit of a delicate situation." Bobbie was hesitant to share her girl problems with her mom. No matter how frustrated she was with Grace, she didn't want her mom to have a bad opinion of her.

"Does it have anything to do with Grace Hammond?" Her mom obviously knew more than she was letting on.

"I'm in a bit of a pickle." Bobbie's eyes welled up as her mom put an arm around her.

"Let's get out of the heat and sit down. We'll figure this out." She led Bobbie into the barn and sat her down on a bale of hay in the shade. Riley sat next to her and rested her chin on her leg.

"She's already completely devoted to you." She smiled at the little dog who had become Bobbie's shadow. "So tell me what's going on. Is this about her being married?"

Bobbie's head jerked up and she stared at her mom in shock. "How the hell did you know she was married and why didn't you tell me?"

"Watch your language, Roberta."

"Sorry."

"I was down at Janice's getting my hair done and she said her mother-in-law saw Grace's mom having brunch at the club this morning. She was excited to remind everyone that her daughter was married to a senator's son and said he was in town to surprise her."

"You got all that information from gossip?" Bobbie was always amazed how quickly information traveled in a small town.

"I take it you saw her at your appointment for Riley?"

Bobbie could tell her mother was trying to give her a chance to talk to her at her own pace. "I did."

"And this is the first you've heard of this senator's son?"

"Could you please stop calling him that? His name is Jake."

"Fine. This is the first you've learned about Jake?"

"Yes, ma'am." Bobbie pulled a strand of hay from the bale and began to pick it apart.

"Bobbie, you didn't—"

"No." She interrupted her mom before she could say more. "We've seen each other a few times, all very innocently. It turns out I thought we were heading in a direction that she didn't."

"Do you think she was going to be unfaithful to her husband? I would hope you would never be party to something like that."

Bobbie tossed the last bit of straw on the ground and stood. She sometimes found it easier to think when she was walking. Riley watched her closely as she paced the floor in front of her mom. "No. I really don't and you know I wouldn't. We have this crazy connection. We always have. When we're together I feel like there's this part of me that I didn't even realize existed and she's the only one who can show me. If I'm being honest with myself I knew something wasn't right. The more we hung out together, the more she seemed uncomfortable. I should have known."

"How could you have known, Bobbie? She should have been up front with you from the start."

Bobbie leaned against the stall door of one of the horses and reached through the bars to rub its head. "She would have. I think she knows that and feels guilty about it, but what's done is done. I don't think I'm even mad at her anymore."

"Bobbie, you can't just roll over and expose your belly every time that girl offers to give you attention."

"Okay." Bobbie chuckled for the first time since she met Jake. "That's super weird, but I think I understand what you're saying."

"Help me up."

Bobbie reached down to help her mom up from the bale of hay. She threaded her arm through Bobbie's as they walked down the center aisle of the barn. "I know you're not going to like this suggestion, but will you do your old mom a favor and go out on a couple of dates?"

"Mama, no. I'm not ready to start dating someone."

"I know you don't think you are, but hear me out. Before Grace came back to town you hadn't been on a date in months."

Bobbie rolled her eyes. "Mama, I have a ranch to run—"

"And a mother to care for and everything else you do every day," her mother said. "I get it, sweetheart. You have a busy life, but it's your life and you can't always put everyone and everything else before that. I think your connection to Grace is so strong you were able to see beyond your duties and think about the things that will make you happy besides cattle."

"I don't want anyone else, Mama." Bobbie's heart ached with the weight of the words.

"I know that's how it feels right now, but there's someone out there for you that can offer you what you need. She might not be the one you think you want, but you just might be surprised."

Bobbie helped her mom up the steps to her house and opened the front door. "I love you, Mom. Thanks for the chat."

Her mom pulled her down to place a kiss on her cheek. "I love you, too, Peanut. More than you'll ever know. I wish I could take this hurt away from you, but that's the curse of motherhood."

"That sounds horrible." Bobbie laughed and kissed the top of her mom's head. "I'll go on one date. That's all I'm promising right now. One date and only because Garret has been trying to fix me up with his cousin for months."

"You're going to be all right, sweetheart."

"I hope you're right, Mama. I hope you're right."

CHAPTER THIRTEEN

Grace slipped on her shoes and took one last look in the mirror before meeting Jake in the reception area of the clinic. She hadn't planned to dress up quite so much, but when she asked Jake to bring her a dress she wasn't specific about which one and he brought one of her nicer ones. He did pick shoes that went well with it so she appreciated that.

She wasn't sure what the appropriate outfit was when your intention was to tell your husband that you wanted a divorce. Was blue the right color dress for that kind of occasion?

When Jake showed up at the clinic the day before she was so shocked and heartbroken over Bobbie's obvious pain, she'd been a wreck ever since. Jake knew something was wrong, but she knew she wouldn't be able to talk to him until she had better control over her emotions. They'd slept in the same bed for the first time in a year. Even before she left Seattle, they'd been staying in separate rooms.

How was she going to get out of this situation? The thought of disappointing either Bobbie or Jake made her sick. She loved them both, although in very different ways. Jake showing up was completely her fault. She'd left things still up in the air when she left for Preston and hadn't exactly been the best communicator while she was there.

She was frustrated that Jake decided to just surprise her and didn't give her any warning that he was coming, but in his defense, he was her husband. Husbands had every right to surprise their wives when they'd been gone.

If she'd had it all to do over she would have made things much clearer when she left, but with the death of her father and all the emotions and paperwork that was causing, she thought talking to Jake was something she could put off. She should have learned you can never put anything off. It will always come back to bite you in the ass.

Jake smiled from ear to ear when she exited her office. "You look spectacular."

Grace knew his compliment should make her feel good, but with the state of their relationship and her intentions for the evening, it just made her feel even guiltier.

"Ready?" She held open the front door for him to exit and locked up behind him.

"You'll have to tell me where to go."

Jake had dropped her off at work that morning so he could run errands for her mom. He really was a great guy, and if either one of them had any romantic feelings for each other it might be a totally different story. They didn't. They'd been great friends from the day they met, and even though they loved each other, it wasn't enough for her anymore. She knew it wasn't enough for him either. Jake never looked at Grace the way he looked at their friend Carla. She wasn't blind. She didn't think he'd ever acted on those feelings, but she knew he had them, nonetheless.

He deserved to be with someone who made him feel the way Bobbie made her feel every time they were together. Grace couldn't give that to him. She knew he would deny it all day long, but she knew he wasn't happy and neither was she.

Jake held her hand as they entered the restaurant and walked to the podium.

"Reservations for Barrington," Jake said to the hostess who smiled an appreciative smile at him as she walked them to their table.

"Hey, fancy seeing you here." Grace looked up to see who Jake was greeting and sucked in a breath when she realized it was Bobbie. "You remember my wife don't you? Are you okay? I was so worried about you, but Grace said you had low blood sugar or something."

Grace wanted to die right there. This was an absolute, red alert, worst-case scenario.

Bobbie's eyes didn't leave Grace as she answered Jake. "Hey, Jake, yeah. Sorry to rush out on you like that. When my low blood sugar hits me, it really knocks me off my feet." The words coming from Bobbie's mouth were polite enough, but Grace found no kindness in her eyes. She looked at Grace as if she'd just been slapped.

"Hello, I'm Jake." Jake shook the hand of the person sitting with Bobbie. Grace pulled her eyes from Bobbie long enough to see who he was speaking to. Grace's stomach did a flip when she saw the gorgeous brunette who was obviously her date.

Grace knew she was giving the woman a dirty look, but she was trying to wrap her head around the fact that Bobbie was on a date. What did she expect? Bobbie didn't have some kind of commitment to Grace. Of course, calling this person a "woman" was being a bit generous. She looked to be barely out of college and had apparently been ordered right from a catalog with a perfect figure and legs for days.

Her date looked from Bobbie to Grace and back to Bobbie before settling on Jake. "I'm Karen Jackson. It's a pleasure to meet you, Jake."

Grace felt like time was suspended. She couldn't decide if she was embarrassed that Bobbie saw her here with Jake or upset that Bobbie was here with another woman. She knew she had no right to be upset but she was. Bobbie was a grown woman and wasn't obligated to Grace in any way. Logically, she knew this to be true, but the sting of jealousy was just as strong, even when she had no right to feel it.

"This is my wife, Grace," Jake continued, completely oblivious to Grace's near mental breakdown.

Grace shook her hand and gave her the best smile she could, under the circumstances. Bobbie wiped her mouth with her napkin, pushed her chair back, and said, "Please excuse me," giving her date an apologetic smile. Grace watched as Bobbie headed toward the restrooms in the back of the restaurant.

She sat stunned for a moment, gathering her thoughts before excusing herself as well. Grace headed for the bathroom and burst through the door. She checked under each stall to make sure they weren't occupied, then locked the main bathroom door. Bobbie was at the sink, splashing water over her face and hadn't looked up when Grace walked in. She tore a towel from the dispenser and turned to Grace, leaning back against the sink for support.

Grace struggled not to let her anger bubble to the surface. "What kind of game are you playing?" she asked through gritted teeth.

"Me? What game am *I* playing? You must be joking. I'm not the one who conveniently forgot to share the fact that she was married. I didn't fail to mention my husband was in town while I was making lunch plans with some other poor sucker. I'm especially not the one who showed up to a fancy dinner, looking like every teenage boy's fucking wet dream, on what is obviously a date with the husband I never mentioned I had."

"Speaking of teenage dates…" Grace snapped back.

Bobbie rolled her eyes and ran her fingers through her tousled hair. God, she was sexy when she did that. Grace's imagination flashed to a picture of what Bobbie looked like after sex so many years ago. Sweat glistening on her sun kissed skin, hair wild and sexy.

Without thinking, she closed the distance between them and pulled Bobbie's head down for a searing kiss. It was everything she wanted to say but couldn't articulate with words.

Bobbie seemed startled for a moment but quickly recovered, opening her mouth to let Grace's tongue slip past her lips. Grace felt warm hands slide down her body to rest on the curve of her ass. This was it. She was kissing Bobbie. Really kissing Bobbie. It had been years since she'd felt those soft lips against her own, but there was something so comforting, so right about it.

As the kiss deepened, she felt her legs weaken and her body go slack as Bobbie lifted her and set her on the counter. The feeling of Bobbie's strong body so close was driving Grace insane. She felt Bobbie's hands on the bare skin of her thighs and realized her dress had been pulled up, exposing her now drenched panties to the cool air.

Grace was on the edge of letting go when her conscious mind slapped her in the face. "Bobbie, I can't, we can't." She gasped, trying to convince herself as much as Bobbie. She knew, at least for herself, it was a losing battle, but she had to try.

Bobbie let out a pained groan and stopped her hands from progressing up Grace's thighs. "What are we doing, Grace?" She sounded like a wounded animal, and Grace knew exactly the kind of willpower Bobbie needed to stop this before it really started.

They were both panting heavily as Grace rested her forehead on Bobbie's broad chest. As they held each other trying to gather themselves, there was a quiet knock on the bathroom door and a disembodied voice said, "I'm not sure. I didn't think this door was ever locked. Should we ask someone?"

Bobbie stepped back and said to the people outside, "One sec, I'll be right there," as she helped Grace off the counter and smoothed down her dress. Her eyes teared up a bit as she gently kissed Grace's cheek, turned, and walked toward the door.

"I'm so sorry, ladies. I had a very upset stomach and needed my friend to hold my hair," Bobbie explained as she passed the confused women waiting in the hallway.

Grace laughed a little and stepped into a stall so she could privately ensure everything was back in its place before she walked out into public. By the time she returned to the table, Bobbie and Karen were gone. Jake set down his glass of wine and stood until Grace was seated across from him. "Are you okay, sweetheart?" he asked.

"You know, I'm not. Would it be terribly rude of me to ask if we can leave?" Grace hoped her guilt and disappointment weren't as obvious as it felt.

"But we haven't eaten our meal. What happened in that bathroom? Bobbie wasn't feeling well when she came back either."

What were they thinking? "I'm not sure. If you don't mind, I'm going to get some fresh air while you pay." Grace stood and gathered her bag as she left the table. The lie left a terrible taste in Grace's mouth. She guessed it must be what guilt tasted like. Grace knew she couldn't continue living like this, but she didn't have the energy to have the talk with Jake tonight. Not when she could still feel a whisper of Bobbie's kiss on her lips.

CHAPTER FOURTEEN

B obbie silently backed out of the parking spot and headed
toward Karen's apartment after leaving the restaurant. She
had no idea how to explain her abrupt change in mood so she decided
it was best to keep quiet.

Karen stared out the passenger side window into the darkness.
"Did you know her?"

"Who?" Bobbie was so lost in her own thoughts she forgot
Karen was even there.

"Grace," she answered. Bobbie could hear the irritation in
Karen's voice but didn't fault her for it. Her behavior had been
embarrassing, and she knew she was lucky Karen wasn't angrier than
she was. It had been a nice evening before Grace showed up. Karen
was a sweet, intelligent woman who deserved a date who was fully
committed to being emotionally present, not just physically there.

"We went to school together. Look, I'm really sorry I've been
such a dud of a date tonight. I promise I'm usually much more
charming." Bobbie gave Karen a little wink and a sly smile, but Karen
obviously wasn't going to let her off that easily. Bobbie knew she had
to be honest with her. This mess was way too complicated to pull yet
one more victim into the web of confusion.

Bobbie let out a slow breath before giving Karen the abbreviated
but honest version of her predicament. To her credit, Karen listened
patiently while Bobbie tried to convince herself her feelings for Grace
were nothing more than excitement over seeing her again after so

many years. When Bobbie explained what happened at the restaurant with enough detail to be honest but not so much it would upset Karen, she finally stopped talking.

When they reached Karen's apartment complex, Bobbie pulled into an empty spot and turned off the ignition. They both sat there in silence for a few minutes until Karen gently placed her hand on Bobbie's. "You are in love with Grace, Bobbie. You can try to convince yourself you aren't, but it won't make it not true. I understand why your mom would want you to date other women because she knows that a love like that can easily lead to heartbreak in the best of situations, but take tonight as a lesson. You are meant for Grace. She is obviously in love with you as well. I think she knows it and isn't sure what to do. She looked like a woman in agony, and I can only guess that's because she feels trapped between two choices that will change her life forever. She will figure it out. I suspect sooner rather than later if the look she had when she saw you and me together was any indication." Karen winked at Bobbie and gave her hand a gentle squeeze. "She'll get there and you will need to be patient. It'll be worth it in the end. Love like that doesn't come around very often."

Bobbie lifted Karen's hand to her lips and gave it a gentle kiss. "You're an incredible woman, Karen. You will make someone very happy someday."

"If you have any good candidates, send them my way." She laughed as she unfastened her seat belt and exited Bobbie's truck. Bobbie walked Karen to her apartment door. "Thanks for an exciting night, Bobbie."

"Thank you, for everything." Bobbie kissed Karen on the cheek and jogged back to her truck. Patience. She hated patience.

CHAPTER FIFTEEN

Grace couldn't pull herself out of her funk after they left the restaurant. Jake had asked her several times if she was okay and she assured him she was only tired. It wasn't a lie, exactly. She was exhausted, but it was the type of exhaustion no amount of sleep could fix.

When they arrived home, Grace's mom asked Jake to help her move one of her bird cages away from a vent. She worried the cool air would give it a chill. Grace couldn't remember one time in her life when her mom seemed half as concerned about her welfare as she did her birds. That thought did nothing to lift her spirits.

As her mom led Jake to the bird room, Grace told them she was going to turn in for the night. Jake gave her a concerned look but continued following her mom when Grace silently mouthed that she was okay.

Once in the safety of her bathroom, she stood at the sink and stared at the reflection of what felt like some other woman. The stress and anxiety was pushing her toward full-blown depression. Grace didn't like the woman she'd become. The Grace she thought she was would be strong enough to talk to Jake about her feelings. The Grace she thought she was would do more than stare at herself in the mirror and think about her shortcomings.

When Grace finished with her nightly routine, she walked into her bedroom to find Jake sitting up in bed. The sight of him in his flannel pajamas with his tousled blond locks already sticking up in the back, broke her heart. She didn't want to hurt this man. He'd been her safe harbor since she was just a girl. They'd weathered so many storms together, but she wasn't sure how they would navigate themselves out of this one.

Grace sat on the bed facing Jake so they could talk. He closed his book and removed his reading glasses, setting them both on the nightstand. "What's up?" he asked. "You've seemed off since I got here."

Grace rubbed the palm of her left hand with the thumb of her right, tracing the line of an old scar. "Why are you here, Jake?" she asked.

"What do you mean, why am I here? You're here. I came to be with you."

"No, I mean why would you come here when we discussed separating before I left?"

Jake leaned back against the headboard with a thump. "I didn't think you were serious."

Grace felt the familiar irritation with him bubble to the surface. Of course he didn't think she was serious. That was part of the damn problem. He never thought things Grace said, or wanted, or needed were serious. He always thought he knew what was best. When Grace would mention she might look for a new car, she found one in the driveway a week later. One that he picked out because according to him, he knew more about cars, and therefore her opinion wasn't important. She would come home late from work, dead tired and in need of a shower and sleep, and Jake would have made a huge meal even though she'd told him earlier she was too tired to eat. When they were first together she thought he was the sweetest, most thoughtful man in the world. She'd felt guilty for not being anything other than grateful for the things he did for her. The very qualities she'd been drawn to in the beginning were now driving her away. Well, they were part of the problem at least. The other being there was absolutely no spark between them.

The questioning look on his face was almost comical, which helped Grace tamp down her frustration before they descended into yet one more argument. "Are you happy, Jake? I mean honestly, truthfully happy?"

Jake couldn't hold her gaze, looking down to worry a thread on the blanket draped across his lap. "I'm not, not happy."

"Really?" Grace knew he hadn't been happy for a long time. He'd told her as much again and again in the heat of an argument. "Look, I love you, Jake."

"I love you, too."

"I know you do and I am so grateful for that love. I never want to lose that love, but you and I both know it isn't the love that anyone dreams of. It's the kind of love that means we'll always be there for each other. It's the kind of love that makes you feel not so alone in the world, but it's not the kind of love that makes you swoon. We both deserve a love that makes us swoon."

Jake leaned forward and took Grace's hand. "It can be. We just need to work on it. Marriages ebb and flow and sometimes they need a little push." He pushed himself forward on his knees and crawled toward her on the bed.

"What are you doing, Jake?"

"Giving us a little push."

Grace abruptly stood and crossed to the foot of the bed. "Jake, this is bigger than a push. I'm not in love with you and I know you're not in love with me, either."

Jake collapsed face down on the bed. "Why are you saying that, Grace? Why would you even think that?"

"Because we're not in love and this isn't the first time we've talked about it. This is exactly why we decided to take a break from each other in Seattle. This is exactly why we spend sixty percent of our time together arguing and thirty percent avoiding each other."

"That's not fair." Jake pushed himself back up to sit cross-legged in the center of the bed.

"Isn't it?" Grace folded her arms across her chest. She wanted to run from the room and never come back, but she knew they had to work through this now or they'd be doing this for the rest of their lives.

"That ten percent where we're together and actually getting along is so, so good. Doesn't that count for something?"

Grace sighed. "Yes, Jake, it counts for a lot and it's called friendship, not marriage. We're not meant for each other. We're meant to take care of each other for the rest of our lives, but as friends, not lovers. Do you not see that?"

She could see the moment Jake let down his guard and allowed her words to sink in. His shoulders relaxed, his expression changed from angry and confused to acceptance. He collapsed backward on the bed, arms tossed out on either side as he released a long and what seemed like an almost relieved breath. "I know you're right," he said.

Grace sat next to him on the bed and took his hand in hers. "Jake, why are you here? We had this conversation before I left Seattle. I'll admit it was a much more abbreviated version, but this conversation nonetheless. We'd decided it would be a good idea to separate. We were living separate lives already. We slept in separate rooms. Our finances are separate. We weren't living as a married couple, at least not the type of marriage I would like to have someday. We decided to separate, and then you show up here, at my mother's house, in my place of work, and act as if nothing has changed. Scratch that, you act as if we've had this perfect marriage and the last few years never happened. What gives?"

Jake stared at her hand, fingers laced between his. "Why haven't you worn your wedding ring for the last ten years?"

The question took Grace by surprise. "It's too hard with my work. You know that. I don't want to get it caught on a dog's nail or have the stone scratch some animal's eye in a struggle."

"Right. That's what you've said."

"Jake—"

"Please be honest with me, Grace."

Grace pulled her hand from Jake's. "Can I ask you a question first?"

"Shoot."

"Why haven't we had sex in more than eight months? We've had plenty of opportunities and yet we've done nothing more than quick pecks on the lips. Why do you think that is?"

Jake rubbed his eyes and Grace's heart ached. She really did love him and would be forever grateful to him for putting her back together when she needed someone the most.

"I get it," he said. "Was I a terrible husband?"

Grace stretched out next to him in the bed and wrapped an arm around his middle. "You were the best husband you could have been under the circumstances. This isn't about you doing something wrong. We just aren't meant to be husband and wife."

Jake slipped his arm under Grace's head so he could hold her. "Where do we go from here?"

"I guess we talk about divorce."

Jake jerked away in surprise. "Divorce?"

"Umm…yeah. What did you think was going to happen?"

He shrugged and moved farther away on the bed. "I don't know. I guess…I don't fucking know."

"Don't you want to be happy, Jake? Don't you want to find someone who can make you truly happy instead of just going through the motions of a passionless marriage?"

"I can't talk about this anymore, Grace. I need some space. I'll go sleep on the couch."

"No. My mom would freak out. I'll go. I have a couch in my office that pulls out. I can sleep there."

"I don't want to—"

"It's fine, Jake. I'll have to be there in just a few hours anyway." Grace stood and pulled on her jeans. "We'll talk about this more when we're not both so raw and exhausted."

"Okay." Jake looked dejected and it broke Grace's heart.

"We'll figure this out, sweetheart. We're both going to be okay. I promise."

He stood and walked over to Grace, wrapping his arms around her. He'd always made her feel safe, and the thought of not having that comfort in her life was scary. She knew she'd never truly feel fulfilled if she didn't leave though so she gently pulled away and stood on tiptoes to kiss his cheek.

"Thanks for being a good man, Jake. Thank you for being my best friend." Grace turned away and walked out the door. Her heart ached, her eyes burned, and she couldn't remember ever being this tired in her life—or so hopeful. When she'd left Seattle it had been more like fleeing the scene of a crime, but this time felt different. Even if they were nowhere near done, and they had a long road ahead to disentangle their lives, at least this part of their journey was finally underway.

CHAPTER SIXTEEN

G race wiped tears from her eyes as she sat alone in her office at three in the morning. She'd been crying for half an hour and knew if she didn't get some sleep, she'd be dead on her feet at work the next day.

"Right," she said to the empty room. The thought of going through the effort of pulling out the bed and putting on sheets exhausted her so she grabbed the blanket from the back of the couch, slipped off her shoes, and stretched out her legs as much as she could. Sometimes being short had its advantages.

The night had been a jumble of emotions that Grace hadn't fully sorted through yet. She hoped the talk with Jake was a step forward in getting her life together. Everything was still so fresh she feared it had all been a dream, or nightmare, depending on how she looked at it.

That kiss with Bobbie, though. That kiss was a completely different story. They'd kissed a million times when they were young. She'd thought about those kisses through the years, but good God, either her memory didn't do them justice or Bobbie had perfected her craft as she aged.

Grace was ashamed she hadn't mentioned the kiss to Jake, but knew things were already too emotionally charged to throw that log on the fire. She couldn't deny that seeing Bobbie had prompted the conversation with Jake, but she wasn't the reason it needed to happen. Their conversation in Seattle had been similar, if not more heated, but she might not have been as strong as she'd let herself believe. She thought she'd been clear about her feelings, but in hindsight, she was still working through things in her own mind at that point.

What's done was done and there was no use in dwelling on things she couldn't change. She'd always been faithful to Jake, which was more than she could say of him. She hadn't brought it up when talking to him that night because the last thing she wanted to do was put him on the defensive, but there had been a time a few years before when Jake had been seeing a woman who worked in his office. He'd never been caught, but after a couple of months he couldn't handle the guilt and he came clean to Grace. She had forgiven him.

In light of recent events, it made more sense why she didn't feel the betrayal or jealousy she thought she should have felt. It had hurt. It wasn't fun to find out someone you trusted was going behind your back and lying to you, but that wasn't the same as jealousy. His infidelity had almost come as a relief on some level she didn't fully understand. At least he'd been passionate about someone. After they'd talked, things between them had improved somewhat. He'd put forth more effort in making her feel attractive and wanted. They probably had more sex in the month following his big confession than they'd managed since their first year of marriage.

As marriages tend to go when the spark isn't there, they'd slowly gone right back to their normal routine. She didn't think he'd cheated on her again, but she couldn't be sure. He'd certainly never shared the information with her if he had, and she hadn't paid enough attention to notice anything amiss. It was all water under the bridge at this point, and she was excited to move forward.

Grace closed her eyes and attempted to clear her mind so she could get a little sleep. The couch was comfortable, but after a few minutes of tossing and turning, she blew out a breath. "Sleep, sleep, sleep." She tried to command herself to let go, but nothing seemed to work. She covered her eyes with her hands and slowly drug them down her face until the tips of her fingers circled the outline of her lips. In the dark she could almost picture Bobbie in her mind. Her short dark hair a mess. Sweat trickling down her face after making love on a hot summer's day. That wolfish smile that made Grace weak in the knees. "God, Bobbie, what am I going to do about you?"

With the picture of Bobbie still in her mind, Grace imagined her legs wrapped around her at the restaurant. Bobbie's large warm hands creeping up her thighs toward the very place she needed her most. God, her lips were pure sex as they possessively pressed against her eager mouth. Lost in her fantasy, Grace slipped her hand across her stomach and into her panties, dipping a finger into increasingly wet folds.

She closed her eyes and imagined her finger was Bobbie's. Her clit throbbed with need as she lazily swept her finger through the wetness and down to her entrance. She couldn't remember the last time she had felt this aroused. She sat up on her elbow so she could reach farther, and slipped her middle finger into her warm center quickly followed by a second digit. The palm of her hand bumped her clit as she gently fucked herself.

She imagined Bobbie was on top of her, fingers buried inside her, claiming her, taking what she needed from her. Her lips were on her neck, whispering something Grace couldn't quite make out, but it didn't matter. Grace could feel her all over, filling the places that had been empty for so long.

She felt herself nearing the edge of orgasm and reached down with her other hand to rub more vigorously on her clit. With the image of Bobbie in her mind, she climaxed with an explosion. As her heart rate slowed, she lay there for a moment with her fingers still buried inside herself while she caught her breath.

Sated, she was finally able to relax and drift off to sleep.

CHAPTER SEVENTEEN

A my escorted the last patient of the day outside, then turned to lean against the front door and let her body limply slide down to collapse on the floor.

"Stop being so dramatic, you big baby." Lena winked at her as she signed the notes on her last file and dropped it on top of the pile. "Grace, you really need to pull this place into the future. I can't believe we're still doing paper files at this point. The trees, woman. You're forcing us to kill trees."

Grace laughed, then helped Amy to her feet and brushed her off. "It's not my fault Doc Randolph is about ninety years old and doesn't trust computers. Why would you want to rely on data that can be backed up in several different places when you have the guarantee that everything will being perfectly safe on a flammable material like paper?"

Lena and Amy laughed as they started the process of ensuring everything was turned off and secured for the night.

"If I have to treat one more dog for fleas, I'm going to scream." Lena removed her white coat and hung it on the hook behind the counter. "Let's go out for drinks, ladies. We don't have to work tomorrow, and I could sure let off some steam. You guys can be my wingmen or ladies or whatever. Some lucky person isn't going to know what a wordsmith they've found tonight."

Grace wrote Jake a quick message to let him know she wouldn't be home until late. She paused before pressing send. Did she owe him a message? Would it be undermining everything they discussed if she then checked in with him like it was still his business? As if he had any say in what she did. She pushed send before she overthought it. Even if he was only a roommate she would give him the courtesy of letting him know so he wasn't concerned when she didn't show up at her regular time. It was a matter of respect.

"Let's go, ladies. First drink is on me." Grace laughed as the other two predictably cheered. She wasn't one to drown her problems in alcohol, but tonight she was willing to try anything.

They all piled into Amy's car for the ride to the bar. As soon as she turned the key, a wall of sound blasted them with New Kids on the Block. Grace burst into giggles in the back seat as Amy frantically messed with the dials trying to hide her shame. "I never pegged you for a New Kids fan, Amy," Grace said. "Not that we all don't secretly love them."

Amy's cheeks flushed. "Secretly is the key word there."

"You're in a safe place, my friend, crank it up," Lena said. Amy hit play and they all rocked out to "Step by Step" as they drove the short distance to the bar.

Two hours and three pitchers of margaritas later, they were feeling pretty good. Lena had already received drink offers from not just one but two separate men, but her sights were set on a cute blond woman sitting at the bar. "How do I look?" she asked her wing-women.

"Beautiful, and she would be an idiot to turn down someone who is not only totally hot but also fixes puppies. Who could resist that?" Grace said as she checked to make sure Lena's hair was perfect. After several margaritas, she wasn't sure if she was helping or hurting Lena's chances.

"At least if she turns me down, I have one of those guys as a backup plan. It's been too long and Dr. Lena needs some lovin' tonight." She sauntered away from them toward the leggy blonde at the bar.

Grace and Amy almost knocked the table over laughing at her "sexy walk" as she left them. "I love that girl," Grace said.

"Me, too. We have such an awesome crew. I love you guys," Amy slurred. "So now that we're away from the office and we have a little social lubricant, I have to ask, what's the plan with Jake? If you are separated, then why did he all of a sudden show up and practically pee on your feet to claim you? That's a little vet humor, by the way." They both burst into laughter, and Grace slipped off her tall chair onto the floor. That only caused another bout of laughter.

"I'm on the dirty floor." Grace frowned as she looked around at the sticky carpet she was sitting on. Amy knelt down to help her back up to her seat. The later in the evening it got, the louder the music was and the more people were crowded into the tiny bar. "Let's get a booth before they're all taken. I'm going to end up injuring myself at this tall table. Should we let Lena know we're moving?"

They both looked over where Lena seemed to be making progress with the girl at the bar. She was whispering something into her ear as the blonde smiled a very pleased smile. "Let's leave her to her hunt. She'll find us later," Amy said. She grabbed her purse in one hand and helped Grace off her chair with the other.

Once they were settled into a booth, Amy asked her question again. "So spill. What's the plan with Jake?"

Grace rested her head on the table in exasperation. "Jake, ugh. I don't even know what to say. We talked the other night, and at least I know we're finally on the same page." Without lifting her head from the table, she turned toward Amy and gave her a weak smile. The coolness of the Formica felt good on her cheek. "I feel like I'm breaking his heart and it makes me hate myself."

"Don't you think remaining in a loveless marriage until one of you finally has enough and you end up hating each other is much worse? Isn't it better to get it all out in the open now and be able to salvage a friendship before it's too late?"

"Yeah." She knew she sounded pathetic, but she needed a minute to feel sorry for herself and her situation and Amy seemed game to listen. Amy rubbed Grace's arm and gave her a sympathetic look.

"Margaritas?" Grace quietly asked as tears threatened to spill from her eyes. Amy raised the empty pitcher toward the waitress and mouthed "Please" when she had her attention.

"I'm in love with Bobbie," Grace mumbled, sliding her warm cheek across the table to find another cool spot.

"I know, sweetie," Amy said with a look of sympathy.

Grace groaned and flipped her head so her other cheek could be cooled. "I don't know what I'm going to do, Amy. I'm like really, really in love with her and she's in love with me, too." Grace sat up and slid her hand across the table to pull Amy's hand to her. "Tell me what to do."

"You need to fix this thing with Jake," Amy said. "I know you've talked to him, but you need to file for divorce. You can move in with John and me if you need to. We have a spare bedroom. John snores so loud you may want to get earplugs though. You can hear it through the walls. There's nowhere to hide."

Grace laughed and Amy joined in as the pitcher of margaritas arrived.

"Next, you need to talk to Bobbie and let her know how you feel but make it clear that you have to take care of this situation with Jake before you can even think about dealing with feelings for her. "

"You give remarkably good advice for someone who can't even sit up straight."

"It's a gift," Amy joked. "What about your mom?"

Grace was confused what her mother had to do with anything. "What about my mom? Jake's too young for her."

"Grace, no, you're disgusting."

"What does she have to do with anything?"

Amy traced a finger down her glass to cut through the condensation. "Grace, do you promise not to get mad and to hear me out?"

"Okay…" Grace didn't like the direction this conversation was going, but she didn't want Amy to not feel comfortable talking to her about anything. "Am I going to hate this?"

Amy smiled. "No, I'm sorry, it's not like that. I just wonder if you think any of these issues you're dealing with have anything to do with your mom."

"Of course." Grace knew without a doubt that many of her issues were directly related to her mom and the rejection she'd always felt. "I've never been good enough for her and it has absolutely held me back from asking for the things that I want, the things that I need in my life. Knowing that doesn't make me braver though."

"Maybe the only bravery you need is to let go of the resentment you feel toward her for what she isn't able to give you and realize that you don't need her approval to live a happy life. You're the one who matters in this equation, not your mom, not Jake, not Bobbie for that matter. You. Beautiful, funny, smart Grace."

Grace sat silently and thought about what Amy had said. It was something she'd thought about a million times before, but Amy's drunken wisdom resonated with her somewhere deep inside. The scared and lonely little girl inside her felt something shift. Of course, it might have just been the margaritas.

"I hear what you're saying, but I'm not sure I can completely process it all right now."

Amy laughed and flagged down another waitress. "I think we're going to need another pitcher."

Two hours later, they had ordered another pitcher of drinks. When the waitress returned she gave them a stern look. "Okay, ladies," she said, "this is the last one. You're both cut off and so is your friend at the bar." They all looked over at Lena who was straddling her conquest like she was going for eight seconds. This sent them into another laughing fit as they poured their last drinks into glasses.

When they were ready to leave, they found Lena who told them she would get a ride with her new friend.

"We need to get an Uber," Amy said. "There's no way we can drive like this." They leaned on each other as they made their way out to the sidewalk in front of the bar.

"I know who will give us a ride," Grace said excitedly.

Amy pulled her phone from her pocket. "John will get us. I'll call him."

Grace waved Amy off as she selected a number from her contacts and put it on speaker so Amy could hear.

CHAPTER EIGHTEEN

B obbie woke from a deep sleep to her phone ringing. She snatched it from the nightstand and looked at the time. She was sure any phone call at this ungodly hour must be an emergency. When she saw who the call was from, her heart sank. "Grace, are you okay?" Panic caused her stomach to roll as she fought through the fog of sleep to understand what Grace was saying.

"It's me, Grace," Grace said through giggles. "You totally already knew that." Bobbie could hear the laughter of someone who wasn't Grace in the background.

"Are you drunk, Grace? Where are you?" Bobbie was concerned now. She knew the bars would all be letting out soon and worried Grace wasn't sober enough to realize she wasn't in a safe situation.

"Can you take us home? To our home? Amy to her home and me to my mom's home?"

Bobbie could hear them laughing, but Grace hadn't told her where they were yet. "Where are you? You have to tell me where you are so I can come get you guys."

"Isn't she the best, Amy?"

Bobbie threw on clothes and headed out the door to her truck. "Try to focus, Grace. Where are you so I can come and pick you up?"

"We had margaritas," Grace answered. "Lena needed wingmen, women, wing-women, and we came here, but she went home with the hot blonde at the bar."

Bobbie knew Lupe's had five-dollar pitchers of margaritas on Saturdays so she suspected they might have gone there. "Are you at Lupe's, downtown?" she asked.

"We're at Lupe's, downtown," Grace answered.

Bobbie couldn't help but smile. Grace was a funny drunk. She hoped she would have the opportunity to experience that Grace in a much safer setting in the future. "I'm on my way. You guys stay right where you are. I'm almost there." Bobbie pulled onto the street with Lupe's and saw them both sitting on the ground, leaning against each other for support.

When she reached the restaurant, she pulled into a spot and jumped out. "Hey, girls, looks like you had a fun evening." She helped them to their feet and into the waiting car.

"You're the best Bobbie," Amy said from the back seat. Bobbie smiled and looked in her rearview mirror just as Amy's head fell back and she started to snore.

Grace laughed at Amy and turned her attention to Bobbie as they drove. "Amy lives in the blue house, but that's all I know for sure."

"Do you know where the blue house is?" The town wasn't big, but she needed more than "blue house" to know where to go.

"Near the firehouse, on the street with the park. It's a woman's name or something." Grace leaned over the center console and rested her head on Bobbie's arm as they drove. "You're really mad at me."

Bobbie sighed and bent to kiss the top of Grace's head. "We'll talk about all that later."

"I'm sorry I didn't tell you about Jake. I didn't know how to explain. Please don't hate me."

The sadness in Grace's voice tugged at Bobbie's heart. She was mad. There was no getting around that, and she knew they had a lot of talking to do, but this wasn't the time or the place to hash that out.

"It's going to be okay, Gracie. You know I could never hate you. You're stuck with me."

Grace smiled, squeezed Bobbie's arm tighter, and closed her eyes. A few minutes later, Bobbie was able to find the Millers' house on Rebecca Way and helped Amy to the porch while Grace waited in the truck. Amy's husband, John, answered the door sleepy-eyed and confused.

"Hey, baby," Amy said. "Bobbie brought me home because I had a margarita."

John took Amy from Bobbie and kissed her cheek. "Looks like you had a couple of margaritas, my love." He helped her up the last step into the house and turned to wave good-bye. "Thanks, Bobbie, I'm John Miller by the way. You don't happen to know where her car is parked, do you?"

Bobbie shook John's hand and looked back to make sure Grace was still okay in her truck. "I picked them up at Lupe's so I suspect it's going to be near there. Sorry I can't give you more details. They were in front of the bar when I found them."

John thanked Bobbie profusely and helped Amy into the house. Bobbie climbed back into her truck to find Grace had fallen asleep. She wasn't exactly sure where to take her, but thought it best to take her to her mother's. The Hammonds' house was the very last place Bobbie wanted to be, but she didn't want to take Grace back to her place and cause more problems if Jake found out.

When she pulled into the large circular drive of the gigantic home, Bobbie flashed back to the sleepovers they had there as kids before her parents found out they were doing more than just watching scary movies and freezing each other's bras. The Hammonds had never been fans of Bobbie and she was pretty confident Mrs. Hammond's feelings for her hadn't changed.

Bobbie turned off her truck and unbuckled their seat belts. She gently reached out and put her hand against Grace's cheek. "Are you okay, sweetie? We're at your house. Are you ready to head in and go to bed?"

"I love you, Bobbie," Grace mumbled, half asleep. "Let's go to bed. I drank too much."

Bobbie's heart jumped, and she realized after a moment that she was holding her breath. She rubbed Grace's cheek with her thumb and whispered back, "I love you, too."

Bobbie wiped the tears that had started to fall just as the porch light came on and the front door swung open. Jake came running out in boxers and a T-shirt with Mrs. Hammond on his heels.

"What are you doing here, Bobbie?" he asked.

Bobbie got out of the truck and walked around to the passenger side to help Grace out. "I got a call from Grace asking me to pick her and her friend up at the bar," Bobbie explained as she wrapped one arm behind Grace's back and slipped the other under her knees to lift her out of the truck while she slept. When she turned toward Jake and Mrs. Hammond, she saw a flicker of agitation cross Jake's face.

"I think we can handle things from here, Bobbie." The coldness in Mrs. Hammond's voice sent chills down Bobbie's spine.

"Why would she call you for help? I didn't even know you were friends." Jake seemed confused as he took Grace from Bobbie's arms.

Mrs. Hammond stepped forward and stood between Bobbie and the others. "I think you've done enough tonight. Please leave."

Bobbie ground her teeth trying to hold back a retort before turning to Jake. "I think she'll be fine, but she's going to have a hell of a hangover tomorrow morning. You're going to want to have her drink as much water as possible so—"

"I got it, thanks. You should probably leave," Jake said. With that, they turned and walked into the house, slammed the door, and cut off the porch light to leave Bobbie standing in the driveway alone and in the dark.

Bobbie shook her head and trudged back to her truck. Seeing Phyllis Hammond brought back anger she thought she'd long forgiven. It was always Phyllis Hammond, both her cold judgment and impossible standards, at the root of Grace's misery. Always had been.

CHAPTER NINETEEN

G race slowly opened her eyes long enough to let a tiny bit of light in before slamming them shut again with a moan. She couldn't clearly remember where she was or how she got there, but fuzzy details of the night before seeped into her foggy mind. Her painful, foggy mind. Oh God, why did she do this to herself?

She remembered going to Lupe's with Amy and Lena. She remembered margaritas. She remembered lots of margaritas. She remembered sitting in front of the restaurant with Amy wondering how they were getting home. Oh no, she remembered calling Bobbie but not exactly what she said to her. She remembered Bobbie picking them up. She remembered Bobbie being sweet and how relieved Grace was to see her. She remembered being in the car with Bobbie. She could vaguely remember Bobbie touching her cheek and how gentle and warm her hands were. She remembered hearing Bobbie say she loved her.

Grace sat straight up with the sheet over her head to block the light. The abrupt movement sent her stomach into a tailspin so she jumped from the bed and ran for the bathroom to deposit last night's margaritas in the toilet. She heaved over the bowl as the memory of her telling Bobbie that she loved her came flooding back followed by her mother and Jake being rude to Bobbie. She didn't remember exactly what they said, but she was certain it wasn't "thank you."

Anger gripped her chest like a fist as she heard Jake walk into the bathroom. He leaned down next to her and wiped her forehead with a warm cloth. "There, there, you're okay now. I'm going to take care of you. You're home." Grace glared at him before lowering her head back into the toilet and vomiting again.

When she thought she had finally emptied her stomach of its contents, she pulled herself up using the wall for support. With a groan, she crawled back under the covers and closed her eyes. A minute later, she felt the bed sink as Jake sat next to her and rubbed her back through the quilt. His kindness frustrated her, or maybe it was that she was frustrated with herself for allowing this to go on for so long. They hadn't been happy for years, but she'd never believed in her own strength enough to control her own destiny. Whatever it was, she couldn't deal with it feeling like death. Grace curled into a ball and allowed herself to fall back asleep.

Six hours later, she heard the door close and the sound of someone walking across the carpet toward her. She wasn't ready to attempt the light quite yet so she stayed under the blanket while she asked who it was. "It's your husband, silly. I brought you some water, Pepto-Bismol, and eggs. Are you ready to face the world?"

"Why are you still here, Jake?" Grace asked with no emotion in her voice. She felt the bed shift as Jake sat on the edge.

"What do you mean, why am I still here? I brought you something for your stomach. Sit up and I'll feed you some eggs." Jake loaded the fork with eggs and pulled the top off the Pepto so she could take a swig.

"I mean, why are you still here after our discussion the other night? Why haven't you gone back to Seattle?" Grace's head felt like it might actually explode, and words at this point hurt more than they were worth.

"I'm here because you obviously can't take care of yourself. I'm here because you think it's okay to just go out with friends and get wasted."

"What the fuck, Jake?" Grace felt dizzy as her anger bubbled to the surface and blood rushed to her head.

She felt him get off the bed, and heard his heavy footsteps as he paced back and forth across her floor.

"What the hell is going on with you, Grace? Why are you doing this?"

"Are you fucking kidding me? Are we going to pretend like we didn't just have this conversation the other night just like we're going to pretend we didn't talk about this in Seattle before I left?" The floodgates had opened and Grace knew there was no stopping it. "I can't do this anymore, Jake. I can't do it. I feel like I'm losing my mind. You aren't listening to a goddamn thing I say, and what's worse, you aren't listening to yourself because a happily married man doesn't see other women. That's just not how happy marriages work."

"Don't talk to me about women when you come home in the middle of the night with some bitch who obviously has feelings for you." Jake was yelling now as well.

"First of all, Bobbie only picked Amy and me up at the bar and brought us home, you know that. Second, don't be a dick. Bobbie was only trying to help."

"Why would you call someone else and not me? I'm your husband, Grace. You need to come home so we can work this shit out." Jake was almost pleading with her.

"You aren't listening to me, Jake. I'm not going back to a loveless marriage. I'm done. I'm done pretending that I don't need love. I'm done listening to you pretend that you're happy. I'm done arguing with you every fucking day. I'm done. I don't have to do it anymore so I'm out."

Between the emotions and the effort of speaking, Grace felt like she was going to die. She really wished she was in better shape when she finally found the strength to say what she needed to say, but maybe she needed to be this low, in this much pain to push her over that edge.

Ridiculously, she was still buried under the covers. She didn't hear anything but assumed Jake was still there because she hadn't heard him leave. She slowly peeked out from under the blanket and squinted to focus on Jake as he silently stood at the end of the bed staring at her.

"Jake? Are you listening to me?" She pulled the blanket all the way off and sat up. "I told you before I left Seattle that things weren't working and that I needed space. I told you I needed space, and once again you completely ignored me by coming down here without any notice, and practically moving into my mother's house. What did you think would happen?"

Jake's face was red with anger and sweat dripped down his forehead. "Well, excuse me if I'm trying to make this marriage work," he yelled. "One of us has to."

"No, they don't. Nobody needs to try to make it work because it isn't going to work," Grace said. "Sure, you're Mr. Wonderful now because you're trying to win me back, but we all know what would happen if I did allow this to continue. We would both go back to living our separate lives. You would work all the time and be out at all hours of the night and I wouldn't care because when you're home we just argue. We argue because we're not happy and no amount of force is going to make this work. We just can't do it. I'm not doing it, Jake. I'm not going to sit around and become my mom, bitter and pissed off at the world."

"I had no idea you thought so poorly of me, Grace," her mother said from the door. "If I'm so horrible, may I ask why you are living under my roof and eating my food?"

"You're absolutely right, Mother. I shouldn't be here." Grace knew things were not going well and would only get worse so she stood on unsteady legs and began placing her things in a bag. She hadn't brought much more than clothes so it didn't take long to empty her drawers and grab her toiletries.

"What do you think you are doing, Grace Anne? Where do you think you're going to go, to live with that perverted rancher?"

"What rancher?" Jake asked, looking completely confused.

Her mother looked like she was going to destroy a building she was so angry. "That damn Roberta Del Ray lesbian," she said through pinched lips.

"Who's Roberta Del Ray?"

Grace shook her head and sat on the edge of the bed. "She's talking about Bobbie, Jake. Bobbie and I were girlfriends in high school. My parents found out and sent me to boarding school. My mother would rather only see me twice a year than have someone find out their perfect daughter was a lesbian."

"A lesbian?" Jake asked. "You're not a lesbian. Tell your mom you aren't a lesbian, Grace."

"I'm a lesbian, Jake," she said. "My biggest regret is not standing up to my mother sooner. It would have saved us both so much heartache, and I'm truly sorry for that. I should have never pulled you into this circus. Please know there was no malice to my actions."

"Grace…" Jake just stood there as Grace gathered her things and walked out the door. Her car was still at the clinic from the night before so she started walking toward Amy's house with her bags in tow. Once she was out of sight of her mother's house, she pulled her phone from her pocket and called Amy.

"Hello," Amy said with a very gravelly voice.

"Can I stay at your house?" Grace asked through tears that were starting to fall faster and faster. "I just left Jake and can't stay at my mother's any longer." She sobbed.

"Of course you can stay with us," Amy said. Grace could tell she was whispering something to John. "Are you at your mom's now?"

"I'm walking down the street toward your house." She knew Amy's house was at least two miles away, but she was walking in the general direction.

"Hang tight, we're on our way."

CHAPTER TWENTY

Grace rested her head on Amy's lap as the tears streamed down her face. John and Amy had found her dragging her bag about a mile from her mom's and brought her back to their house. That had been hours ago and Grace still couldn't stop crying.

"Why does all this stuff have to be so hard?"

Amy ran her fingers through Grace's hair. "Hey, at least the ball is rolling, right?"

"I know and I really am glad. I don't regret anything I said, but it's just been such an emotional few days. I feel like a rag that's been wrung out and left to dry."

"Well, drink some water and take a nap. I know I should do the same. I'm too old to drink like we did last night, but it sure was fun."

"Was John mad at you?" Grace asked.

"No, why would he be mad? He thought it was funny and was very happy that Bobbie got us home safely, but he isn't mad."

Grace sat up and leaned back against the pillows propped on the headboard. "You're a lucky woman, Mrs. Miller. You have a good man there. Even if he is a lawyer."

Amy laughed and shoved Grace. "Even lawyers know how to love sometimes."

They both giggled and then sat in comfortable silence for a minute before Grace spoke.

"Tell me some of your problems so I can try to fix them and we can pretend I don't have any of my own."

"John wants to try to make a baby."

Grace grinned but did her best to control her excitement. "And how do you feel about babies?"

"I really, really want a baby. I've always wanted to be a mom, and John would make an incredible dad. I really want to, but…" Amy pushed out a breath and collapsed against the pillows. "I'm not sure I'm ready to give up my freedom, and let's be honest, you're a slave to those little suckers for at least eighteen years. My more immediate concern is lugging that thing around for nine months and then pushing this fucking bowling ball out of my pussy. And cussing, I won't be able to cuss anymore. I love cussing. I love my pussy. I love all the things about my life just the way it is, but I also really want this other life where I can be a mom and teach them to play ball. John sucks at sports so thank God they'll have a sporty mom. I want to take them camping and teach them all about music…"

"You may want Auntie Grace to teach them about music. Their mom listens to New Kids on the Block a bit too enthusiastically." They both cracked up at that.

"Okay, Auntie Grace, you're in charge of music. I want all that so much, but I'm scared."

Grace reached out her arm so Amy could rest her head on her shoulder. "Listen, I totally get it. That is a massive decision, but I've never talked to anyone who wanted to be a parent that regretted having kids. It's obviously difficult and isn't for the weak of heart, but you guys will be the best parents and you and the baby will have the absolute best support system ever. I expect auntie time with Baby Miller so their parents can catch their breath, and I get my baby fix without having to push a bowling ball out of my pussy."

"Thanks, asshole," Amy squealed. That set them off into another round of laughter. They heard a soft knock on the door as John poked his head in. "Are you girls okay in here?"

"We're talking about how you want to ruin my pussy," Amy said.

John looked from Grace to Amy, obviously not sure exactly how to respond.

"She means by making her push a baby out it, you weirdo." Grace laughed and threw a pillow at him.

"Phew," John dodged the fluffy object. "I wasn't sure what exactly you guys were talking about, and I was a little concerned I had done something wrong."

Grace and Amy laughed and invited him to sit on the bed with them. "You do all the right things, but unfortunately, that is something I have to do on my own. Trust me, if I could give that task to you, I wouldn't hesitate."

John frowned and gave Amy a sympathetic look. "I'm sorry, baby. It's not something I want to do either, but I would take one for the team if I could. I feel bad that all I have to do is have a few orgasms and then you have to do all the hard stuff. I promise to make it up to you with back rubs and I'll wait on you hand and foot."

"And don't worry about the clinic. We'll for sure struggle without your awesomeness, but you take as much time as you need," Grace added.

"You two are making it difficult to talk myself out of this baby." Amy laughed.

Grace and John gave each other a knowing smile as he stuck out his hand for a sly high five.

"Grace needs help divorcing Jake so she can live happily ever after with Bobbie Del Ray," Amy blurted out.

It took John a minute to catch up. "Um, okay. I can help you with whatever you need, Grace. Have you served him divorce papers yet?"

"Nice deflection, buddy," Grace said as she gave Amy a dirty look. "I haven't served him anything. I was hoping it would all just go away, but apparently the law doesn't work that way."

John laughed. "No, thankfully, or I would be out of a job."

Grace picked at a string on her shorts as she talked. She knew the battle ahead was going to be difficult, and she wanted to avoid as much frustration as possible. "What do I need to do to get the ball rolling and how can I make it go easily?"

"I can't guarantee that it will be easy, but I will help you through the entire process. You won't be alone."

Grace hugged John and pulled out a paper and pen to take notes. "Where do I start?"

"First, you need to decide how much you're willing to give up. If he's an ass, you're going to have to fight him for absolutely everything you want."

Grace wrote on her paper.

"I don't care about much. I want my stuff of course, but he can have most of the rest. I really don't want to make this a big fight. At the end of the day, I love him and hope to salvage some sort of friendship from the mess we've created."

"Okay, well, things like your house, cars, stuff that was most likely purchased with joint money are open for negotiation."

Amy squeezed Grace's hand. "Everything will be fine, Grace. Figure out what's important to you, and then John will prepare the paperwork so you can file."

Grace jotted a few things that came to mind that she wanted to ask for.

John smiled at her notes. "Lists keep me from freaking out," Grace said. "I'm starting a list for Amy. One, no more margaritas until after baby is born."

John and Grace busted up laughing at that, but Amy's eyes went wide. "I forgot about that part of making babies. No margaritas or pot until after the silly thing is done feeding off me like a little tick. That's it, John, we're figuring out how you're going to make this baby."

"Technically, I will be making the baby since it's my sperm—" John began but was cut off with a pillow to the head.

"You aren't making shit, mister. You're fucking coming in my vagina and then walking away until it's a fully created human. The butter doesn't brag to the baker about how he made the cookies. I'm the fucking baker in this scenario and your sperm is the butter."

John looked like a scolded puppy. "I got that part. You're right, my liege. I will be your slave as long as you need me to be."

"That's right you will." Amy folded her arms over her chest and gave Grace a wink.

"I think I'm going to go for a drive now that the alcohol is out of my system. Can I borrow your car since mine is at the clinic?"

"You bet," Amy said. "Take your time, John and I might start trying to make a baby."

Grace slipped on her shoes and quickly walked toward the door. "Text me when it's safe to come back. I really don't want to accidentally witness any shenanigans between you two."

CHAPTER TWENTY-ONE

Whoa there, cow, you're okay." Bobbie slowly approached the animal where it was tied up in a stall. While checking the herd that morning, she had noticed this one was lame and brought her back to the barn for care. Cattle became lame for one reason or another all the time, and one of the most important aspects of Bobbie's job was to notice problems quickly and remedy them before infection set in.

It had been a long day, and Bobbie was finding it difficult to focus on her duties after the events of the night before. Grace had said she loved her. As in present tense, loved her. Not that Bobbie had her heart or that she would always hold a special place in her life, but that she *loved* her. She doubted Grace would remember the admission through her alcohol soaked haze, but Bobbie would never forget. "What am I going to do, Riley?" Her constant companion wagged her tail at the mention of her name.

Bobbie leaned her shoulder against the cow to force her to take weight off the bad hoof so she could pull it up for inspection. She was careful to stay on the animal's side and not get too far behind her where she could possibly be kicked and suffer real damage. As she inspected the interdigital space on the hoof, she noticed a fair sized rock jammed in there deep. She pulled her hoof pick from the back pocket of her jeans, and carefully began to pick the rock out.

What was she supposed to do about Grace now? It took everything she had to not call her to make sure she was okay after her night on the town. Bobbie smiled at the memory of Grace and Amy laughing their fool heads off on the phone. It was stressful last night when it was happening, but now that Grace was safe, Bobbie allowed herself a chuckle at their antics.

She loved to hear Grace laugh. It filled her soul in a way she just couldn't explain and she wanted it in her life all the time. Why did she have to be married? How could the Universe be so cruel?

"Whoa, cow." Bobbie steadied herself as the cow stepped sideways and pushed her closer to the wall of the barn. Once the animal seemed to settle, she continued working to dislodge the stone.

Bobbie's stomach clenched as she thought about the fact that Jake had taken care of Grace all these years. Jake had been there to hear her laughs, he'd wiped her tears when she cried, he'd been the one to make love to her... Bobbie realized she'd let herself get too far behind the cow the moment she saw the leg jerk toward her and immediately felt an intense pain in her side before being thrown through the air toward the barn wall.

Darkness. Bobbie felt like she was being woken from a deep sleep but couldn't remember ever going to bed. The smell of hay and dirt helped pull her from the fog and let her focus on her surroundings. She realized her limp body was pressed against the wall of the barn and registered an excruciating pain in her side, and in the back of her head as Riley licked her cheek. "I'm okay, girl. Thank you for trying to fix me." She weakly reached up and put her hand on Riley's head to reassure her she was okay.

She attempted to move but was too dizzy and couldn't seem to catch her breath. She rubbed the back of her head and, feeling something sticky, realized she was bleeding. With a groan, she admitted defeat and pulled her cell from her pocket. She squinted her eyes to make out the blurry numbers as she called her lead ranch hand. He picked up after a couple of rings. "What's up, Bob?" he asked.

"I'm an idiot," she answered, wincing in pain. "Can you come over to the barn and help me get in my ATV? I'm going to need you to take over looking after this cow for me as well."

"No problem, boss," Jensen answered with concern in his voice. "Are you sure we don't need to call out an ambulance? You sound pretty shook up."

"I'll be just fine." The last thing Bobbie wanted was a bunch of attention and a trip to the hospital. She hated hospitals. "I just need some anti-inflammatory meds and ice and I'll be good as new. You know it's going to take more than some ol' cow to keep me down."

"I know it and that's the problem. You're just as stubborn as your old man." Jensen didn't mean it as a jibe, but the comparison stung anyhow. Bobbie's dad was so stubborn he'd kept working through the pain in his chest until the horses were safely put away in the barn, protected from the impending storm, before finally walking into his house, removing his wet jacket and boots, and collapsing in the hallway of a major heart attack. When Bobbie's mother found him on the floor, she hadn't wasted any time calling an ambulance. But help came too late. He'd been gone for several minutes by the time the paramedics arrived. Bobbie struggled to not be angry with him for refusing to take better care of himself. Maybe she was more like her father than she cared to admit.

"I promise if it seems like something major, I'll give you or Mom a call." Bobbie knew he wasn't satisfied, but she had no idea what to else she could say to make him trust that she was just a little banged up.

Jensen arrived a few minutes later and helped her to her feet. "How in the world did this happen?" he asked as he walked her to the ATV. He knew as well as Bobbie that being aware of where you were and how the animal could potentially hurt you was basic ranching and should be instinctual at this point.

"I let my mind drift off and wasn't paying attention. Rookie mistake that I won't be repeating anytime soon. That old girl gave me a swift reminder to keep my head out of the clouds." Bobbie was embarrassed and glad Jensen didn't press for details. They were friends, but he wasn't someone Bobbie would share girl problems with. "Can you finish up with that cow for me? She looked to be lame in her right rear hoof, and I found a good size rock caught in there. I was fishing it out when she decided she didn't like me messing with her and kicked me away."

"Will do." Jensen buckled an unsteady Bobbie into the seat. "You let me know you're okay once you're settled. Are you sure I can't take you to the hospital?"

Bobbie smiled at him. "I'll be okay. I appreciate the concern. If I have any doubt, I won't be an idiot. I'll get straight to the doc." She knew he wasn't comfortable letting her drive, but the longer she sat, the more painful her side and head felt, so with a weak wave she and Riley headed home.

As they approached her house a few minutes later, Bobbie could see her mom waiting in the driveway. She knew right away Jensen had called ahead to warn her. She didn't want to make her mom worry but had to admit the thought of her being there was a relief.

"Looks like Jensen ratted me out," she joked as she turned off the ATV and her mom came around to help her into the house. Moving was difficult, and she found that she was gasping for breath. She couldn't tell if her dizziness was from slamming her head against the barn wall she'd used to stop the trajectory of her airborne body or the pain of her possibly broken ribs.

Her mom looked concerned as Bobbie leaned on her more and more for balance. "I think we need to get you to the hospital, Peanut."

"I'm okay, Mama. I just need some rest."

"Dammit, Bobbie, don't try to be a hero. You and your brothers are all I've got."

Bobbie struggled to catch her breath as her legs grew weaker. She knew if she could just get into the house and sit down she'd start feeling better. Her mom was helping her up the front steps when she heard a car pull up behind them. She turned to see who had arrived, and as her body pivoted, a stabbing pain shot through her and the world began to spin. With stars swimming in front of her eyes, she felt herself being lowered to the ground as her mother's worried voice called for help.

CHAPTER TWENTY-TWO

Grace rolled down the windows and took a deep, cleansing breath as she drove toward the coast. The last couple of weeks had been stressful and the crisp air was like a shot of adrenaline. It was time to get her house in order, and she decided to start by apologizing to Bobbie about the night before.

She turned off the freeway and headed toward Bobbie's ranch. She knew she wasn't going to just make everything better by apologizing for the pain she'd caused, but she had to start somewhere. Bobbie deserved an explanation, and even though Grace wasn't exactly sure what she would say, she had to try to make her understand she never meant to hurt her by not telling her about Jake.

As she approached Bobbie's house, Grace saw her and her mother on the porch. She parked her car and was getting out when she saw Bobbie turn in her direction. Then, to Grace's horror, Mrs. Del Ray stepped forward to catch Bobbie in her arms before slowly lowering her limp body to the ground. She rushed to Bobbie's side.

"Bobbie? Sweetie? Can you hear me?" Grace's stomach rolled as she fought back panic.

With a deep breath, she gathered her nerves and relied on her training to slip into doctor mode. She pulled her sweater off to place under Bobbie's head and began a cursory check for injuries. "What happened to her, Audrey?" she asked when Bobbie's mother knelt beside her.

"Jensen called and said she'd been kicked by a cow in the barn and was on her way to the house. He said she wouldn't let him call the doc."

Grace could hear the fear in Audrey's voice and reached out a hand to comfort her. "She's going to be okay. You and I are going to take care of her together."

"Can you help me into the house?" Bobbie's eyes fluttered open, their blue depths clouded by pain.

"We're going to the hospital, baby. You can't just sit in your house. We have to get an X-ray to make sure you didn't puncture something important when you were kicked. Did you hit your head?" Grace ran her fingers through Bobbie's hair and found a little patch of dried blood on the back of her skull.

"Gracie?" Bobbie asked, eyes cloudy with confusion.

"It's me, sweetie. What have you done to yourself? It looks like I got here just in time. It's going to take two of us to force you to get help it appears. Let's put you in the car so we can get you checked out."

Now that Grace was confident Bobbie could be moved safely, she wanted to get her to the hospital as fast as possible. She couldn't see what was going on inside her body and Grace didn't want to take any chances. Things could rapidly get worse if something internal was damaged.

They loaded Bobbie into the back of Grace's car and sped down the dirt road toward the freeway as Bobbie faded in and out in the back seat. "It hurts when I breathe. Mama, I don't feel good," Bobbie said. Audrey pulled a plastic bag out of her purse and handed it to Bobbie just in time for her to vomit into it instead of the car Grace had borrowed from Amy.

"Thanks for that, Audrey," Grace said. Bobbie was obviously uncomfortable in the back seat, and the sight of her broke Grace's heart. "We're almost there, and they'll give you some pain medication at the hospital that will help."

"Is that you Gracie?" Bobbie asked. Audrey looked at Grace with definite concern in her eyes.

"She'll be okay, Audrey. She's showing signs of a concussion. I felt a little dried blood on the back of her head. Do you know how that happened?"

"Jensen didn't mention anything, but I don't think he was there until after all the action." Audrey looked scared to death, and Grace knew she needed to stay calm and confident for her sake.

"I suspect she has a concussion and at least a couple of broken ribs. They're very likely going to do some X-rays of her ribs and a CT scan of her head just to make sure everything is where it's supposed to be, and then she'll be off her feet for a few weeks while she recovers," Grace told Audrey with more confidence than she felt.

Grace parked in a space next to the ER door, then got out to help Audrey with Bobbie.

"Hey, Gracie," Bobbie said.

Grace smiled and carefully wrapped an arm around her middle. "Hey, Bobbie."

"I'm really glad you're here."

"I'm really glad I'm here, too."

Grace supported Bobbie's weight as they entered the ER. Once the automatic doors slid open, she called for help which caught the attention of the nurses at the front desk. They quickly appeared with a wheelchair. Grace helped Bobbie sit and relayed all the information she had regarding the accident. She could hear the fear in her own voice as she spoke, but the nurses assured her they would take good care of Bobbie and then whisked her down the hall for tests.

Grace felt completely alone as she watched them roll Bobbie away. When she was out of sight, Grace turned back toward the waiting room where she found Audrey sitting in a hard plastic chair near a fish tank, filling out paperwork. Ridiculously, Grace felt a pang of jealousy that it wasn't her responsibility to do essential things like that for Bobbie. She searched her jeans pocket and found enough change for one cup of coffee from the vending machine.

"Here you go, Audrey." She handed Bobbie's mother the warm cup of caffeine and sat in the chair next to her.

"Thanks. I filled out the paperwork to get her checked in," Audrey said.

Grace gave her a weak smile and nodded. "Thank you," she said. She took the clipboard from Audrey and walked it up to the desk. She wasn't exactly sure why she was thanking her since it wasn't like

Bobbie belonged to her, but it felt natural to say it. The pain of her situation shot through Grace at the thought of how badly she wanted Bobbie to belong to her.

Once the nurse confirmed that she had what she needed, Grace returned to the seat next to Audrey. She wasn't sure what to say to her. Now that they weren't actively caring for Bobbie, the tension between them was palpable. As the minutes passed, the waiting room filled with people waiting for word of their loved ones and then emptied, only to be filled and emptied again. Grace and Audrey sat in an uncomfortable silence until finally a doctor stood in the doorway.

"Roberta Del Ray's family?" the doctor called out, reading the name on the chart.

They stood and walked over to her. "That's us. I'm her mother, Audrey Del Ray."

"Hello, Mrs. Del Ray, I'm Dr. Fran Bishop. Let's sit and we'll talk about Roberta's status."

The doctor gestured toward an empty bank of chairs at the far end of the waiting area and Grace and Audrey anxiously sat across from her, desperate for an update.

"Roberta is doing well. She sustained two broken ribs on her right side and a concussion. I was told she was kicked by a cow?"

"That's right. She also goes by Bobbie," Audrey answered.

"Okay, Bobbie." The doctor made a note on the chart. "She isn't going to feel like it for the next few weeks, but she's lucky. We've had people come in with much worse injuries from similar accidents. She's going to be in quite a bit of pain for a week or two so you'll need to make sure she stays up on her anti-inflammatory pain medications. It's important to allow her to take deep breaths, so please don't put any kind of tight clothing or wrap around her body. For the concussion, rest. That's going to be the best medicine for all of her injuries, but especially the one to her head."

"Any chance you can lend me one of those beds with the restraints? I think I'm going to need it to convince her to rest," Audrey said.

Dr. Bishop chuckled. "I got that impression when I was talking to her. She seems to think she'll be up and about in a week, and I think that could be true to a certain extent, but she's going to find it difficult to breathe until those ribs heal, and she might suffer from bouts of dizziness. Someone will need to keep a close eye on her for the next twenty-four hours, waking her up occasionally and speaking to her. The brain will repair itself, but she has to rest to allow it to do that. If you notice any kind of slurred speech or anything else that concerns you, please call us immediately. The nurse will give you paperwork that will explain in more detail what to expect and what to look out for."

"Thank you, Doctor. May we see her now?" Grace asked.

"She's pretty out of it from the pain meds, but I'd be happy to take you to her if you would like."

Grace and Audrey followed the doctor down the hall to where Bobbie rested behind a curtain. "You can see her for a few minutes, and then we'll need one of you to come to the front desk to discharge her," the doctor told them.

Audrey walked up to Bobbie's hospital bed and wrapped her arms around her. "You ol' dummy. You scared the crap out of me. What if Grace hadn't shown up and I couldn't get you in the car by myself? You need to admit defeat sooner, you stubborn kid."

Bobbie gave Grace a surprised look over Audrey's shoulder as she let her mom vent her frustration. "I'm sorry, Mama. I didn't realize how injured I was at first. I knew I was in pain but just didn't know the extent of things until I tried walking up the stairs to the house. I'm sorry I scared you." Audrey planted kisses all over Bobbie's face before stepping back to give her space. "I'm going to take care of the bill while Grace stays with you. We're getting you home and you're sitting in your chair until I say it's okay for you to get out. Got it?" Audrey meant business, and Grace could see Bobbie knew there was no use in arguing with her about it.

"Yes, Mama," she said. After one more kiss on her forehead, Audrey turned and left Grace and Bobbie alone.

They looked at each other for a moment without moving or saying a word. Finally, Bobbie reached out her hand and Grace moved closer to take it. "You okay?" Grace asked.

"I'm fine. I'm sorry you had to be pulled into all of this."

Grace raised Bobbie's hand to her lips and kissed her open palm, savoring the warmth she found there. "I'm just glad you're okay. It could have been bad, Bobbie. I know I don't have to tell you that, but I just have to say it. What exactly happened?"

"I was in the stall, working a stone from a cow's hoof, and let myself get in a position where she could kick me."

"How in the world did you let that happen? I remember you scolding me when we were kids for doing that very thing."

"I wouldn't say I exactly scolded you but, yeah…I knew better. I just wasn't paying attention to what I was doing. My mind wasn't on what I was doing."

Grace worried she knew the answer but asked the question anyway. "What was on your mind?"

Bobbie gave Grace a weak smile. "You."

"Oh, Bobbie, what am I going to do with you?"

"Why were you at my house? I thought you were a dream at first."

"I came out to talk to you and apologize about last night. Jake and my mom were way out of line, and there's no excuse for the way they treated you. They were rude, especially when you actually came to my rescue, which I also want to apologize for." Grace covered her face, embarrassed. "I don't drink often, and I almost never get that drunk. I can't imagine what I must have said. I remember some things, but I'm still foggy on the details."

"You told me you loved me." Bobbie pulled Grace's hand from her face. "You said you loved me and I told you that I loved you."

A tear ran down Grace's cheek as she stared into hopeful eyes. Bobbie reached up and wiped the tear away. "You were funny, too. You guys are a handful, I can tell."

Grace smiled. "Amy and Lena are a bad influence."

"Sure, Amy and Lena are corrupting poor innocent Gracie." They both laughed, but Grace could tell the effort was causing Bobbie pain.

"Bobbie, Jake and I—" Grace started before she was interrupted by a nurse with a wheelchair ready to help Bobbie out to the car. "Okay, Ms. Del Ray, are you ready for your chariot?" Bobbie gave Grace an apologetic smile as the nurse helped her into the chair.

The ride back to Bobbie's was quiet. As they pulled up to the house, Grace could see Jensen waiting for them on the front porch. He stepped down and opened the back door as soon as the car rolled to a stop. "I knew you should have gone to the doctor. Why'd you scare us like that, you stubborn old goat?" His words were playful, but Grace could see real concern on his weather worn face.

"I know, I know. I've had an earful already. I don't need you mother henning me as well." Bobbie allowed him to help her out of the car. Grace pulled the folder with Bobbie's hospital paperwork from the front seat and followed them as they slowly made their way toward the front door.

"I've got it, Grace." Audrey gestured for the folder in her hands. "You don't need to stay. I think we can handle it from here. I can't thank you enough for your help today. I don't know what I would have done if you hadn't shown up."

Grace wanted to offer to stay longer, but she didn't get the impression Audrey would welcome her presence, no matter how thankful she was for the help earlier. "Okay. If you're sure there's nothing else I can do. Please let me know if there's anything at all you or Bobbie need. I'm happy to help in any way I can."

"You're very sweet, but I think we can handle it from here. I'm sure your husband will be wondering where you've gone off to." Audrey gave Grace a look that spoke volumes about her opinion of the situation.

"Right. Have a nice day, Audrey." Grace bit her lip to hold back the tears that threatened to fall as she climbed into her car and drove away.

CHAPTER TWENTY-THREE

Jensen carefully lowered Bobbie into her recliner as Riley resumed her post on the footrest. "Is there anything else I can do for you, Bob?" he asked as he tucked a blanket around her legs.

"You're quite the caregiver. I'm going to have to remember that the next time I'm sick." Bobbie closed her eyes and leaned back in her chair.

"This is a one-time deal. Don't get used to it. If you're done abusing me, I should head back out to finish what I was doing." Jensen squeezed Bobbie's arm and left her in her mother's capable hands.

"Where's Grace?" Bobbie asked.

"She had to go home but said to tell you good-bye," her mother said over the clank of ice cubes in the kitchen.

"That's weird she didn't tell me good-bye in person."

"I'm sure she had somewhere to be. Your brothers are never going to let you live this down." Her mom returned from the kitchen with an ice pack and ibuprofen.

"Let's just not tell them. Evan is already talking about setting up a drone system to monitor the land and check the fence. He's going to have me sitting at a desk if he gets his way," Bobbie said. She winced as she adjusted the pillow in her chair so it stopped pressing on her ribs.

"You'd never be satisfied at a desk. I suspect you'll be riding around double-checking everything from horseback when you're so old they have to tie you to the saddle. You're like your dad that way."

Bobbie laughed but knew her mother was right. She hadn't been able to sit still since she was a kid. She was always smart but struggled to stay in her seat and listen to someone lecture her. She loved most of the subjects and would read and study them on her own, but being trapped in a classroom without the ability to move around was torture. The inactivity required to recover from these injuries was going to be hell.

"You're going to sit here and keep this ice on your ribs until I tell you otherwise, and you're going to tell me what set your mind to wander when you should have been paying attention to what you were doing."

Truth be told, her distraction was part of the reason Bobbie had refused help when Jensen asked. She knew she would be questioned about what happened, and she was too embarrassed to confess she was daydreaming about a girl like a lovesick teenager.

Her mom sat patiently as she waited for Bobbie to explain. She knew there was no way around coming clean, but she did her best to delay the inevitable by swallowing her medication one at a time, inspecting each pill before popping it into her mouth.

"Enough stalling, daughter, let's hear it."

Bobbie rolled her eyes and set down her glass of water. "Are you seriously going to force me to talk about it?"

"Of course I am. You scared the dickens out of me, so the least you owe me is an explanation—although I'm pretty sure a certain veterinarian has something to do with it." Her mom leaned back on the couch, folding her arms over her chest in frustration.

"It's not her fault, Mama. I knew better than to let myself get distracted. You can't fault Grace for my inability to keep my head in the right place." Bobbie knew her mother would automatically want to place the blame on Grace, but it wasn't fair. If she couldn't keep her mind on her task she should have contacted Jensen and asked him to take over.

"Did something specific happen or is this just general lovesickness?" There was a hint of frustration in her mother's voice.

"Geez, Mama. You do know I'm an adult, right?" Bobbie felt her head throb as her anger threatened to bubble over. "I can't deal with this right now. I'm in pain all over, including my heart, and I don't need you lecturing me on my job or my love life." Bobbie pressed her fingers into her temples in an attempt to will her head not to explode.

"I'm sorry, sweetheart. You're right, you aren't a child and I have no right to question you. I love you, Bobbie, and it just hurts my heart to see you like this." She stood and walked toward the door. "If you decide you need someone to talk to, I'm here. I won't judge you or Grace, and I'll try to keep my opinions to myself. If you need anything, I'll be at the house."

Bobbie let out a deep sigh and grabbed her mother's hand as she walked past her chair. "Please sit down, Mama. I'm sorry I'm so grumpy. My head feels like I got shoved into a wall by a cow."

Her mother chuckled as she turned to sit back down on the couch, but Bobbie knew she didn't find humor in any part of what had happened.

"Grace and some friends went out drinking last night at Lupe's. They had a really good time, and several margaritas later, they weren't in any shape to drive home so Grace called to see if I could pick them up."

Her mom sat forward on the couch and placed her face in her hands. "Why wouldn't she call her husband? Why does she have to pull you into these situations?"

"Mama, I can't help but want to protect her, and when you do this, it just makes it more difficult. I know you're my mom and you love me, but I really need you to just be my friend right now. If you can't, I totally understand and don't have to talk to you about her. If you're willing to listen and not make this about Grace and the mistakes she's made, I could sure use a friend right now." Bobbie wanted to talk to someone about it and hoped her mom would understand.

"I'm sorry, Peanut. You're absolutely right. I promise I'll keep my trap shut." She leaned back against the couch cushions in defeat.

"I picked them up and dropped her friend Amy off before taking Grace to her mother's house. As I was trying to get her out of the car, Jake and Phyllis came out of the house asking where she had been and why I was the one she called to pick her up." Bobbie looked at her mother to see if she would keep her word and stay quiet. The effort was evident all over her face, but she held her tongue so Bobbie continued.

"Before we had gotten out of the car and all the drama had started, Grace told me she loved me. She was drunk and I don't think she meant to say it at the time, but she said it and I know she meant it. She loves me and I love her. She's married, and I'm not going to do something stupid and get involved with a married woman, but I know she doesn't love him. She's all I want in this world, and she's not mine to have. I should have asked for help today because I knew I was distracted, but I'm just not used to having distractions like this. I never lost focus when Dad died or when we were raising Evan or any other time in my life. Not like this. It was my fault and I knew better. I won't let it happen again, and I'm awful sorry I worried you."

Her mother wiped a tear from her cheek as she stood to kiss Bobbie on the forehead. "I love you, sweetheart. I was once in love myself and I remember how distracting and overwhelming that can be. I don't know what to say about the Grace situation other than you're going to have to have the patience of Job if she's the one. There are a lot of obstacles in front of you, but if you love each other as much as you say, nothing will be able to keep you apart. That being said, if she truly does love you, she'll move heaven and earth to be with you, including taking care of her business and getting out of the marriage she's already in. You deserve someone who will do whatever it takes to be with you."

"I know," Bobbie conceded. Knowing her mom was right didn't make the idea of staying away from Grace any easier. She would just have to trust that Grace wouldn't make her wait forever because, deep down, she was afraid she'd be willing to.

CHAPTER TWENTY-FOUR

Jake picked up on the third ring when Grace called a couple of nights after their argument. "Hello?"

"Hey, Jake, do you think we can get together to talk?"

There was a pause on the line and she worried they'd been disconnected. "Jake, are you there?"

"Where do you want to meet?"

She wasn't sure if he was still at her mom's and she wasn't ready to deal with mother-daughter issues yet so she decided to suggest a neutral place where they could talk without distractions. "How about the coffee shop at the country club?"

"Fine. I'll be there in an hour." Without so much as a good day, the call was disconnected.

An hour and a half later, she waved him over as he walked in the door of the coffee shop with a scowl on his face. "I got you a caramel latte, but we may want to ask them to heat it up at this point."

"It's fine." Jake sat across from her and took a sip of his drink. "What do you want to talk about, Grace? Should we start with how you've lied to me for our entire marriage or should we skip right to your affair with the rancher?"

Even though the accusations weren't technically true, they still cut deep, and Grace felt terribly guilty for having put Jake through a marriage that was essentially a lie. "You're right about me not being honest with you about being a lesbian. In my defense, I wasn't intentionally misleading you as much as telling myself I could live without happiness if it meant my parents would accept me."

"Goddamnit, Grace. You avoid conflict to the point you leave a trail of misery in your path. Get a fucking backbone. Be honest with yourself and maybe you'll stop breaking everyone's heart." Jake was getting angry, but at least he was keeping his voice down so he didn't draw too much attention.

"You're right. I need to learn to stand up for myself, and that is what I am doing now. I want a divorce, Jake."

His laugh sent shivers down her spine. "Of course you do. I suppose you and the rancher are going to ride off into the sunset and make lots of babies. What a fucking joke. Your mother isn't going to be happy. I hope you know what you're doing. She warned me this might happen."

"You're still living at my mom's house?" Grace was a bit surprised he would still be there.

"Where am I going to go? I didn't want to go back to Seattle until I knew what was happening with our marriage. I guess now that I know, I can go home and throw the rest of your shit in the garbage." Jake's face turned dark red as sweat trickled down his temple.

"This isn't about Bobbie."

"Really? It's not?"

Grace took a deep breath to control her frustration. It wasn't only about Bobbie, but she couldn't deny Bobbie was on her mind and a part of her motivation. The feelings Bobbie had stirred in her helped her realize how unhappy she was in her marriage and how much more she needed from life than Jake was able to offer. It wasn't Jake's fault. There were aspects of her failed marriage that greatly involved him, but a big part of her discontent was that she would never feel about him the way she felt about Bobbie.

"I haven't been having an affair with Bobbie. I'm not going to lie and say I don't have feelings for her because I do. I always have, but nothing has really happened between us."

"You don't sound very convinced," Jake said with a smirk on his face.

"We kissed," Grace admitted, embarrassed by her behavior.

"Of course you did." Jake shook his head. "I just don't understand, Grace. I don't understand why you would agree to marry me and then live with me for years as husband and wife when you were not only in love with someone else, you weren't attracted to me at all. How did you convince yourself that was okay?"

Grace knew she could remind him of the fact that he had done more than just kiss another woman but she decided to take the high road. This wasn't the time to bring up any more old wounds if they were going to move forward without obliterating any chance of salvaging a friendship. "You're right, and I have no excuse other than I was raised to put my own desires aside and be the person I was expected to be. It breaks my heart that you're feeling the brunt of my mistake, but I can't turn back the clock. You're wrong if you don't think I have and always will love you, Jake. I love you very much. I'm just not in love with you and for that, I'm sorry." Grace tentatively reached out a hand to place over his on the table.

"What are we supposed to do now?" Jake asked.

"Well, now I file for divorce and we split up our belongings. If we can work everything out and come to an agreement, then we can keep this out of the courts."

"Here we go. What is it that you want, Grace?" Jake pulled his hand off the table and looked like he was prepared for a fight.

"The fact that you would even ask, tells me you don't know me at all and a divorce is the absolute right thing for us to do." Grace was offended by his reaction. She had never been materialistic and didn't think he was going to want anything she asked for anyway.

"You're fucking taking my boat." Jake seemed to be grasping at the easiest thing to get angry about.

"I'm not taking your boat, Jake. We can discuss the value of all community property and divvy it up. I'm not looking for an exact dollar split. I don't want to be taken advantage of, but I also know there are things that are important to you and things that are important to me. Let's figure out what those are and put a value on them. That will make the things that are less important easier to split."

"You can have the convertible. I bought it for you and you can take it," Jake said. He seemed to be calming down a bit, and Grace was relieved to see they might actually be able to get through this without blood being spilled.

"How about this, I'll keep the convertible and you keep the boat. Deal?" Grace wanted to show that she was willing to be reasonable in hopes of inspiring him to do the same.

"Deal," Jake said with a smile, holding his hand out to shake.

"Things didn't work out between us, but we don't have make this any more difficult than it has to be." Grace kissed him on the cheek.

"I love you too, Grace, and I'm sorry I wasn't a better husband to you when I had the job. I know it couldn't have been easy for you when I was so distant." Jake seemed regretful. "I know part of this is that you're being true to yourself, but I also own the fact that I've known for years that you weren't happy and I waited until you were leaving before I tried to do anything about it. I know now that there wasn't anything I could have done to make our marriage work, but maybe if I'd tried harder before now, we both could have moved on sooner. I'm sorry."

"Let's start from the beginning and be friends," Grace suggested.

"Friends sounds good."

Grace felt silly for delaying talking to Jake as long as she did. With this first hurdle down, she felt like things were starting to come together.

CHAPTER TWENTY-FIVE

Grace leaned back in her office chair and stretched her arms above her head. The muscles in her back burned as she forced them into a different position. She'd been sitting at her desk doing paperwork for the better part of the afternoon and the words on her computer screen were starting to blur.

"What's up, Doc?" Amy walked into the room and stretched out on the couch in the corner. "My ass is killing me. We've got to get a better chair out there. I have no idea how Doc Randolph's front office lady sat there for thirty years and was still able to walk at the end of the day. No wonder she retired."

"I think she actually took her chair with her. She'd never sit in that piece of crap. It'd kill her back."

Amy groaned. "Why the hell am I dealing with it then? Don't you love me?"

Grace sat on the couch, pulling Amy's feet into her lap. "These socks are adorable."

Amy wiggled her toes at the compliment. "I know. I love cool socks. It's my thing."

"I thought shoes were your thing?"

"They're related items. Shoes and socks. It's a combined thing." Amy moaned her pleasure as Grace massaged her foot. "Damn, I really needed this. When are you going to be single because you give much better massages than my husband?"

"You couldn't afford me."

Amy laughed. "You're probably right. Have you talked to Bobbie lately?"

Grace sighed and switched to Amy's other foot. "We've texted a few times. Her mom has been taking good care of her and she seems to be feeling much better. It's always tough to tell with the stoic ones, but I think she's good."

"You haven't been out to see her?"

Grace was embarrassed to admit how much Bobbie's mother's dismissal of her after the hospital had scared her off. She understood that Audrey was merely being protective of her daughter but it stung just the same.

"After her mom told me to take a hike, I haven't been brave enough to go. Besides, between the clinic and dealing with Jake, I've had plenty on my plate."

"You've filed, though, and Jake is back in Seattle. So isn't that pretty much all over but the crying."

"It's a little more complicated than that." The last month had been a rollercoaster of emotions for Grace, but she and Jake had finally worked out most of the details and he'd gone home to Seattle to file for the divorce. Grace planned to follow him once Doc Randolph was back at the clinic, but in the meantime, she felt a little adrift.

Amy pushed herself up to sit cross-legged in front of Grace. "What's on your mind?"

Grace blew out a breath and stretched across the couch, resting her head in Amy's lap. "Is this okay?"

She needed comfort and Amy seemed happy to give it. "It's more than okay. I'm here for you, pal. Tell me what's causing the cute little wrinkles on your forehead."

"I feel like I'm trapped in the middle of my old life and my new life. Jake and I talked a lot. We talked more than we've talked in years. It reminded me of when we were first together and we would sit on the fire escape of my dorm room and smoke pot. We were such good friends then and I saw shadows of that old relationship for the first time in what feels like forever. Enough to make me think we might actually get out of this with a decent friendship."

"That's great." Amy threaded her fingers through Grace's hair and gently scratched her scalp.

"That feels good." Grace closed her eyes and let her body relax into the touch.

"So what's got you down?"

Grace rubbed her temples as she tried to put her thoughts into a coherent order.

"You don't regret the divorce, do you?" Amy asked.

"No, nothing like that. For sure nothing like that. I just don't want to allow myself to go running into Bobbie's arms." Grace had spent the bulk of her life looking to someone else to validate her existence. She knew Bobbie would welcome her without any hesitation, but she felt like she had a second chance at life and wanted to start off on her own two feet.

"You don't want to even date her?" Amy asked.

Grace sat up, and took her time thinking over the question. It was something she had thought about often in the last few weeks but not something she'd completely decided on yet. "The idea of finally being able to date Bobbie, out in the open where everyone could see, fills me with so much joy I'm almost scared to think about it. On the other hand, I could easily lose myself and fall right back into old habits. I don't know what to do."

Amy pulled tissue from a box on the desk and gently blotted the tears from Grace's cheeks. "Hey now, none of that."

"I can't help it. I feel so fucking pitiful sometimes."

"You're not. You're human and you're a human who has spent her life living by someone else's plan. I completely understand wanting to be cautious no matter how much your heart tries to convince you it's a good idea to jump in feet first."

Grace appreciated the friends she'd made since she'd come back to town more than she could express. She had friends in Seattle. Good friends, but she'd never felt the connection to any of them that she felt after only knowing Amy for a few months.

"I really don't know what I'd do without you, Aim. I love and appreciate you so much."

Amy smiled, slipping an arm around Grace to pull her closer. She rested her head on Amy's shoulder and soaked up the affection. "Ditto. So what's the plan?"

Grace pulled another tissue from the box and blew her nose. "Well, I think I need to start by talking to Bobbie. She may be done with me for all I know. I can't say I'd blame her."

Amy smacked her leg. "Stop it. That girl has it bad. I'm sure she's just waiting for you to reach out. It is possible to maintain your independence within a loving relationship. Share your fears with Bobbie and tell her what your expectations are. You guys will work this out and find balance."

"I should go talk to Bobbie."

"Why are you still here?"

Grace kissed Amy's cheek. "Thanks."

"Get out of here," Amy said, shooing her away. "Don't worry about the clinic, I'll lock up."

Grace grabbed her bag and walked toward the front door. "See you tomorrow. Thanks again, Aim."

The day was still warm as she climbed into her car and pulled her phone from her bag. She found Bobbie's number in her contacts and placed the call before clipping the phone into its cradle.

"Hello." Bobbie's groggy voice worried Grace she'd woken her up.

"Hey, did I wake you?"

"No, not at all." Bobbie cleared her throat. "I was just resting my eyes. I'm getting a little too used to this relaxing thing. I might need to become a kept woman so I can spend my days eating popcorn and watching my stories."

Grace laughed and started her car. "Good luck with that, Del Ray. I was wondering if you might be up for a little company."

The silence on the other end of the line was unsettling. "Bobbie?"

"Yeah, sorry, I'd love some company."

"Is something wrong? I don't have to—"

"Nope," Bobbie said. "Nothing like that. I'm not used to the idea that you can just come to my house and hang out. It's still a little hard to believe. It's nice."

Grace smiled. She understood what Bobbie was saying and it was a little hard for her to believe, too. In all the best ways.

CHAPTER TWENTY-SIX

G racie is coming to visit," Bobbie told Riley as she carefully stood and began to gather the dishes and various things that had collected by her chair while she was recovering from her broken ribs. Her mom did a great job of taking care of her while she was out of commission, but she hadn't felt well the day before so Bobbie insisted she take care of herself and get some rest. Bobbie worried caring for her these past weeks had taken a toll on her poor mother.

Once the majority of the mess was stowed away, she stuck Riley in the backyard for a potty break and started up the stairs toward her room to get presentable. Halfway to her goal, she heard Grace's car on the gravel driveway outside. She looked down at her outfit realizing she had no time to change. Hopefully, Grace would look past the Star Wars pajama pants, Superman slippers, and shirt with a beaver on the front. Grace was getting the full "Bobbie Experience" and she prayed that wouldn't just scare her away.

Bobbie brushed the chip crumbs off of her shirt before answering the knock at the door.

"Hey, I'm glad you could stop by."

"Mind if I come in?" Grace asked.

"Yes, sorry, I'm just a bit out of it. I don't get many visitors." Bobbie moved so Grace could enter. "Can I get you a drink?"

"That would be great. Water?" Grace followed Bobbie into the kitchen and climbed onto a stool at the counter. "I can't get over how much you've done to the place since we were kids."

"Wyatt was an animal so I've had to pretty much gut it and start from scratch, but it's coming along. I would give you a tour, but I still get out of breath when I climb the stairs." Bobbie wasn't used to not being healthy so her injury had been difficult both physically and emotionally.

"How are you feeling? How are you really feeling?" Grace asked with a look that said she wanted the honest truth.

"Well, I could use some meds, but I'd rather go the natural route if you're interested." Bobbie pulled a rolled joint and lighter from a bag in her kitchen drawer.

"You have no idea how much I need that right now." Grace climbed off the stool and grabbed their glasses of water as she followed her out to the back deck.

Riley greeted them as they stepped outside, and Bobbie led Grace over to a couple of Adirondack chairs with a small table in between. Bobbie handed Grace the joint and lighter before carefully sitting down in a chair. She held her breath against the pain of her ribs until she was settled against the pillow.

"I'm sorry you're in so much pain, Bobbie. I can't believe you functioned as well as you did before your mom and I were there to help. How is your mom?" Grace lit the joint and took a deep drag, holding it in for a few seconds before exhaling and coughing the last of the smoke from her lungs. Her shoulders noticeably relaxed as she handed it back to Bobbie.

"I think the adrenaline kept me from feeling it right away. It all happened in slow motion, and I knew I was in for a world of hurt so when I came to, I was just so freaked out I think it delayed the pain." Bobbie took a much smaller drag since her ribs were already hurting. "My mom is…not great. She's so strong and would never let on that she's struggling, but I can see it. She's been waiting on me hand and foot, and I could tell yesterday that it was taking a toll on her. I told her to stay at home which is why I had to quickly put away all the dishes and chip bags before you arrived. I had tortilla chips and salsa for breakfast, then salt and vinegar chips and onion dip for lunch. I think I might do Cheetos for dinner. Mix it up a bit."

They both laughed as they passed the joint back and forth. "I'm going to make you dinner. Two meals of chips in one day is sad, but three…that's pathetic." Grace smiled and gave Bobbie a wink.

"I'm not going to argue if you're willing. I like to eat so I'll never turn down a meal." Bobbie laid her head back against the chair and let her muscles relax as the pot did its job. "Why are you here, if you don't mind me asking?"

Grace reclined into the chair and soaked up the remaining sun of the day.

"Can I ask you a question?"

"Sure." Bobbie carefully turned in her seat to face her.

"Will it bother you if I talk to you about Jake? I know there are things between us that still have to be talked about, but the root of all this is my relationship with Jake."

"We can talk about Jake. I'm not a big fan of his, but he's a part of your story and me not liking him doesn't make that go away. I want you to feel comfortable talking to me about anything. Above all else we're friends and I'm always here for you."

"Thanks. Well, when I came out the other day to find you had been wrestling a cow, I was not only going to apologize for Jake and my mom's behavior but also tell you that I asked him for a divorce. We had a massive blowout the morning after you picked us up, and my mom not only outed me to him but told him you and I had a history."

Bobbie's heart ached for Grace, and the position her mom put her in. "Jake didn't know you were bisexual?"

"I think I'm closer to lesbian than bisexual technically, although I do find some men attractive so maybe. My tastes seem to lean closer to the boyish lesbian type though." Grace winked at Bobbie, which made her heart skip. "Anyway, no, Jake had no idea I was ever attracted to anyone other than him, apparently. Especially not another woman. Once he figured out that the Roberta my mom was talking about was you, let's just say it didn't go over well."

"Sorry, Gracie."

"Don't be sorry. It's not remotely your fault. It's not even Jake's fault. I take full responsibility for the havoc I've caused and am doing my best to extricate myself from the situation as easily as possible." Grace accepted the joint from Bobbie and took another drag before continuing with her story. "Anyway, Jake and I had coffee a couple of days later, and after he vented his frustrations a bit, we actually came to what I think is an amicable plan."

"That sounds positive," Bobbie said. "Is he still in town?"

"He isn't. He went back to Seattle to file for divorce and start figuring how to disentangle our lives."

"So he's the one who's going to file? I thought it would have been you."

"If I was in Washington, it probably would have been me, but I'm not so he's going to get the ball rolling. I think he wanted to do it anyway. He's feeling pretty fragile right now and I think the idea that he was filing made him feel like he was taking back some of the power in our relationship."

"What the fuck is that about?"

Grace brushed ash from her pants. "I wouldn't call him controlling or anything, but Jake has always been the one to make the decisions in our relationship. I think in the beginning I was just so afraid to speak up because I'd never been taught that my opinion mattered. As I got older I would occasionally try to communicate my needs, but by that time he'd gotten used to having things his way."

"What a dick."

Grace shook her head. "No, he wasn't a dick about it. It was just the way it was and I didn't push hard enough to make anything change. I don't know what he would have done if I'd really pushed so I don't want to assume that he'd be a dick. I think that's why it was such a shock to him when I said I was going to divorce him. I'd never really asked for what I wanted like that. It should be interesting when I have to go back to Seattle."

"Back to Seattle?" Bobbie sat up but quickly regretted it when pain shot through her like a freight train. "Fuck." She grabbed her side and tried to catch her breath.

Grace was up in a flash, kneeling next to her chair to make sure she was okay. "Easy does it there, chief. You're not ready for excitement yet."

Bobbie weakly laughed as she tried to catch her breath. "Would you mind helping me back into the house and onto the couch?" she asked between short gasps.

"Absolutely. I'm sorry for making you move around this much. Did they give you something to work on your breathing?"

Bobbie groaned as Grace helped her to her feet. "They did. It's next to my chair." Grace wrapped an arm around her back to support her as they walked. The sudden movement had taken her breath away and left her dizzy.

Once they were back in the house, Grace helped her lie on the couch and sat next to her as she placed Bobbie's head on her lap. Bobbie's breathing evened out as Grace gently stroked her hair.

"Thanks for looking out for me. Sorry I'm so much trouble."

"You're no trouble at all. It's kinda soothing to take care of you like this. It feels good to be useful," Grace said.

Bobbie closed her eyes and soaked in the affection. No one other than her mother had ever made her feel so safe and loved. Between the pot, the comfort, and the exhaustion from trying to breathe, Bobbie let herself drift off to sleep.

The sound of Grace's voice pulled Bobbie from her nap. She stretched her legs to work out the cramps from sleeping on the couch. She heard Grace in the kitchen talking on the phone. She didn't want to eavesdrop but she couldn't help overhearing Grace's part of the conversation.

"I just can't believe it. Did they say how much? Holy shit." Bobbie heard Grace pull a dish from the oven and set it on the counter. "So when is this supposed to happen? Right. Shit. I know, I know. I'm still in California." She heard Grace pull plates from the cabinet. "I don't know. Not for a few weeks, at least. Okay. I am excited. Very excited. My life is just a little complicated right now. I know, Debbie. Look, give me a couple of weeks to figure this out. I know. I won't tell anyone yet. I will. I promise. Tell Gary I said hello and he still owes me twenty dollars." Grace laughed. "Okay. Bye, Deb."

Bobbie heard Grace end her call and watched her stare at her phone a few seconds before slipping it into her pocket. She wanted to ask what that was about but part of her was afraid to find out. She decided to let Grace think she was still sleeping.

"Bobbie, sweetie?" She opened her eyes to see Grace kneeling next to her. She leaned forward to plant a delicate kiss on her forehead "Hey." Her voice was so soft Bobbie almost didn't hear her.

"Hey." Bobbie fought the urge to kiss the lips that were only inches away from her own. "Did I fall asleep?"

"You did so I took the liberty of scrounging some things together for a meal while you rested. I hope you don't mind."

Bobbie smiled as her stomach growled, voicing her appreciation of the smell that came from the kitchen. "Are you kidding? I'm starving. A girl can only live on chips for so long."

Grace laughed and pulled over a TV tray with a plate of food and set it in front of her. "I hope enchiladas and rice casserole will work."

"Holy shit, these look good, Gracie. What's in the enchiladas? There isn't tofu or something is there?" Bobbie looked at her food suspiciously.

Grace laughed as she walked back to the kitchen and returned with some for herself. "Well, I didn't go anywhere and since you don't already have tofu in your house, you're safe. These have black beans, cheese, grilled onions, corn, and peppers. I hope you like them. What would you like to drink?"

"Beer? They smell amazing so I'm sure I will." Bobbie closed her eyes and moaned when she took her first bite. "These are crazy good." She dug into the food like she hadn't eaten in days. When she finished, she sat back against the couch to rest her ribs as well as gather her thoughts. "Earlier you said something about going back to Seattle. I didn't realize that was your plan."

Grace picked at the label on her bottle of beer. "I haven't decided what I'm going to do. I have to go back no matter what to get moved out of the house, but I haven't decided beyond that."

Bobbie wanted to fall to her knees and beg Grace to stay, but she knew that wouldn't be fair to her. "Do you want to talk about it?"

"Let's talk about us."

"About us? What about us?"

Grace traced her finger around the mouth of her beer. Bobbie could see she was struggling but didn't know what to do or say to make it easier for her. "We don't have to—"

"No, I'm sorry, I'm just trying to figure out exactly what to say without sounding like a complete loser."

"Okay…try me and I'll keep an open mind."

Grace stood and gathered their dishes. "Did you want more enchiladas?"

"Grace, sit and talk to me." Bobbie watched as Grace placed the dishes in the dishwasher and put away the leftovers. When the kitchen was back in order, she sat next to Bobbie on the couch. Bobbie picked up her hand and cradled it between her own. "You can talk to me about anything, Gracie."

Grace blew out a breath and squeezed Bobbie's hand. "I know. I'm still trying to figure out how to sort through my feelings, let alone communicate them in a way you'll understand."

"Try me." She just wanted Grace to tell her something at this point. She could figure out what to do with whatever was causing her so much heartache after that.

"I like you a lot."

"I like you a lot, too, Gracie." Bobbie smiled and brought Grace's hand to place a gentle kiss on her palm.

"I know you do and I don't want to hurt you."

"Why are you going to hurt me?"

Grace withdrew her hand from Bobbie's and moved to the chair facing her. "I'd never intentionally hurt you, but there are so many reasons why I can't give you what you want right now that I'm afraid I'm just going to hurt you."

"What is it you think I want?" Bobbie asked.

"A wife, a family, someone who has their shit together."

"Why do you think that's what I want?"

"It's what you've always wanted, Bobbie. Are you telling me those dreams have changed?"

Bobbie sat back against the cushions and rubbed her eyes. "No, that's not what I'm saying. I do want those things, but I don't have to have them now. I realize you're going through a huge, life changing thing and I'm a very patient person."

Grace smiled and they both laughed.

"Well, I can try to be a very patient person. Tell me what you need. If we communicate our needs, we can work this out."

"I need you to understand, and I mean really understand, that I haven't decided if I'm staying in Seattle or not. My life is there. I have a job waiting for me there. My friends are there."

Bobbie wanted to point out she had friends and a job here, too, but kept it to herself and just nodded her head. "I get it. What else?"

Grace stood and paced in front of the large, stone fireplace. "I want us to date and I think you do, too, but I need you to understand how important it is to me that we take things slowly. I need you to be patient with me. I know that's asking a lot. I know it's probably unfair—"

"It's not." Bobbie expected Grace would want to start with baby steps if they were ever able to date so she wasn't surprised. She was so happy to possibly get the opportunity to be in Grace's life that she was willing to go as slow as she needed. "It's not unfair. I want you to be happy, Grace."

"I know you do. I want the same for you." Grace reached out and took Bobbie's hand. She turned it palm up and rubbed her soft fingers across the callused surface. "I can't offer you any promises. I can't tell you for sure that I will stay here. I can't tell you for sure when I'll be ready for more than casual dating. I wish I could say that I lost myself and need to find my way back, but the honest truth is I'm not sure I've ever really known who I am because I've spent my entire life trying to live up to other people's expectations."

"I'm so sorry."

Grace gave Bobbie a quick smile. "No need. I've led a privileged life and am proud of what I've accomplished. I need the space to do a little self-discovery and then I'll be good. What about you? How are you feeling about all this? I've just made all these demands of you without asking what you want. You can't say you just want me to be happy because that's not what I'm asking."

Bobbie laughed and pulled Grace back onto the couch with her. "I do want you to be happy. I also want the happy ending. I want someone to come home to. I want someone to share my dreams with and take vacations with and to hold me when I'm sad. I want all those things and can be patient while you decide what you need to be happy. I know I can't be the one who does that for you. Let's take this one step at a time, without expectations, and we'll see where we land. What do you think?"

"I think that sounds like a great idea. How are you feeling? Are you still up for company? I don't feel like going back to Amy and John's yet. They are the best, but I feel bad I'm always in their space."

"I would love to have you here as long as you want." Bobbie turned on the TV. "What should we watch? Do you watch *The Great British Baking Show*?"

"I have no idea what you're talking about, but if it has cakes, I'm in."

"This is the best therapy ever. You'll love it." Bobbie cued up the show.

"Sounds like it's a must then." She gestured for Bobbie to lay down with her head on Grace's lap.

"Thanks for hanging out with me." Grace gently ran her fingers through Bobbie's hair. "I really missed you."

Bobbie gazed up into the face that she'd dreamt about for so many years. "I missed you, too."

CHAPTER TWENTY-SEVEN

Two weeks later, Bobbie backed the ATV up to a fallen tree limb and carefully stepped out to secure the rope from it to the hitch so she could pull it to the wood pile and out of the path of the cattle. Six weeks without working on the ranch had almost driven her to madness, but her mother had finally cleared her to work as long as she didn't lift things and spent most of her day in the ATV.

She knew she was an adult and her mom wasn't her boss, but she also knew she wasn't a good judge of when the appropriate time to go back to work was. She would've resumed her normal duties within a week or two and most likely would have made things even worse. She learned long ago to trust her mom to keep her safe. Besides, if she defied her mother's wishes by getting back on the proverbial horse too soon, injuring herself even more, she never would've heard the end of it.

Riley was certainly glad to be back to work. She sat next to Bobbie in the passenger seat surveying her area. Riley had completely healed from her injuries other than little patches of missing hair. Bobbie and Riley had fallen into a comfortable schedule. It was hard to believe it had only been a few months since she rescued her from the wire.

"Let's get this limb over to the pile and then get home for a shower before we head into town for your checkup with Grace," Bobbie said.

She was excited but also nervous to see Grace again. She hadn't seen her since the day she stopped by the house. They'd texted back and forth and talked on the phone a few times, but Bobbie was doing her best to give Grace the space she requested. Everything they'd done that evening had been very innocent, but she hadn't stopped thinking about the way Grace's fingers gently stroked her hair while they watched TV.

She didn't recall one thing that happened on the show they watched, but she remembered every minute of Grace touching her. She'd never known contentment like she had in that moment, and every stitch of clothing stayed on. She wasn't sure she would survive if things went any further.

Unfortunately, the phone conversation she overheard was still a mystery. Bobbie wasn't sure how to ask her about it, or even if she should. As far as Grace knew, it had been a private conversation, and Bobbie wasn't sure she was ready to admit she'd listened. In addition to that, she'd heard Grace reassure the person on the phone she wouldn't tell anyone the details of whatever they were talking about. It wouldn't be fair of Bobbie to press her to share the information. She'd have to be patient and allow Grace to tell her on her own, if she ever did. Add this to the list of things Bobbie didn't know about Grace.

The past couple of weeks had been difficult, not only because she felt she should be out working her ranch, but also because she didn't have the distraction of work to keep her mind off of Grace. Logically, she knew Grace needed time to process everything that had happened, but logic meant very little to her heart.

Bobbie's heart told her to stand below Grace's second-story window holding a radio over her head that played a ridiculously romantic song. Her heart told her she should profess her undying love, hopefully followed by Grace climbing down the trellis outside her window to a waiting Bobbie who would carry her to the car, take her home, and make love to her until they both couldn't take any more pleasure for fear they would permanently damage some vital body part.

Bobbie smiled at the fantasy, but it scared her how much she wished it were true. She had never wanted anyone as much as she wanted Grace, and she was quite sure she would never want anyone else as much. Grace wasn't just the one she had chosen to love. It was more like the Universe had chosen them to need each other and she wouldn't be complete without her. God, she was such a sap.

"Come on, girl," Bobbie called Riley out of the ATV when they finally finished their chores and arrived safely home. She tried to act casual about going to see Grace, but she knew it was a lie. The fact that she'd been thinking all day about what she would wear to the stupid veterinarian checkup appointment was a pretty dead giveaway that she cared deeply.

❖

"Hey, Bobbie. I'll let our new tech Dani know you're here," Amy said when they arrived at the clinic. Bobbie found a chair in the back of the waiting room and did her best to get comfortable in the hard plastic. She felt well enough to be back at work, but after a long day in the ATV, her ribs were starting to throb.

As she thumbed through a *Family Handyman* magazine, she realized her cheeks were starting to hurt from smiling in anticipation of seeing Grace again. She knew she was going to have to get control of herself if she wanted to maintain any shred of "cool" she hoped she still had.

A few minutes after they arrived, a cute Hispanic woman in scrubs called Riley's name. Bobbie and Riley stood and followed the tech into an exam room.

"You must be the famous Bobbie and Riley Del Ray?" she said as she began taking Riley's vitals.

"I don't know how famous we are, but you're right about the Del Ray part." The thought of Grace talking about her enough to earn her the title of "famous" made Bobbie's heart jump into her throat.

"The way Doc tells it, you're something special. But you didn't hear that from me." Dani winked as she jotted something in the chart. "She'll be right with you guys."

Once Dani left the room, Bobbie took the opportunity to stand and do a little ill-advised happy jig that her ribs weren't ready to experience. When she was done, she held her side and grimaced as she gingerly reclaimed her seat on the bench.

Riley perked up at the sound of someone pulling the chart from the slot on their door. "Me too, girl, but we have to play it cool, man." Bobbie's nervous energy matched Riley's excitement, and she couldn't guarantee she wouldn't hug Grace when she walked in the door.

With every last bit of willpower she had, Bobbie stayed seated as Grace entered the little room looking more beautiful than ever. Bobbie's heart skipped when Grace raised her eyes to hers and smiled.

"Good morning." Grace was cool as a cucumber. "How's Riley doing?" She reached down to pick Riley up for a snuggle before setting her on the exam table.

"She's good. She's been super excited to see you again," Bobbie said. "It's all she's thought about for days."

"Is that so?" Grace asked with a knowing smile. "I'm glad she's been thinking about me. I've thought a lot about her as well."

As Grace ran her slender, delicate fingers through Riley's fur, Bobbie almost swooned remembering those same fingers in her own hair. That night she'd wanted nothing more than to reach up and pull Grace's head down so she could capture her soft lips in a kiss but never found the nerve to follow through with the urge.

"Bobbie?" she heard Grace say.

"Yes." Bobbie snapped back to reality.

"You with me?" Grace asked.

Bobbie rubbed her face with her hands. "I'm here, sorry. I was thinking about something else."

"I was saying that Riley looks really good. Her weight is getting better so I assume the goldfish cracker people are wondering what the hell happened."

Bobbie laughed and scruffed Riley's fur. "She's making jokes about our addiction, girl. What a mean, mean lady."

"Poor babies," Grace said with mock sympathy. "Hey, I really have to get to my next appointment, but Sunday I'm looking for a place to rent. Would you like to come with me? It sounds pretty boring now that I'm saying it out loud so don't think you have say yes if you're busy."

"I'd love to," Bobbie said. She realized too late that she sounded a little too enthusiastic to be cool and casual. "I mean sure, that would be great."

Grace laughed at Bobbie's attempt at nonchalance. "If you're interested you could pick me up at Amy's around noon and we can do lunch before we go?"

"That sounds great," Bobbie said.

She couldn't tell if things were getting more or less complicated, but she didn't really care.

Chapter Twenty-eight

How do I look? Do I look okay? This dress is silly. I probably look like I just came off the farm in Kansas. I don't have time to change." Grace turned around and around in the mirror scrutinizing her dress as Amy watched with amusement.

"You're totally hot. Looking like you're fresh off the farm is always good, but especially when you're being picked up by a farmer." Amy handed Grace a pair of adorable white sandals.

"Technically, she's a rancher, not a farmer, but I get your point. Thank you. I have no idea why I'm so nervous. We're just going to lunch and then to look at houses."

Amy leaned down to help Grace with her sandals as she tried to calm her nerves. "I remember that new love feeling. I still get it occasionally with John when he's not farting or snoring. Sometimes he looks at me and I just start laughing because I can't believe this totally hot guy married dorky old me."

Grace laughed and pulled her into a hug. "He's just as lucky as you. You're smart and funny and adorable, and I would totally do you if you were into chicks and I wasn't already about to pass out with lust for another woman."

"I get your point, and if I were into chicks you would be at the top of my list other than the fact that you're kinda like my sister at this point and that's just weird, but thanks for the sentiment." They laughed and Grace appreciated the effort to distract her.

"Your date's here, Grace," John called from the front room.

"Honey," Amy scolded him in a loud whisper. "You can't call this a date yet. They still aren't technically calling this a date. You don't want to pressure Grace."

John looked confused but shrugged as he turned back to the model he was building on the kitchen table.

Grace and Amy stood at the kitchen window watching Bobbie check her hair and clothes before walking up the path. "Good luck, buddy. It's going to be great." Amy gave Grace a peck on the cheek and nudged her out the front door.

"Wow." Bobbie paused mid-step as she took in the white sundress with little blue flowers Grace had been so worried about only minutes before. Her hair was pulled back into a ponytail, and she had chosen a soft pink lipstick to complement the color. "You look...amazing," Bobbie said. She looked down at her plaid shirt and jeans. "I hope I'm not underdressed. I look slovenly next to you."

"Don't be silly," Grace said although she couldn't help but smile at the compliment. "You look adorable. I'm probably overdressed for looking at houses. I might have been a little too excited to see you again."

Bobbie took Grace's hand and walked with her to her truck. "I have an idea." She held the door open for Grace to climb in. "Come to my house tonight and I'll make you dinner to repay you for all the care and attention you've given me over the last few weeks."

"It's a trap," Grace answered with her best Admiral Ackbar impression.

Bobbie stared at her for a minute before leaning into the truck and giving Grace a gentle kiss on her lips. "You keep quoting *Star Wars*, Grace Hammond, and you're going to make me fall in love with you."

"You're too easy," Grace said.

Bobbie laughed as she shut Grace's door and walked around to climb into the driver's seat. "That's what she said."

Grace laughed. "How are your ribs and noggin?"

After punching the address to their first house into the GPS on her phone, Bobbie started the truck and pulled onto the street. "I'm feeling okay. I'll occasionally turn the wrong way or bump against something and it will hurt, but for the most part I'm well on my way to full recovery. You never answered about dinner."

Bobbie looked anxious and Grace resisted the urge to kiss away her worry. "Sorry, yes. Dinner sounds great."

"When you come over tonight, I'll let you examine my rib injury, Doctor." Bobbie punctuating the tease with a wink.

"You're an impossible woman," Grace said. "Now when are you feeding me? I'm starving."

"Let's check out one place on your list that's super close and then we'll eat. How do you feel about a picnic? I'd hate to waste this beautiful day being indoors."

"Perfect. Word of warning though, I'm about forty-five minutes from hangry so this house visit better be quick."

"That sounds terrifying, Doc. We'll for sure have food in your tummy in less than forty-five minutes, promise."

❖

Forty minutes later, they laid a blanket on the grass in the shade of a beautiful oak tree. Grace was in awe as Bobbie placed their bounty in front of her. Hummus, carrots, sliced apples, warm pita bread, roasted garlic, dried fruits, roasted red peppers, and an assortment of cheeses were spread out before them.

"I don't even know where to start. This is like some kind of food dream that I don't want to wake up from."

"I pretty much grabbed everything that didn't have meat at the little market. Thankfully, they had quite a few options. What did you think of that house?"

Grace thought for a minute and then scrunched up her nose. "Not so much. It was cute, but it was a fancy house in a crappy neighborhood. Someone put a bunch of work into it, but it's surrounded by a bad area."

Bobbie nodded. "I agree. It doesn't matter how nice the inside of the house is if you're afraid to step out the front door. What is it that you're looking for in a rental?"

"Hmmm…I want a nice neighborhood. Near a park would be a bonus. Not too far from work, and it has to be a short lease since I'm not exactly sure how long I'll be in Preston. Month-to-month would be perfect, but those are difficult to find. I thought I might be able to talk Lena into renting it when I have to leave, but I haven't discussed it with her, yet. I wanted to see what kind of rental I found first."

"So, when do you think you're leaving?" Bobbie asked.

Grace popped a piece of dried apricot in her mouth and chewed before she answered. She knew any talk of her leaving was difficult for Bobbie and not something she was excited to talk about either.

"I'm not sure, yet. I talked to Doc Randolph the other day and they believe they've removed all of the cancer from Carol, but she's still very weak. She's a strong woman though and I think she'll be back on her feet before too long."

"That's great to hear," Bobbie said. The words were sincere but Grace detected a hint of sadness she knew was because Bobbie didn't want her to leave.

"Hey," Grace said, rubbing Bobbie's arm. "I'm here now. Let's make every moment we have together count and we'll worry about the rest of it later. Deal?"

"Deal." Bobbie dipped bread into the hummus and stacked olives on top until it was almost too big to fit in her mouth.

"You don't date much, do you?" Grace teased.

Bobbie smiled around her mouthful. "There's not a big market for boyish girls who spend most of their time smelling like a cow."

"You can't tell me you don't have offers."

Bobbie shrugged. "I have offers but none of them ever feel right." She cleared her throat and wiped her mouth with a napkin. "Out of curiosity, let's pretend you knew you were going to stay here and you were in the market to buy a house. What would you want?"

"Hmmm…Something small with a porch for a rocking chair and window boxes full of daisies. I would really love a yard for my future dog."

"What kind of dog? Big dog, little dog?" Bobbie asked.

"Big dog. I want a Great Dane. Kelly Barnes had one in high school named Diesel, and he was the sweetest dog ever. You remember Kelly, don't you?"

Bobbie laughed. "Um, yeah, she totally threw herself at me when you left. She pretended like she was comforting me, but it quickly escalated to her trying to get into my pants."

"That bitch. She was one of my best friends so your pants should have been off limits. I can't believe she would go after my woman as soon as I left. She was one of only a couple of people I told about us. Is nothing sacred to a teenager?" Grace was disgusted by the floozy who had claimed to be her friend.

"Easy there, Hammond. Nothing happened between us. I resisted her advances because it felt dirty with her being your friend and all." Bobbie put away the food containers since they both had stopped eating and stretched out on the blanket.

Grace cuddled up next to her and looked up at the sky. "Did you date anyone else from high school that I would know?" she asked even though she wasn't sure she wanted to hear the answer.

Bobbie rolled on her side facing Grace and reached out to brush her fingers against her cheek. "Are you sure you want me to answer that question?"

Grace took Bobbie's hand and pressed it to her lips before threading their fingers together. Bobbie's big hand felt so strong and warm wrapped around hers. "How about the abbreviated version?"

Bobbie rolled onto her back and let out a breath. "Well, I didn't date anyone for a while. The news was out that I was a lesbian, and although lots of girls were suddenly curious, none of them were brave enough to approach me, except Kelly of course. I was a bit of a pariah for a bit."

It hurt Grace to know she had left Bobbie to face the school alone after she left. Her fault or not, in some ways she was the lucky one to have been whisked away to a new life where she didn't have to deal with the real consequences of that night. "I'm so incredibly sorry. I wish I could have been here with you."

"I'm glad you weren't. It might have been worse because I would have felt the need to protect you. I didn't really care what they thought of me, but I very likely would have been involved in more than one fight if someone had said something hurtful to you."

Grace smiled. She knew it would have been ill-advised if she had, but the thought of Bobbie protecting her was quite romantic. She was sure her teenage self would have been even more impressed.

"So who did you date when people started speaking to you again?" Grace asked to get them back on track.

Bobbie laughed and covered her face with her hands in embarrassment. She turned to face Grace and very seriously asked, "You'll tell me if any of this bothers you, right?"

"It's been twenty years and I married a man. There's nothing you did that I haven't done," Grace said.

"I've never been with a man so..."

Grace smacked Bobbie on the arm. "Shut up, Del Ray, and tell me."

"Geez, nosy. After you left I worked at the pool giving swim lessons on Tuesdays and Thursdays. Several kids from our class worked there with me. Jennifer Dodson, Dillon Jenkins, and Samantha McGrath among them."

"Sam McGrath, the head cheerleader; Dillon Jenkins, the quarterback; and Jennifer Dodson, the most popular girl in school worked with you at the pool? Wow, that's...quite a group." Grace shook her head picturing what that was like.

"Tell me about it. After the few months I'd had, I wanted to quit the first day but my mom said I made a commitment and had to see it through. She wasn't aware of my social issues or I'm sure she would have let me quit, but I didn't want her to worry about me so I didn't tell her. Anyway, the four of us actually became very close and we hung out quite a bit. Dillon and Jen started dating a couple of weeks in, so Sam and I were often left alone together as the love birds snuck off to have sex somewhere."

"I think I see where this is going," Grace said with a smile.

"Want me to stop?" Bobbie asked again.

"Hell, no. You're getting to the good part. I'm blocking out the fact that this would be you doing things with someone for the first time after being with me. I'm focusing on hot Bobbie doing dirty things with the head cheerleader." Grace blushed and covered her face while they both laughed.

"Okay, you pervert, you asked for it. One Saturday, the four of us spent the day having a picnic by the lake on the ranch. That evening, Dillon and Jen rowed the canoe to the other side to probably have sex while Sam and I relaxed on our towels staring at the stars. How much detail do you want?" Bobbie was obviously checking in to make sure Grace was still cool.

"Stop stalling, you're killing me." Grace scooted closer and rested her head on Bobbie's outstretched arm.

Bobbie laughed and continued her story. "So we were staring at the stars and Sam asked me if the rumors of you and me were true. We hadn't really talked about it before so it had all just been rumors as far as she knew. I told her some of what she heard was probably true and some wasn't. She asked me which parts were true. I asked her which parts she thought were true."

"Jesus Christ, I'm remembering how infuriating you could be back then," Grace said.

Bobbie gave her a big grin. "Anyway, she said she thought you and I were probably really girlfriends and we probably had sex. I asked her if she ever had sex and she said no. She scooted closer. I asked if she had ever kissed anyone and she said millions of times. I asked if she had ever kissed another girl and she said no. I asked if she wanted me to kiss her and she said yes." Bobbie turned on her side toward Grace and leaned in for a kiss.

Grace felt Bobbie's tongue touch her lips as if asking permission, and she opened them to welcome her in. Bobbie's hand slid down Grace's side to rest on the dip of her hip as she pulled her closer and deepened the kiss. Every time she and Bobbie kissed she thought surely it couldn't get any better, and then it happened again and surpassed her wildest expectations.

Grace's heart was pounding in her chest, and just when she was ready to climb on top of her right there in the park, Bobbie pulled back.

"Holy shit, where did you learn to do that? If you say Sam McGrath I'm going to murder you dead," Grace said. They both burst into laughter. "Did you guys have sex that night?"

"Yes, but you'll have to wait until we aren't in a public park to hear that part of the story."

"You're going to be the death of me. We should probably pack up. We're supposed to meet the agent at the next house in fifteen minutes and I'm going to need at least fourteen to catch my breath after that kiss."

CHAPTER TWENTY-NINE

What's the next place?" Bobbie asked as Grace checked her list. She called out the address so Bobbie could enter it into her GPS, and they pulled away from the park leaving their temporary sanctuary behind.

"Thanks for the picnic," Grace said.

Bobbie stole a quick glance at her before pulling onto the street. "Thank you. I love spending time with you, Gracie. You make me happy."

Grace smiled and placed her hand on Bobbie's arm. "You make me happy, too."

The words were what she wanted to hear, but Bobbie detected a hint of sadness in them she couldn't help but be disappointed about.

When they reached the next house on their list Bobbie turned off the ignition and looked at Grace. "We have a few minutes before the agent is supposed to meet us so let's talk. I can tell you're struggling. We can talk about it if you're willing to share."

Grace sighed and stared out her side window. She slid the hand resting on Bobbie's arm down to entwine their fingers. Bobbie gave her a moment to gather her thoughts. She knew the same feelings she was dealing with were a hundred times more confusing for Grace. Rushing things between them would only cause them both pain, and the last thing Bobbie wanted to do was cause her any more pain.

After a couple of minutes, Grace took a deep breath and spoke. "I don't want this to be a recurring thing every time we're together, but I'm struggling. I know how I feel when I'm around you and while it thrills me, it also sends me into a panic."

"I'm sorry, Grace."

"Nothing to apologize for. You aren't doing anything wrong. This is totally my issue."

Bobbie brushed a strand of hair from Grace's face and tucked it behind her ear. "Look, let's enjoy the time we spend together and not focus on what's going to happen. I know where you stand and even though I wish you were ready for more, I understand why you aren't."

"Things are just so complicated right now."

"I know. It's okay, Grace. We'll figure this out together."

Grace smiled and kissed the back of Bobbie's hand. "Thanks. I'm sorry I keep bringing this up."

"It's totally fine. We can talk more over dinner tonight."

Grace shook her head. "No, let's just have a nice evening and enjoy what we have right now. I can worry about the other stuff later."

"Deal. If you—"

"Hellooo." Grace and Bobbie jumped when the Realtor appeared out of nowhere and knocked on the window of their truck.

Bobbie put a hand over hear heart. "Kathy, you just about gave me a heart attack."

"Hey, Bobbie, good to see you. I hope you two are well fed and rested after lunch because we've got four houses to look at this afternoon. We're going to find you girls something that will work if I have to show you every rental in town," Kathy said.

"Well, this will only be for Grace so she's the one we have to convince. We'll find her something though. Won't we, Kathy?" Bobbie gave her a wink as she swatted her arm.

The house was adorable with two bedrooms and two baths, near a park with a pond and only five minutes from Grace's clinic. As they walked through the front door, Grace's eyes lit up with all the detailed trim and beautiful wood floors. It was older but full of character and well maintained.

"I love it." Grace wasn't able to hide her excitement. As she walked around and looked into each space, she made appreciative noises.

"You may not even have to show her those other houses after all, Kathy." Bobbie laughed. It was hard not to get excited when Grace was excited.

Bobbie was checking to make sure the gas stove worked when she heard a gasp from the back porch. She followed the sound of voices and found Grace taking photos of the yard with her phone. She knew it was pretty much a done deal. "I think we have a winner, Kathy."

CHAPTER THIRTY

The sight of Riley's excited little face looking out the window as they pulled up to Bobbie's house made Grace laugh. "She is such a happy dog. She's lucky you found her."

"I usually think I'm the lucky one except when I leave an ink pen out." Bobbie laughed. "For some reason that crazy dog loves to destroy ink pens. You should have seen her a week ago. I came back from a trip to the store and she was covered in red. I thought she had murdered something until I got closer and realized it was a shade closer to pink. There were tiny pink paw prints all over the floor leading away from a pile of broken red pen remnants on my leather couch. I just about tossed her out."

Grace was laughing so hard she had to hold on to Bobbie as they walked. "At least ink doesn't cause issues when ingested."

"I googled it to make sure, but my couch wasn't as lucky. It came off of the leather for the most part, but the white thread on the seam has a definite pink tint to it even still." That sent Grace into another fit of laughter. Bobbie unlocked the door and led her into the house.

"Sounds like you have your hands full." Grace knelt down to greet Riley when she ran up to them. "You keep your mommy busy don't you pretty girl." Riley gave Grace the toothiest grin she could manage.

"She really hates being alone. We spend most of our time together, but I can tell she's sad when I'm not here. I thought about getting her a friend to hang out with, but I'm not entirely sure she would welcome the competition for love. Can I get you a drink?"

"Wine if you have it," Grace said.

"Have a seat on one of the stools and I'll grab us some wine and snacks to hold off starvation until I can rustle up something to eat." Bobbie pulled the wine glasses from the cabinet. "Sorry I didn't plan for dinner better. I wasn't expecting a guest, but I'm certainly glad I have one."

"Don't go through a bunch of trouble for me. I'm easy."

"It's no problem." Bobbie poured the wine and set out their leftovers from lunch. "I have frozen homemade pasta sauce I can heat up, and I soaked enough polenta for two last night so I could make that if you like. Luckily, I like to make extra in case my mom stops by or I want leftovers for my lunch the next day."

"You have many talents." Grace watched Bobbie put on an apron with a Viking ship embroidered on the front.

Grace admired the way Bobbie moved efficiently around the kitchen. She was more agile than Grace expected. As Bobbie prepared their food, Grace took the opportunity to study her while she was distracted. Bobbie's jeans weren't tight, but they were tight enough to outline a strong, muscular body underneath the denim. Grace imagined what it would feel like to slip her hands into the back of those jeans and massage her perfect ass.

Grace jerked her head up when she realized Bobbie was talking to her. She did her best to pick up the conversation before she caught on that Grace was ogling her and not listening.

"The kitchen still needs work, but I've updated most of the rest of the house," Bobbie said.

Grace looked around taking in the honey oak cabinets and tile countertop. It looked exactly as she remembered it from when they were kids. "Will I get a tour of the rest of the house this time?" Grace asked.

"Absolutely, I can't leave the polenta so let's do the grand tour after dinner if that works for you. Please ignore any socks or pants that are possibly left in public areas. I'm not used to having company, and I don't like socks or pants so I tend to leave them in odd places." Bobbie smiled and looked a little embarrassed at the admission.

Grace laughed and shook her head. "I don't think I want to know why there would be pants anywhere other than a bathroom or a bedroom."

"Because pants, or leg prisons as I like to call them, are tools of the man." Bobbie punctuated her statement by lifting her wooden spoon in the air as if she was leading a revolt.

"You crack me up," Grace said. "Can I help with anything?"

Bobbie thought for a moment then pointed toward the frozen bag of sauce she'd pulled out of the freezer a few minutes earlier. "Would you mind putting that into this pan on the burner next to me and heating it up?"

"With pleasure." Grace jumped up to help. Even though the kitchen was older, it was efficiently designed. Grace could tell Bobbie spent a lot of time in this space. "It looks like you really enjoy cooking. I don't remember you doing much of that when we were kids."

"I kinda had to learn to do it by necessity. When Dad died, Mom went into a pretty severe depression for a couple of years. Wyatt did what he could to take care of us but he was left to do most of the work on the ranch. Things like making sure Evan and Mom had food on the table and clean clothes to wear were left to me. Mom eventually recovered, and with help from a therapist, came back stronger than ever. I had to learn to be the parent in the interim."

Grace could tell it was difficult for Bobbie to talk about that time in her life. She slipped her hand under the hem of Bobbie's shirt and rubbed her back to comfort her as they stood side by side at the stove. "I'm so sorry I wasn't here for you during all of that."

Bobbie smiled and shook her head at Grace's apology. "You had your own stuff going on. I can't imagine being plucked from my life and shipped off against my will away from my friends and family. I'm sorry I couldn't be there for *you*. I tried to find you, but by the time the internet was a thing to use to find someone you must have been out of school and living in Washington. I searched for you on Facebook but never found you."

"I know." Grace felt so much guilt for not trying to find Bobbie. "I should have looked for you. I wanted to look for you, but I think I was afraid of what it would do to me if I found you and you were happily married. Pretty ironic, right?" Grace shook her head as she stirred the sauce. "I believed for years I was in an impossible situation. On top of that I was afraid you would hate me."

"Hate you? Why would I hate you?"

"Hate me for leaving you like I did. We had just made love for the first time and I was whisked away," Grace said.

Bobbie set the spoon down, turned Grace toward her, and looked deep into her eyes. "You listen to me carefully, Grace Hammond. Nothing that happened that day was your fault. Your parents would have eventually found out and once they did, it was inevitable they would tear us apart. We both suffered that day. You especially since you lost everything. Please don't beat yourself up one more minute over something that was not in any way your fault."

Grace reached up and slipped her fingers through the hair on the back of Bobbie's head and pulled her down for a deep, searing kiss. When they stepped back to tend to their pots, they were both still a bit dazed.

"This is done." Bobbie's grin made Grace smile. "Is yours heated up?"

Grace stirred the sauce and laughed. "It's heated up all right. The sauce seems warm, too. Let's eat. I'm starving."

Bobbie dished them each out a serving of polenta and sauce before carrying them onto the back deck with Grace and the wine right behind her.

The night was absolutely perfect after the warm day. The sun was just setting over the hills in the distance and they sat down to enjoy their meal.

"Holy shit, Bobbie. How can you not be married? If any of the girls in this town realized you could cook like this you would have been off the market years ago," Grace said through a mouthful of food.

Bobbie laughed. "I've never cooked for anyone else other than my brothers, my mom, and Jensen now and then. I don't usually bring girls back to my house. I've never wanted anyone to get that close. It's always seemed easier to keep them at a distance."

"Have you dated much?" Grace asked.

Bobbie squirmed in her seat a little, obviously hesitant to answer. "I've dated some. The ranch keeps me pretty busy so I'm usually too tired to date, but occasionally I've gone out for a beer or two and found company."

"I'm sorry. It's none of my business."

"It's okay, I don't mind. I don't want you to think I'm some kind of player, but I'm also not inexperienced. Please feel free to ask me anything. I'm an open book when you're doing the asking."

Grace swirled her spoon in her food, hesitant to say anything else.

"Can I ask you a personal question?" It was Bobbie's turn to probe. When Grace looked up, Bobbie asked, "Have you been with other men besides Jake?"

Grace laughed nervously. "I wasn't expecting that one." She smiled to make sure Bobbie knew she wasn't bothered by the question. "I dated some in both boarding school and college. I thought I was going to eventually have to make my parents happy and marry a man so I dated around."

"How personal can I get? What are the boundaries here?" Bobbie asked as she leaned back in her chair.

Grace thought for a minute and decided she felt comfortable sharing anything Bobbie wanted to know. She wasn't ashamed of the things she had done, other than marrying someone she wasn't actually in love with and then not being brave enough to talk to him about her feelings years ago. Sexually though, before Jake she had a life and wasn't ashamed that she lived it.

She held out her empty glass to Bobbie. "Pour me another glass and ask away, no boundaries."

Bobbie poured them both more wine and held out her hand to help Grace up from the chair. "Let's take this inside where we can be more comfortable. I'll get the dishes later." Grace followed Bobbie into the living room where they both sat on the couch. Grace didn't understand why she was nervous but suspected it was more excitement than anything else. Sometimes it was difficult to separate the two emotions.

"Before we go any further, I need to ask you a question." Grace reached for Bobbie's hand.

"Okay…"

"Nothing to be concerned about. I just feel things moving in a direction that I'm excited about but I also want to just check in to make sure we're still on the same page as far as relationship stuff and what I'm willing to offer at this point. I just don't want you to feel like I'm leading you on."

Bobbie nodded her agreement. "I'm really enjoying the time we're spending together, but I know the score. Thanks for checking in, but we're good."

Bobbie pulled Grace's hand up to her lips and gave it a gentle kiss. "Now, back to the dirty things you're going to tell me that you've done. What happened after you got to this all girls boarding school?"

Grace laughed and smacked Bobbie on the leg. She slipped off her shoes and placed her feet on Bobbie's lap where they were immediately grabbed up for a massage. "You're good with your hands, cowboy." Grace smiled at the blush that flushed Bobbie's face.

"Stop stalling. I want to hear about the slumber parties and experimenting and all the crazy stuff that happened."

"You're a nut. It wasn't *that* crazy. The other girls were pretty boy crazy and talked constantly about them. I mostly kept to myself in the beginning. I had friends, but I wasn't really interested in going out looking for guys on the weekends like most of the other girls. A couple of my friends were major bookworms and spent their weekends in the library so I ended up spending a lot of my time there with them. I became a really good student in my seclusion. One weekend my friend Liz got a joint from her older brother and we found a spot in the woods near the school to smoke it. It was the first time for us both and we got stupid silly. We stretched out on a blanket next to each other. For some reason we both started rolling from one end of the blanket to the other playing 'steamroller' which seemed much funnier at the time, although I'm sure with the right high I would totally play it again." Grace winked at Bobbie as she laughed.

"I'll keep that in mind," Bobbie said.

"So we were rolling back and forth, and before I knew it we were rolling over the top of each other, which seemed even funnier. On one pass I rolled on top of her and I have no idea what came over me, but I leaned down and kissed her. She was taken aback at first but quickly got right on board. Liz was the first person I had kissed after you so I had mixed emotions about the whole thing. We ended up messing around a little that day and several times after that. Not that I ever truly got over you, but she helped me take those first steps to getting on with my life. It was hard."

Bobbie picked up Grace's other foot to massage it and gave her a sympathetic smile. "I know the feeling. Sam was my transition as well. We fooled around the first semester, but when school started again after Christmas break she began dating a football player and we slowly drifted apart. I see her now and then here in town. She became a beautician and has her own shop."

Grace had absolutely no right to feel jealous but knowing the girl who helped Bobbie get over her was still in town irritated her more than she wanted to admit. "I'm glad she was there for you."

"Uh-huh. Is that a little jealousy I see?" Bobbie asked with a smile.

Grace laughed and covered her face with her hands to hide her embarrassment. "Let's just say I won't be letting her cut my hair."

Bobbie laughed and flipped over so they were lying side by side on the couch. "So how about guys? What's the story there?"

Grace ran her finger across Bobbie's eyebrow and kissed the top of her nose. "You're awfully curious about my sex life," she said with a sly smile.

"Does it bother you?"

"Not at all. Just teasing you."

Bobbie leaned forward and delicately kissed Grace on the lips before sliding her hand between them and popping open the top button of her jeans. "Is this okay?"

Grace nodded her approval as she bit her lip. In the small space of the couch, she felt surrounded by Bobbie. There was a tug when Bobbie slowly slid her zipper down and pushed her warm hand into her jeans. Grace squeaked as Bobbie grabbed a handful of her ass and pulled her hips toward hers.

"Jesus, Bobbie, I don't know how many more stories I can tell you when you do that."

A deep groan escaped Bobbie's lips as she whispered in her ear. "You feel so good, Gracie. I feel like I've been waiting a lifetime to touch you again." Their breathing had become ragged as they ground against each other. Grace was sure her heart would beat out of her chest as Bobbie's hand moved forward and one thick finger slid inside.

"Don't make me come on the couch, baby. I want you naked and on top of me when we do that for the first time. Or again, I guess." Grace laughed but was having a difficult time not shoving Bobbie's hand deeper into her panties.

Bobbie pulled away from Grace and stood. "Let's move this party upstairs. If I'm able to walk, we'll be more comfortable in my bed."

"I bet you say that to all the girls."

"You're the only one that matters," Bobbie said with so much sincerity Grace's heart melted right there on the spot.

CHAPTER THIRTY-ONE

Bobbie led Grace upstairs and into her bedroom. "I don't want you to get your hopes up and think I'm someone who makes her bed on a regular basis. Full disclosure, I put on clean sheets this morning so you are getting the four-star service this evening of a made bed."

Grace laughed nervously. "We're just going to mess them up anyway, so the bed won't stay made for long. Before we go further, if something happens that hurts your ribs please let me know. Don't be a stoic idiot and let me hurt you. Got it? I'm a doctor and I took an oath to do no harm."

"Oh, we're playing doctor? I like it. My normal doctor never undresses me."

"I like to be very accommodating," Grace said. She gently kissed the newly exposed skin revealed as each button of Bobbie's shirt was undone.

"You're gifted with your hands, Dr. Hammond, but now it's my turn." Bobbie pulled Grace's shirt and bra over her head and backed her toward the bed. "You sit right here and let me take care of you for a minute."

Bobbie fell to her knees on the floor between Grace's thighs. The last time she had seen Grace's body they were only girls. The stunning woman before her now took her breath away. Her skin was the most beautiful porcelain she'd ever seen. Her breasts were perfectly proportioned for her body, not big but not small with dark, pink, erect nipples begging to be kissed.

She leaned forward and took one tight bud into her mouth. Grace let out a gasp and pulled Bobbie's head to her breast even tighter. "That's fucking hot." Grace moaned.

Bobbie slipped her fingers into the waistband of Grace's jeans, and pulled her pants down and off. Grace lifted her hips to help, leaving her in only a pair of panties. Bobbie pushed Grace to lie on the bed and kissed down her body toward her center.

"I've dreamt about this for so many years I can't believe it's actually happening." Bobbie ran her finger along the elastic band of the panties on her inner thigh. She could see Grace squirming on the bed as wetness appeared on the thin material covering her pussy. "Is this making you wet, sweetheart?" Bobbie ran a finger against her slit before pulling the panties aside to get her first look at the wet folds beneath. "So beautiful." She leaned forward and placed a delicate kiss there before pulling the final barrier off and tossing the panties across the room.

"This is all for me, isn't it, my love?" Bobbie swirled a finger through the wetness.

Grace nodded and moaned when she used her thumbs to spread the lips open and delicately touch her labia with the tip of her tongue.

"You taste so good. I can't wait for you to come all over my mouth, sweet girl."

"Please, Bobbie," Grace begged her.

"Don't worry, I'll take care of you," Bobbie reassured her as she pushed farther, working the folds with her tongue. This wasn't the first time she had licked someone's pussy, but she couldn't remember ever doing it with such care. Oral sex had always seemed like something someone did to get to the next part, but she would have been happy to only do this the entire evening.

"I'm so close." Grace groaned as she grabbed handfuls of the sheets. "You feel so fucking good." Bobbie's tongue ministrations sped up. She slid one finger into Grace's tight hole.

"God, you're so fucking tight," Bobbie ground out. She slid one more finger inside. "I know you already feel full, but will you take a third finger for me, sweet girl?" Bobbie placed a third finger at her opening, waiting for permission.

Grace nodded. She ground her hips toward the contact in an effort to pull her even deeper. Bobbie took her distended clit into her mouth, curled her fingers toward Grace's G-spot, and began to fuck her in a deep rhythm.

"Don't stop, please don't stop."

Bobbie moaned when Grace's pussy walls clenched her fingers and milked them as she came. She was so happy in that moment she never wanted to remove them from her.

Bobbie kissed her mound. Grace reached a hand down to push Bobbie away, but she wasn't ready to give up her position just yet. She pushed her fingers deeper into Grace's center, and gently licked her clit until one last orgasm wracked Grace's body. She cried out Bobbie's name, and reaching down with force this time, shoved her away, toppling her over and onto the floor where she let out a groan of pain.

Grace jumped off the bed and ran over to check on her. "Holy shit, I'm so sorry."

"I can't believe you just did that." Bobbie laughed and looked up at Grace who fell to her knees next to her on the floor.

"I can't believe it either, I'm so sorry. I felt like I just needed to make it stop or I might pass out, but I pushed a little too hard."

"I got the hint," Bobbie said with a grin. Grace tried to check Bobbie's side to see if she hurt her, but the angle with her on the floor wasn't good. "I was totally supposed to be careful with your ribs and you distracted me with your skills."

"I do have mad skills," Bobbie said.

"Come on, stud, let's get you into bed." Grace put out a hand to help Bobbie off the floor.

"I've waited twenty years to hear you say that."

Once she was on the bed, Grace gently bent down and kissed her still sore ribs. "Does that help?"

"That helps a lot," Bobbie said. "I think I might need more of it, Doc." Grace laughed and kissed her again, rolling Bobbie onto her back. She unbuckled her wide leather belt and popped open the buttons of her jeans. "Grace" was the only coherent word Bobbie could remember as her back arched toward her touch.

Grace scooted down to pull off Bobbie's boots and dropped them next to the bed. "Let's get these off, cowboy." Bobbie lifted her hips and helped Grace pull her jeans off leaving her in nothing but boxer briefs. "You're sexy as hell, Bobbie Del Ray."

Grace climbed back onto the bed and straddled Bobbie's thigh, soaking it with her wet pussy. It was too much for Bobbie and she realized she was tired of sitting on the sidelines. She flipped Grace onto her back and took control of the situation.

"Hey, that was a dirty trick," Grace said.

"I like to be in control." Bobbie smiled before taking a nipple into her mouth. Grace moaned and reached up to twist her other nipple with one hand while threading her fingers through Bobbie's hair with the other.

"I want to feel you." Bobbie was breathless with need. She pulled Grace's hand from her nipple, and put it where she needed her most. Grace's long, delicate fingers penetrated her wet center as Bobbie rode them from above her.

"That's right, you feel so fucking good," Bobbie said.

"Do you like that? Did you like being inside of me? Did you like it when I came all over your fingers?" Grace moved her thumb up to rub Bobbie's hard, swollen nub.

Bobbie felt herself climbing quickly toward release faster than she ever imagined she would. She couldn't remember ever being this turned on so it wasn't a complete surprise. "You're being such a good girl. You're so good at getting me off. Don't stop."

"I won't stop. Come for me, Bobbie."

Grace's soft fingers caressed Bobbie's core and made her dizzy as she felt her muscles tighten. Just when she thought she couldn't take any more, Bobbie's orgasm hit her like a freight train. She rode Grace's fingers so fast and deep she knew she would feel it the next day. Finally spent, she collapsed on the bed next to Grace barely able to keep her eyes open from exhaustion.

"Poor baby, did I wreck you?" Grace joked as she snuggled up next to her.

"Holy shit, sweetie. That was crazy fucking good. I think I saw stars there for a minute." Bobbie was fighting to stay awake. "I love you, Gracie," she whispered before drifting off to sleep.

CHAPTER THIRTY-TWO

Grace woke up early with what felt like a gorilla draped over her. When she opened her eyes she realized Bobbie's large frame was wrapped around her. She was hesitant to move and spoil the connection, but her bladder demanded she make a pit stop.

Grace slid from Bobbie's warm embrace and picked up a blue plaid button-up shirt draped over the back of a chair and slipped it on. Her panties were ruined from the night before so she didn't bother with them.

Riley, who migrated to the foot of the bed once the action had stopped the night before, lifted her head to see what Grace was doing but quickly drifted back to sleep when she realized Bobbie wasn't awake yet.

After using the restroom, Grace washed her face to freshen up. The wine and sex from the night before left her feeling completely relaxed but a bit sticky. The wood floor was cold beneath her feet so she slipped on Bobbie's Superman slippers and wandered downstairs in search of something to drink.

The kitchen was colder than the bedroom had been and Grace felt her nipples harden to sharp points under Bobbie's shirt. They were sore from the night before and the material from the shirt rubbed against them reminding her of Bobbie's attention. The memory made her knees weak as she felt a fresh flood of wetness to her pussy. She wondered how long she should let Bobbie sleep before waking her up for another round.

Grace smiled as she thought about Bobbie and what they had done the night before. She'd had good sex before and was physically sated, but last night was something altogether different. Last night she and Bobbie connected in a way she had never known possible. She wasn't sure where she ended and Bobbie began.

Everything had been wonderful about the night before until Bobbie's confession as she fell asleep. Grace tried not to make too much of it, but a thread of fear worked its way up her spine. She loved Bobbie, too. She knew that. She wasn't even going to deny it but she wasn't ready for that yet and worried even though Bobbie had told her repeatedly she understood the rules, they were just words. She needed Bobbie to understand there were no guarantees.

Grace thought about her life in Seattle and what it would mean to leave it behind to stay here. She wouldn't be married to Jake but he wasn't the only thing she had in Seattle. Other than being unhappy in her marriage, she'd loved living in Seattle and after the call she'd received the other day, Seattle wasn't something she could so easily walk away from.

She missed her friends and regretted that she hadn't taken the time to contact them more since she'd left. The only thing Seattle couldn't offer her was Bobbie. She knew Bobbie would never be able to leave the ranch, which meant if they were together, Grace had to be very sure she was willing to give up something she'd spent her entire adult life working toward.

Northern California had been the backdrop of her happiest memories, but it was also the scene of some of her worst. Could she live in the same town as her mother and not let her coldness and disapproval bother her? At least in Seattle Grace was able to push thoughts of her mother aside and live her life without letting it bring her down. Was loving Bobbie worth that? Was the fact that she even had to ask that question a sign that she wasn't? Her instinct was to believe she was worth it and so much more, but Grace's instincts hadn't always been her best guide.

Grace poured herself a glass of orange juice from the fridge and sat at the kitchen counter. She pulled out her phone to check her messages. Amy knew she'd spent the day with Bobbie so wouldn't be worried about her, but she sent a quick message just to make sure.

Grace: *Just wanted to let you know I'm okay. Spent the night at Bobbie's*

Amy: *SPENT THE NIGHT AT BOBBIE'S.*

Grace: *I didn't expect you to be up this early*

Amy: *Don't change the subject. I want all the deets*

Grace: *Lol. I'm not sure you could handle all the deets ;)*

Amy: *OMFG*

Amy: *John says congrats*

Grace: *LMAO ummm...thanks?*

Amy: *He's a dork*

Grace: *I should be home later. Don't wait up ;)*

Amy: *I'm so happy for you, my friend*

Amy: *Bobbie better be treating you well*

Grace: *Yeah, she's treating me super well ;)*

Amy: *You're killing me, woman.*

Grace: *Hey, do you have time to talk later?*

Amy: *All the time you need. :)*

Grace closed her phone and turned to go back upstairs running smack into Audrey.

"I'm so sorry. I didn't see you there." Grace was a little shocked to be standing in a shirt and nothing else in front of the mom of the girl she'd just spent the night doing dirty, dirty things with. Awkward.

"Hello, Grace." Audrey walked past her and into the kitchen with two baskets of fresh vegetables. "I was up early in the garden and thought I would drop some stuff off for Bobbie. I expected her to be awake by now, but it looks like you two had a busy night." Audrey's smile didn't reach her eyes.

"Yeah, Bobbie made me dinner last night." Grace wasn't sure if she should run away or try to come up with more of an explanation.

Audrey stared at Grace with what she assumed was a protective mom look. Her mom didn't have a protective bone in her body, but she imagined the look on Audrey's face was exactly that. "Well, I shou—"

"Why don't we sit and chat for a minute, Grace. I'll make us a cup of coffee. Do you drink coffee?" Audrey asked.

RED ALERT. RED ALERT. Grace did not think this was going to be a friendly talk and wasn't exactly sure how she could get out of it. She knew Audrey was only concerned for Bobbie, and since she was the one who very likely dealt with the fallout of Bobbie's heartbreak before, she owed her this talk.

"I'm actually good with the orange juice, but I'm happy to sit and talk if you would like." Grace took a seat at the kitchen bar which felt strange with her warm, bare pussy touching the cold hard wood of the chair. The feeling was incredibly uncomfortable while sitting across from Bobbie's mother, but she put on a brave face and tried to relax.

Audrey busied herself with the coffee pot as Grace watched. "Bobbie tells me you're working at Doc Randolph's clinic. Sounds like you're planning to stay a while."

"I am," Grace said. "I don't have a firm plan at the moment, but I'm here until he returns from his leave of absence for sure. He needed someone for a few months and I needed to come back to take care of my late father's affairs. It was very fortunate timing on my part."

"Where were you before you came back to Preston? If you don't mind my asking."

"Seattle." Grace was skirting around the "Jake" issue and she was sure Audrey knew it.

Audrey poured herself a mug of coffee and sat across from Grace. "That was awfully nice of you to drop everything to see after your mom." She smiled, but Grace knew she was waiting for her to come clean. She took a deep breath and decided to just be honest. She knew Audrey's questions were coming from a place of love for Bobbie. Grace didn't blame her for protecting her child so there was no use not telling her the truth.

"It wasn't completely altruistic. My husband and I were having marital issues, and it gave me the perfect opportunity to extract myself from an increasingly difficult situation."

Audrey looked sincerely sad for Grace. "I'm so sorry. It's unfair that decisions we make at a young age can seem like such a mistake when we're older. Are the two of you still married?" The question was casually delivered, but Grace knew this was what the whole song and dance was building toward.

"We have filed for divorce and are just waiting for things to be finalized. He has gone back to Seattle at this point. I haven't seen him in a few weeks." Grace wished everything was completely done with Jake so she could move on, but life didn't always move as quickly as you wanted it to. She was anxious to get it over with, but this was as close as she'd ever been so she just had to be patient.

"Just like that then?" Audrey asked.

Grace smiled. She knew Audrey wasn't talking about the legal aspect of the situation.

"I'll be heading back to Seattle when Doc Randolph returns to deal with the divorce and whatever joint property we'll need to separate."

"So this thing with Bobbie is only temporary?"

"I don't mean to be rude, but these are pretty personal questions."

"Can I be frank with you, Grace?" Audrey asked. Grace's stomach clenched with fear at where the conversation was going.

"Yes, please."

"Bobbie was destroyed when you left for boarding school. I am well aware that you were only a child and the decision to leave was not your own, but I assume the fact that you did not contact her one time in the twenty years since was your choice. Bobbie has never let anyone get close to her, and I suspect part of that is because of you. Bobbie is my baby and I would be lying if I said I wasn't a little hesitant to welcome you home with open arms. I like you, Grace. I always have liked you, and my saying this has nothing to do with my opinion of you. I'm a protective mother and I'm asking you, as someone who loves Bobbie with everything I am, please be careful with her heart. I could say I can tell she's falling for you now, but I don't believe she ever fell out of love with you before. You take care to treat my daughter with respect because I don't think she can handle another heartbreak like the one you gave her before."

Grace wiped a tear from her cheek and nodded at Audrey. "I understand." Nothing was said that Grace didn't already know, but Audrey had just voiced her biggest fears. What if she did break Bobbie's heart? Would either one of them survive that loss again?

Audrey squeezed Grace's shoulder and walked toward the door. "Take care of yourself, Grace. Thanks for hearing me out. I hope you take the time to really do some soul searching and know exactly what you want and how much you're capable of giving before moving forward."

"I understand. I won't make promises I can't keep. I'll be careful with her heart."

"What's going on with my heart?" They both turned to watch a very sleepy looking Bobbie walk barefoot down the stairs with Riley in tow. Grace's heart melted as she took in her disheveled hair, an Indigo Girls T-shirt, and Doctor Who pajama pants.

"Good morning, sleepyhead." Audrey kissed Bobbie's cheek. "Grace and I were just having a chat."

"Uh-oh." Bobbie gave her mother a look before wrapping her arm around Grace and kissing the top of her head. "She wasn't mean to you was she, sweetheart? She can be a protective mama bear sometimes." Audrey swatted Bobbie's arm and winked at Grace.

"We just had a nice chat. I don't think I said anything Grace didn't already know. I better let you two get on with your morning. Are you going to do your chores? You're up a bit late."

"I called Jensen and he's going to feed the cattle for me. The rest can wait a couple of hours until I'm ready," Bobbie said with a sleepy yawn.

Audrey walked toward the door. "I'm off then. I left some veggies in the kitchen for you. Have a good day, daughter. I love you."

"I love you too, Mama." Bobbie shut the door behind her.

"Sorry about that." Bobbie shook her head and walked into the kitchen. "By the way, you look sexy as hell." Grace blushed remembering she was still only wearing Bobbie's shirt and slippers.

"It was quite a surprise to turn around and find your mom standing there when I've just spent the night fucking her daughter and am wearing her shirt and nothing else." Grace put her hands over her face as the full extent of her embarrassment sunk in.

"And my slippers," Bobbie added.

"What?"

"You're also wearing my slippers." Bobbie pouted. "I'll get you a pair of slippers for here." Bobbie wrapped her arms around Grace, pulling the shirt up to caress her ass. "Holy shit." She looked at her, wide-eyed. "When you say nothing else, you mean NOTHING ELSE. You're totally not wearing panties."

Grace laughed and then moaned as Bobbie rubbed her warm hands over her bare ass. "I told you." Grace held onto Bobbie's strong frame to keep from collapsing into a lusty puddle on the kitchen floor. "I came down to get orange juice and wasn't expecting company."

"I need to change my locks. I've decided this is pretty much your new standard uniform when you're here, and we can't have anyone walking in seeing things they can't un-see." Bobbie smiled, but Grace saw the hunger in her eyes. "You've got me so hot I'm ready to put you on the kitchen counter and take you right here."

Bobbie's words sent an immediate flood of wetness to Grace's pussy. She could feel it slicking her thighs as she closed her eyes and tried to regain her composure. Grace was losing focus, and she had to rein this in before things got out of hand. The talk with Audrey had only amplified her anxieties. She knew she needed to talk to Bobbie about it, but she was in a constant state of arousal, and convincing her they should stop was like convincing a compass not to point North.

"We shouldn't do this, Bobbie." The words came from Grace's mouth, but she wasn't convinced of them any more than Bobbie was.

"Please let me have you, Gracie. I promise I will make you feel good." Bobbie sounded delirious. She kissed Grace's neck and chest, working her way down to a very willing nipple.

"I can't hold myself up. Bobbie—" Grace thought she might come just from Bobbie's kisses when she was lifted and cradled in Bobbie's strong arms. She carried Grace into the living room and gently laid her on the rug. "We really need to talk, Bobbie." Grace half-heartedly tried once more.

Bobbie balanced herself above Grace with one arm but stopped before she touched her. "If you want me to stop, baby, I'll stop and we can talk. Tell me what you want me to do."

Grace pulled Bobbie down for a kiss. "We really need to talk, but I want you so much I can't think."

Bobbie smiled and slipped two fingers over her soft folds. "You're so fucking wet already. I'll take care of you and then we'll talk." Bobbie kissed Grace again before pulling back long enough to look her in the eyes. "I promise, okay? I hear you and we can talk as much as you need to, but right now I have to have you or I'm going to break into a million pieces."

"That seems a little dramatic, but I understand. I want you, too." A moan escaped her lips as she dug her nails into Bobbie's back, holding on to her sanity by a thread.

Bobbie laughed but followed orders, slipping first one then two of her fingers into Grace's wet, slightly sore pussy. "I'm going to make you feel good, my love. Do you like to feel my fingers spreading your tight little hole?" Grace's need was almost blinding. The feel of Bobbie above her, taking her was driving her closer to the edge. She wanted this to last because she wasn't sure when it would happen again. She felt guilty taking pleasure from Bobbie when she knew she was going to disappoint her when they talked after, but she didn't have the will to make her stop.

Grace pushed those thoughts from her head and tried to savor what they had this very moment. She just needed space to figure things out and hopefully Bobbie would understand.

"You have such a greedy little hole, sweetheart," Bobbie whispered in her ear with the most possessive tone Grace had ever heard from her. "You're such a good girl giving me your pussy like this."

Grace could feel the walls of her center contract around Bobbie's fingers. "More," she ground out and saw a devilish grin on Bobbie's face.

"More? You think you can take another finger in that tight little hole?" Bobbie taunted her as she pulled out enough to add a third and slowly pushed back in. "You like it when I get your pussy ready for me, don't you?"

Grace felt herself get impossibly wetter at that as Bobbie straddled her thigh to find her own relief. Looking into Bobbie's blue-gray eyes, she saw so much love it almost made her cry. "Take your pants off, sweetheart. I don't want anything between us when you come on me."

Bobbie let out a deep groan and with Grace's help, used the hand not buried in Grace's pussy to pull off her pants. Bobbie straddled her thigh once again and continued her strokes into Grace's pussy but this time adding a thumb to her hardened nub. Grace could feel herself quickly climbing toward relief.

"You feel so good, sweet girl. You get so nice and wet for me."

Grace grabbed Bobbie's hand and shoved it deeper into her pussy as she came in wave after wave.

"I'm so close," Bobbie said.

Grace pulled Bobbie's hand from her pussy faster than she would have liked, but her blinding need to taste Bobbie sent her quickly crawling down between her legs.

Bobbie lay back on the carpet as Grace took her clit into her mouth. "Oh my God, Gracie. You feel so fucking good. Suck it. Suck me off, baby. I'm going to come in your mouth. Will you swallow everything I give you?" Grace rubbed her tongue across the nub as fast as she could.

Bobbie threaded her fingers in Grace's hair as she pressed her mouth harder against her clit and came with a roar. Grace could feel the power in Bobbie's tight body, and she let out a guttural yell that shook her limbs like jolts of electricity shooting through her veins.

When she was spent, she lazily reached for Grace and pulled her up into her arms. They were both covered in come and completely sated.

"That was fucking amazing, Gracie. You're a fucking amazing lover."

Grace pressed her head to Bobbie's chest and listened to the strong rhythm of her heart.

"I know I'm not supposed to say this, but I really don't want you to leave," Bobbie said.

Grace closed her eyes and wiped a tear from her cheek. She knew what she had to do but wasn't ready for the pain that would follow.

CHAPTER THIRTY-THREE

Bobbie fell back into a boneless heap and pulled Grace over to snuggle into her side. "At some point we're going to actually have to put clothes on," Grace said.

"Boring."

Grace laughed, but Bobbie could tell she had something on her mind. She kissed the top of Grace's head and asked, "What's up, buttercup?"

"As much as I hate to say this, would you mind if we get cleaned up and dressed before we talk? I'm having a difficult time thinking when you don't have your clothes on."

Bobbie smiled but knew she was right. She would never be able to focus on what Grace was saying when the vision of her naked body writhing underneath her as she came was playing on repeat in her head. Putting clothes on wouldn't stop that, but it would at least remind her she was supposed to be listening.

"No problem." Bobbie stood and reached down to help Grace to her feet. "I will do my very best to not think about your boobs. I promise."

"You're like a fifteen-year-old boy." Grace laughed. "Mind if I use your shower? I'm pretty much covered in come from head to toe at this point."

Bobbie groaned like a feral animal. "That's not going to convince me to let you get dressed, Gracie." Bobbie leaned down for a passionate kiss that almost had them back down on the rug.

"Nope." Bobbie stood up straight and averted her gaze from the object of her distraction. She grabbed Grace's hand and led her upstairs to her bedroom. "You get de-comed and I'll make us brunch while we talk. Pancakes?"

"Ummm, yes please," Grace said.

Bobbie's master bath had a beautiful giant tub and a shower built to comfortably accommodate two. She wanted to suggest they bathe together but knew that wasn't what Grace wanted right now. "How about I run you a bath with lots of boob covering bubbles so there's nothing to distract me, and you can soak for a bit while I make breakfast. I suspect you haven't had much alone time in a while after living at your mom's and then at Amy and John's."

Grace gazed longingly at the tub, but finally shook her head. "I can't. I'm sorry, Bobbie. It's a very sweet offer, but I think it's best that I just take a shower." Bobbie watched as she walked around the bedroom gathering her clothes from the night before, depositing them on the counter, and looking at her expectantly.

"Sorry. I'll just make us breakfast and I'll meet you downstairs?" Bobbie pulled a fluffy towel from the cabinet and set it on the counter next to her clothes. "If you need anything else just let me know."

"Thanks, Bobbie. I'm sorry I'm—"

"No, no problem. It's a lot. I'll just give you some privacy."

Grace pulled the shirt a little tighter across her chest, and suddenly Bobbie felt like the worst person in the world. "Grace, if I've done anything—"

"Bobbie, no, you've been wonderful and you haven't done anything that I wasn't more than willing, and practically begging you to do." She sighed and turned toward the shower. The forlorn expression on her face broke Bobbie's heart.

"I'll just..." Bobbie pointed over her shoulder with her thumb.

"Yeah, thanks."

"No problem." Bobbie turned and made her way downstairs to make breakfast.

She ran through the events of the night before and that morning in her head, trying to figure out where she could have gone wrong. Things between them seemed so easy. An image of Grace below her, sweat dripping down her cheek, eyes tightly closed, begging Bobbie to take her flashed through her mind, and sent a shiver down her spine. They'd had the best sex of Bobbie's life. Every moment with Grace had been almost overwhelming.

Bobbie froze mid-step and lowered herself to sit on the last stair. She covered her face with her hands and blew out a breath. "Fuck." She suddenly knew exactly what was wrong and they were both to blame. They'd agreed to take things slowly and in the beginning they really had. Bobbie realized too late that she'd been treating Grace like someone who was completely ready and willing to jump in with both feet.

She'd said all the right things when they'd talked, but when it came down to actually putting those promises into practice, she'd walked all over them and charged full speed ahead. She completely realized she wasn't totally at fault. She hadn't forced Grace to do something she wasn't willing to do, but she knew they were now dealing with the aftermath of those decisions.

She knew Grace was very likely taking one hundred percent of the blame and worried about how she was going to break the news to Bobbie that she needed to step back. It was the right thing to do.

Bobbie walked into the kitchen to pull out the things she needed to make breakfast. She knew what she had to do and the thought of it twisted her stomach in knots.

Fifteen minutes later, Grace came down the stairs wearing jeans and one of Bobbie's shirts. She was adorable and Bobbie's heart swelled with love for her which made it all so much worse.

Grace sat across the counter and poured herself a glass of orange juice from the carafe she'd left there.

"Feeling better?" Bobbie set a plate of pancakes in front of her and pulled a bowl of warm syrup from the microwave.

"A little. Bobbie—"

"Wait. I owe you an apology."

"Me? Why do you owe me an apology?"

Bobbie poured syrup over her pancakes and took a few seconds to organize her thoughts. "I owe you an apology for making a promise that we would take things slow and then completely steam rolling over that promise and taking you to bed."

"I'm a big girl, Bobbie. That was my decision."

"I know that. I know you are responsible for your own actions, but I'm sorry I didn't hold up my part of the deal. I got excited."

Grace smiled as she picked at her pancakes. "I'm sorry I've blown up your life like this, Bobbie. I never meant to hurt you."

"I know you didn't. We have something, Gracie. We always have. I feel it and I know you feel it, too. I know there's much more going on and you have so many decisions to make let alone the emotions you're trying to puzzle out. I get it. I'm going to step back and give you the space you need. I'm here if you need to talk, but I'm going to leave it up to you to reach out to me."

Grace stood and walked around the counter, collapsing into Bobbie as she sobbed into her shoulder. Bobbie wrapped her arms around Grace and held on for dear life. "It's all going to be okay, Gracie. We'll figure this out. No matter what, we're in each other's lives again and that's never going to change."

Grace pulled back and wiped at the wet spot she left on Bobbie's shirt. "I got you all wet."

"That's quite all right. I'll always be here to wipe away your tears."

Grace giggled and rolled her eyes. "You're a complete cheeseball, Bobbie Del Ray."

Bobbie kissed the top of Grace's head. "I thought that's what you loved about me?"

"One of the many things I love about you." Grace rested her head on Bobbie's chest and released a sigh of contentment. "I'm so sor—"

"Stop it." Bobbie stepped back and held Grace at arm's length. "No more of that. You're doing what you need to do to take care of yourself and I'd be one hell of an asshole if I didn't support that one hundred percent. As it turns out, I'm not an asshole and there's no need for you to apologize. You've done nothing wrong. Let's eat these pancakes before they get cold and then I'll drive you home. Amy's going to think I kidnapped you."

"I texted her this morning to tell her I was okay."

"What did she say about that?"

Grace smiled and gave her a wink.

"You told her?" Bobbie was a little surprised Grace had shared what happened between them with her friend.

"Not details or anything, but she deduced what happened and I didn't correct her. You don't mind do you?"

Bobbie picked up their plates and placed them in the dishwasher. "Not at all. As long as you exaggerate about my prowess in bed, you can tell anyone you like."

Grace fanned her face in a mock hot flash. "Oh, Bobbie, there's no need to exaggerate. You did not disappoint."

Bobbie puffed out her chest and smiled ear to ear.

"You're a dork." Grace laughed.

"Yeah, yeah, let me throw on some pants and boots and I'll get you home. By the way, are you planning on keeping my shirt?"

"Yep."

"Just checking. You look sexy as hell in it so I'm more than fine imagining you wearing it when I'm not around."

Bobbie was emotionally exhausted. She knew the drive to drop Grace off would be sad but also looked forward to getting home and getting on her horse. Nothing in the world grounded her like riding around her property and she needed that stability more than anything at the moment.

CHAPTER THIRTY-FOUR

Grace parked in front of Amy's house and pulled out her phone to let her know she was waiting. It had been a busy few weeks since she'd last seen Bobbie, and Amy asked her to dinner to check in. They saw each other every day, but there hadn't been a good time to really talk.

She'd moved into the little house she found with Bobbie and although it had been nice to have her own space, she missed talking to Amy. Grace checked the time on her phone once again and wondered if she should get out of the car and knock on the door. Just as she reached for her keys to turn off her ignition, Amy came scrambling out the door. Grace laughed when she saw a scantily clad John waving at her before going back inside the house.

"Hey, I'm so sorry." Amy climbed into the passenger side of her car and tried to catch her breath.

"Hey, Aim, what were you guys doing?" Grace knew very well what they were doing but she liked to tease Amy anyway.

"Shut up. I'm ovulating and my man is on a baby making mission."

Grace laughed and pulled onto the street. "I'm sure he's very brave and dedicated."

"He's been a trooper, all right. So, what are we doing today? I have this going on a date excitement happening that I'm a little confused about so you better live up to the hype."

"Well, I don't want to disappoint you or anything, but I thought we'd have a nice dinner and chat."

"Where's dinner?"

"Fratellis."

"I'm in."

Grace pulled her car into the parking lot of the restaurant and they both got out. Fratellis had been a favorite when she was a kid, and on the rare occasion they ate out as a family, she'd always asked to go there.

Once they were seated and drinks were ordered, Amy got right to the point.

"So, what's going on other than work? Have you talked to Bobbie?"

Grace decided to order her childhood favorite, spaghetti, so she folded her menu and set it to the side. "I haven't talked to Bobbie since she dropped me at your house. I've been tempted to, but I'm afraid of falling into that rabbit hole again. I tend to completely lose my mind when she's around."

Amy smiled and placed her menu on Grace's. "I get it and I think it's very strong of you to realize that and be able to resist. Have you talked to Jake?"

The waitress walked up before Grace was able to answer and they ordered.

"I have talked to Jake a few times. We're still in the waiting period for the divorce and he's asked to buy me out of our house in Seattle."

"That's good, right?" Amy asked.

Grace dipped a bread stick into the bowl of warm marinara and took a bite, giving herself time to think. "Yeah, it's really good in some ways. He's actually dating a woman at his office that he's been great friends with for a long time."

"That was quick."

Grace smiled at Amy's instinct to protect her, even when it was misguided. "Not really. He's been good friends with Carla for years. I could be wrong, but I don't think anything has happened between them other than friendship before now. She's actually a much better fit for him than I ever was. She was married for many years, but her husband died in a motorcycle accident a couple of years ago. She's a sweetheart and it really broke my heart to see her struggle after his death. Jake was a great friend to her during that time and I guess with me out of the way, it blossomed into something more. Good for him. He deserves to be happy."

"You're much more evolved than me, my friend."

The waitress showed up with their food and they both moaned at their first bite. "Christ, I forgot how good this place was. I was afraid grown-up Grace was going to realize kid Grace was an idiot and this place sucked."

"Oh no, John and I come here about once a month. It's amazing. Try my lasagna."

Grace accepted the bite Amy offered her and almost melted into the seat. "That's fucking—"

"Grace?"

She turned to see Doc Randolph standing next to her. She quickly swallowed the bite of lasagna in her mouth and wiped her face with her napkin. "Hey, Doc, how are you, how is Carol?" She slid from the booth and wrapped him in a big hug. She'd worked for him in high school and he'd always been a source of warmth and comfort for her when her parents hadn't. She loved him like a grandfather and was sad to see the once vibrant man grow old.

"I'm just fine, sweetie. How are you and the clinic? Widow Carrington hasn't driven you to drink with her snakes, has she?"

Grace and Amy both laughed. "Not yet. I've never met an eighty-year-old woman so obsessed with pet snakes."

Doc Randolph placed his warm hand on Grace's shoulder. "She is a character."

"Doc Randolph, do you remember Amy Miller? She's the office manager you hired right before you left."

Amy stood to shake his hand. "It's a pleasure to see you again, Doc Randolph."

"I do remember Amy. How are you liking the clinic? This one isn't working you too hard, is she?" He winked and checked the watch on his hand.

"She's quite the task mistress but I'm surviving somehow," Amy said.

"Would you like to sit with us?" Grace scooted to allow him room in the booth.

"No, no thank you," he said. "Carol is waiting for me to bring home her favorite spaghetti."

"She has good taste. It's my favorite, too."

Doc Randolph's smile faded a bit and he squeezed Grace's shoulder. "Grace, would you mind stopping by my house next week so we can have a chat?"

She placed her hand over his and patted it. "Of course I can. Is there anything I can bring with me?"

"Scotch," he said without hesitation. "Carol doesn't like me to buy it, but I certainly can't stop you from bringing a bottle."

Grace smiled. "It would be no fault of yours, that's for sure. I've been wondering what type of Scotch to bring, should I decide to surprise you with a bottle."

He smiled and patted her cheek. "If you were to bring a bottle of Monkey Shoulder Scotch, I would be a happy man."

"It's a deal. Will you give Carol my love? I haven't seen her since I was in high school."

A young man with a red apron walked up and handed him a bag of food. "Thanks, Jared." He turned back to Grace and kissed the top of her head, just as he had done when she was a kid asking him a million questions about what it was like to be a veterinarian. "She'll be so happy to see you." He reached out his hand to Amy. "Amy, again, it was a pleasure to see you. Gracie, I'll see you next week."

"See you next week, Doc."

He gave a quick wave good-bye and slipped out the door. Grace watched him go with a heavy heart. It was hard to see him getting older. He'd always meant so much to her and even now, in her time of need he simply handed her the keys to the clinic and let her take over. She knew that was mostly due to the fact that his wife needed him, but still, it showed how much he believed in her.

"You okay?" Amy's voice pulled her from her thoughts.

"Yeah, sorry, just sad. He's always meant so much to me."

"I can tell. He seems like a lovely man."

Grace thought about his request for her to pay him a visit and hoped everything was okay. "I wonder why he wants me to stop by."

"Do you think he's going to offer to let you buy the clinic?"

"No, I doubt it. Do you think? No, I'm sure that's not it. His son Clint is a vet in Walnut Creek and I'm sure he will take over the practice when Doc retires. Besides, he's older but he's not ready to hang up his stethoscope. He's too young for that."

Amy soaked up the last bits of lasagna on her plate with a breadstick and popped it into her mouth. "Whatever you say. I bet you ten bucks he wants to sell you the clinic."

"Well, he can't. I can't. I haven't even decided what I'm going to do yet. I can't just buy the clinic. I still have a life in Seattle and a job."

Amy wiped her mouth with her napkin and unbuttoned her pants. She leaned back in the booth and took a deep breath. "Holy Christ, that was a mistake."

"Too much?"

"And then some. I'll bet you a crisp ten dollar bill that he's going to offer to sell you the clinic. I'm just saying, you need to think long and hard before you go over there so you aren't thrown off-guard when he asks."

Grace sighed and pushed her plate of food away, no longer in the mood to eat.

"You okay?" Amy asked.

"Yeah, I just have a lot of thinking to do."

Amy groaned as she pushed herself out of the booth. "Take me home, woman. I need to take my pants off before I bust out of them."

Grace laughed and left money on the table for the bill and a generous tip. She had a lot to think about before she met with Doc Randolph. "Let's get you out of here, Mr. Creosote," she said, referring to the man in the Monty Python movie who exploded after eating too much food.

"If you only knew how close that is to happening," Amy said. "Way too close."

CHAPTER THIRTY-FIVE

A week later, Grace stood on Doc Randolph's porch with his favorite bottle of Scotch in her hand. She knocked on the door and was greeted by the barks of what sounded like hound dogs.

"Back," she heard Doc Randolph command from the other side of the door. "Sit. Stay." When the commotion settled, he opened the door and greeted her with a hug. "Come in sweetheart, Carol's sitting on the back porch getting a little fresh air."

Grace presented him the bottle of Scotch. "I hope you don't mind that I brought you a thank-you gift."

He smiled conspiratorially and cradled the bottle to his chest like a child. "Oh, you shouldn't have, Grace." His voice was just loud enough to carry through the back door for his wife's benefit.

"No problem, it's the least I can do."

Doc Randolph grabbed three glasses, dropped an ice cube in each, and gestured for her to follow him out onto the back porch. Grace had forgotten how stunningly beautiful the view was from the Randolphs' back porch. She'd had dinner with the family many times growing up and had always gravitated to the back porch when she was there.

"I'll never get enough of this view. How are you, Carol?" Grace leaned down and carefully wrapped her arms around her. She was so much frailer than she'd been when Grace was young, and the sight of her made Grace sad she'd missed so much time with these loving people. "Doc tells me you're feeling a little better."

"I am," Carol said. "As good as an old woman is allowed to feel at least. Don't go getting old, Gracie. It's not all it's cracked up to be, although I guess it's better than the alternative."

Grace smiled and kissed the back of her hand.

"Look what little Gracie brought us," Doc Randolph said. He held the bottle up so Carol could see.

"Did she now? What a coincidence that she would happen to bring a bottle of your favorite Scotch. You must be a lucky guesser, Gracie." She winked at Grace who smiled at their banter.

"I wouldn't say I'm lucky, but maybe this purely coincidental gift is a sign of good fortune in my future."

Carol laughed and patted the spot next to her on the couch for Grace to sit. "Tell me about your life, young lady. It's been way too long since I've seen that sweet face of yours. You've grown into a beautiful woman. I'm sure you've had to beat the suitors off with a stick."

Grace was surprised Doc Randolph hadn't told his wife more about her life, but he'd never been much of a gossip. "My husband and I are actually getting a divorce."

"I'm so sorry to hear that," Carol said.

"It's all my fault. I wasn't a very good wife to him."

Carol turned so she could look directly at Grace. "I can't imagine that's the whole story."

"It's not, but I wasn't completely honest with him, or myself, from the beginning so it was doomed from the start." Grace pushed back tears that threatened to fall.

"Would this have anything to do with you being a lesbian?" Carol was so matter-of-fact about the question it took Grace by surprise.

"How did you know I was a lesbian?" she asked.

"Oh goodness, sweetie, we knew that the first time you brought that Del Ray girl over for dinner. You looked at her like she'd hung the moon. We had secretly hoped you might take a liking to our boy Clint, but we knew the moment that tall, lanky rancher's daughter walked in that he'd never be able to make you happy."

Grace wasn't sure what to say. She couldn't help but wonder how different her life would have been if she had stayed in Preston. She'd loved this town and loved the people. Would she have settled down with Bobbie and had a whole brood of children? Grace blew out a breath and accepted the glass of Scotch from Doc Randolph. "Thanks."

"You bet."

She watched as he swirled the ice cube around in his glass and took a slow, appreciative sip. He closed his eyes and smiled as he swallowed the smooth liquid.

"What did you want to talk to me about, Doc?" Grace hated to interrupt his moment, but the curiosity was killing her.

He set his glass on the table and picked up a file folder from the desk in the corner before handing it to Grace. She opened it and read the first page. "What is this?"

He smiled at Carol as she took Grace's hand in hers. "Sweetheart, we can't afford to just give it to you outright, but if you're interested in buying the clinic we think we've come up with a pretty fair price."

Grace was confused by what she was reading. "This says you're offering to sell me the clinic and all its contents for a fraction of what it's worth."

"Yes, I'm sorry we have to ask for anything, but we tried to make it reasonable."

Grace was speechless. "Reasonable?" She shook her head and closed the folder. "I can't let you do this. It's a drop in the bucket of what it's actually worth."

Doc Randolph sat forward and took her glass, setting it on the table. He held her hands between his much larger ones. "We don't want more. You were like a daughter to us, Grace. We love you very much and were heartbroken when your parents sent you away. We had no idea where you'd gone and your parents refused to tell us."

"You don't have to do this, Doc. You both only ever showed me love and acceptance and that meant more to me than I could ever say."

He wiped a tear away and nodded his head. "We aren't doing this out of a sense of guilt or anything like that. I've run this clinic my entire life. I've looked after generations of this town's furry family. It's very important to me that someone I trust takes over the care of my clients' best friends. I trust you, Gracie. I've always known how special you are, and it would be an honor for you to take my place."

Grace couldn't stop the tears from falling. What was she supposed to do now? "What about Clint? Shouldn't you be leaving it to him?"

Carol handed her a tissue and rubbed gentle circles over her back. "He's got his own clinic in the East Bay and isn't interested in coming back here."

"I don't know what to say."

"Say you'll do it. All you have to do is say yes and we'll work out the details later."

Grace buried her face in her hands and sobbed. Doc Randolph pulled her into his arms and held her tightly. "Why the tears, sweetheart?" he asked. "Shouldn't this be a good thing?"

She sank into the comfort of his embrace. She wanted it to be as easy as just saying yes, but she knew she couldn't make a commitment at that point. She pulled back and wiped her eyes. "It's a wonderful thing and you're both so kind to offer, but I haven't decided if I'm staying here or going back to Seattle so I'm going to have to say no."

"I knew you initially told me it was temporary, but when I heard you moved into that little house I assumed you'd decided to stay."

Carol sat next to Grace and wrapped an arm around her. "Talk to us, sweetheart, what has you so upset?"

Grace picked up her glass of Scotch and swirled the liquid around before taking a sip. The burn felt good as it made its way down her throat and helped focus her thoughts. "I'm stuck between two lives and I'm not sure which one to choose. My life in Seattle is great. I have good friends. I love the city. I loved my job there. My life with Jake is ending, but there's so much more there that isn't so easy to walk away from, especially professionally. I've spent my entire career wanting to make a difference. I enjoy working in clinics but always thought my ultimate goal was to lead a research team and make a name for myself at a higher level."

She looked at Doc Randolph who smiled and nodded. "I remember wanting the same things when I was your age."

Grace smiled, relieved he understood. "I took a leave of absence from the hospital, and then you called and asked me to run the clinic so you could care for Carol. It was the least I could do after all you've both done for me."

"We appreciate it more than you know. I'm not sure what I would have done if he hadn't been able to be by my side." Carol reached out and squeezed her husband's hand. The look that passed between them made Grace think of Bobbie, and she smiled.

"It was my pleasure." She kissed Carol's cheek. "So, here's where it really gets complicated. A few weeks ago, I got a call from a conservation group studying the short-eared dog in Peru. It's a very rare species that has turned out to be quit elusive, but they'll occasionally catch it on motion detecting hidden cameras in the jungle. I spent a summer with the group and used my research as the basis for my thesis. My work was published in the *Journal of Conservation Sciences*."

"That's wonderful, Grace." Doc Randolph seemed truly excited to hear of her success.

"Thank you, Doc. It was a very exciting time in my life and I've always thought I would eventually be part of the team again, so when they contacted me to tell me they'd gotten funding from National Geographic and asked me to lead the team, I couldn't believe it. I told them I'd need time before I could give them an answer. They aren't scheduled to leave until next year so I knew I'd have time to take care of the clinic until you were back from leave and then go home to Seattle and take care of separating my life from my ex-husband's."

"If the research is in Peru, why can't you just leave from here? Why do you have to be in Seattle if you're just going to Peru anyway?" Doc asked.

"My team is based in Seattle and we'll be preparing for a minimum of three months before we leave. When we return from Peru we'll be processing all the data and I'll need to be with my team for that. It could potentially mean at least two to three years before I'd be able to leave."

Doc Randolph poured them each more Scotch and handed Grace her glass. "Here's to your success, Gracie. You deserve all of it and more."

She knew he was trying to give her an easy out, but there was more she needed to share. She clinked her glass to his and downed the drink in one gulp. The strong liquid caused her to cough and Doc patted her back and chuckled. "Easy there, young lady."

Grace took a deep breath and laughed along with him. The alcohol wasn't enough to make her drunk, but it was enough to help her relax and she appreciated it in the moment. "Thanks, Doc"

Carol handed Grace another tissue. "So now we understand what's pulling you toward your life in Seattle, what makes you want to stay here? I imagine there's more than just the clinic you're hesitant to leave."

Grace wondered how much to share. Carol had already said she knew she was a lesbian and seemed fine with it, but her instinct was to be guarded with that information when it came to people who knew her when she was a girl. When she looked at Carol, she only saw compassion in her eyes. She reminded herself she was an adult and no longer had to hide who she was, so she pressed on with her story.

"Mostly, Bobbie. I know it sounds ridiculous to make major life decisions because of someone you haven't seen in twenty years, but when I'm with her it feels like I'm where I belong. She makes me laugh. She makes me feel loved like no one ever has. She's everything I want in a partner, but I can't have her without completely walking away from this life I've built."

"Did you question whether you wanted to go home to Seattle before you saw Bobbie?" Carol asked.

Grace took a moment to think back to her first few weeks back in town. She'd always loved it here and those feelings of comfort she felt when people waved at her as she drove by or chatted with her in the line at the grocery store were welcome. She had questioned whether she wanted to go back to her old life before Bobbie.

"I did. I think part of what I'm struggling with is the moment I saw her, I felt like the decision was made. Like my heart sent a message to my brain that said there was no use in fighting it, this was happening no matter what your life in Seattle offered. That's what scares me. I'm not someone who makes rash emotional decisions. I think about them carefully and weigh the pros and cons. I'm big on making lists."

Doc laughed. "We remember that about you, Gracie. The first time you came in to my clinic and asked for a job you had a little notebook and took notes about everything I showed you. I was always impressed that you seemed so organized at such a young age."

Grace smiled at the memory. She knew she'd been quite the pest, bringing in a list of questions to ask Doc, and the other people that worked at the clinic, on a daily basis. She wanted to soak up all the knowledge she could from these adults who were living a life she had only dreamed of. She loved the idea of being such a huge part of the community. Everyone in town respected Doc Randolph and thought of him as a compassionate man that they trusted with their pets. She wanted to be that type of person when she grew up.

She couldn't remember when her focus had gone from small town vet to research team leader. Both were valid careers and both could make her happy in very different ways. She had to decide which path would fulfill her in the long run.

Doc took her hand and squeezed it. "Look, Gracie, we understand this isn't something you are ready to give us an answer for at the moment. The good news is we don't need you to. We've made the offer and if it's something you decide to take we'll be tickled pink. If you can't and you need to go back to Seattle we understand that, too. We've got time for you to think it over and let us know."

Grace stood and hugged them both. "I love you. I can't tell you how much I appreciate this offer and will get back to you as soon as I've made a decision."

Doc and Carol walked Grace to the door. "You don't be a stranger, young lady. Bring that rancher around to visit. We both grew up with her mom. She's a good woman. It's a shame what happened to that family after Frank died. They had a rough go of it. I did what I could to help out, but they're a proud bunch and wouldn't accept much."

The thought of her not being there for Bobbie when her father died broke her heart. They'd missed so much of each other's lives. She wished she could go back to hold her and tell her everything was going to be okay.

With one more hug and wave good-bye, Grace headed to her car. They'd given her one more thing in the pro column for staying in Preston. She wasn't sure if that made things easier or more difficult.

CHAPTER THIRTY-SIX

Spring was usually Bobbie's favorite time of year. The winter rains were starting to taper off and everything was green and beautiful. This winter had been a particularly difficult one not only due to the buckets of rain but also because she missed Grace. It had been a couple of months since they'd last seen each other and every day seemed a little bit lonelier than the one before. She had lived twenty years of her life apart from Grace, but now that she was back in town, Bobbie couldn't think of anything else.

As she released a seven-hundred-and-thirty-pound calf she and her horse pulled from a mud hole, her mother's voice came over the walkie-talkie attached to her saddle.

"Peanut, you there?"

"I'm here, everything okay?"

"It's fine. We have a visitor. Can you come up to the house?"

"Who is it?" Bobbie's heart skipped with the hope the visitor might be Grace.

"It's your brother here to visit."

Slightly disappointed, she climbed into her saddle. "On my way." She wasn't sure the ache of not being with Grace would ever dissipate, but she knew she had to rejoin the world of the living and stop moping around. The trick was figuring out how.

Once her horse was back in the pasture, Bobbie and Riley went to the big house where her mom lived. She entered through the side door, toed off her boots, and hung her hat and jacket on a peg. She followed the sound of voices toward the kitchen. "Hey, big brother,"

Bobbie said. Wyatt stood up and wrapped his arms around her. "What brings you out here?"

"I came to check on you guys and get a good home cooked meal."

Bobbie suspected there was more to the story than he was saying. She knew Wyatt talked to their mom at least once a week so she was sure he was aware of her situation over the last few months even though she hadn't talked to him about it herself. She appreciated him driving all the way up from San Francisco so she thought she at least owed him dinner.

"How about I cook chili and cornbread for us this evening and you can come over to my place," Bobbie offered.

"That sounds perfect. What time? Mom has a few things she wants help with and then I'm free."

"Will six work?" Bobbie asked.

"Mom?" Wyatt looked at his mom who was sitting on the floor with her lap full of puppy and not paying attention. "Mom, will you be done with me by six?"

"That should be fine, sweetie. Peanut, my grandpuppy is looking a little thin." Riley flopped on her back as if to give her a better look at her belly wasting away.

"She's not skinny, Mama. She's just right. We've been working on it so don't start trying to fatten her up again. I'll get in trouble with Grace at her next checkup if she goes off her diet." Bobbie felt a little flutter in her stomach just mentioning Grace's name. She hadn't even thought about the fact that Grace was her vet.

The look on the others faces told her they hadn't missed the mention of Grace's name either and were waiting to see what came next. "So, I'll see you at six?"

"Six it is. Can I bring anything?"

"Beer and an appetite."

Wyatt laughed. "You got it. See you this evening."

Bobbie called Riley who reluctantly left her grandma's lap and followed Bobbie outside. "You need to stop telling Grandma I'm starving you," Bobbie scolded her. The pup wagged her tail unapologetically as they both climbed into the ATV and headed toward the house.

❖

She was pulling the pan of cornbread from the oven as Wyatt walked into the kitchen with a six-pack of beer. "Hey, brother, just in time. What did you bring me?"

"Fat Tire Amber, that's your favorite isn't it?"

"You can stay." Bobbie gave him a playful wink and put the beers into a cooler she had already filled with ice. "Why don't you take this out back to the deck? I'll dish up a couple of bowls of chili for us and be right behind you. Sour cream, cheese, and onions?"

"You know it." Wyatt lifted the cooler and walked out the back door with Riley on his heels.

Their conversation over dinner was pretty typical. When were the Giants going to start playing better? Hadn't this last season of their favorite TV show been amazing? Bobbie caught Wyatt up on the ranch and the lives of the people who worked for them. Wyatt talked to Bobbie about a girl he'd been dating and how they were thinking about moving in together.

"That's a big deal, brother. I have to say, I never thought it would happen. You can be quite difficult to live with sometimes." Bobbie softened the comment with a wink and handed Wyatt another beer.

"Very true, but for some reason Georgia makes me want to not be a dick. She makes me want to go to stupid flower shows because I know she'll be holding my hand while we're there. She once asked me to attend some baby shower where there was only one other guy. Why in the world would she ask that? I went, of course, and the husband was super nice so it all worked out, but later that evening we were having dinner and it dawned on me what I had spent the day doing. And the worst part, I enjoyed it."

Bobbie laughed and leaned back in her chair, propping her feet up on the deck railing. "I hear you. Love makes you do crazy things."

"I think I'm going to ask her to marry me," Wyatt casually said.

Bobbie almost fell out of her chair in shock, spilling her beer on herself in the process. "Easy there, Peanut."

"Don't call me that." Bobbie gave her brother the evil eye. "Mom gets a pass but nobody else."

Wyatt just laughed and pulled Bobbie another beer from the cooler. "I know it's shocking and I know it's probably too soon, but she's the one. I know it deep in my heart."

"I know the feeling, but unfortunately, the object of my affection is on a bit of a walkabout."

Wyatt laughed. "I respect that she's taking time to get herself right before jumping into another relationship. Even if that isn't what you want."

Bobbie felt a flash of anger at his words but quickly recovered. She knew he was right. Grace was doing what she needed to do for herself and that's what mattered.

"Have you heard from her at all?" He asked.

"No. I respect what she's doing, but it's hard not to feel like she's decided she doesn't want anything to do with me. My head says that isn't what's happening, but my heart worries."

"I understand what you're saying, but from what I hear, she has a lot to deal with. Not that you need my advice, but I wouldn't count her out just yet. Grace is special and worth the wait."

"I know you're right. Patience has never been my strongest quality."

Wyatt cracked up at that and shoved Bobbie in the arm. "Sister, patience isn't one of your qualities at all. I remember when we drove to Crater Lake as kids and Mom and Dad threatened to tie you to the roof if you asked one more time when we would get there. You thought they were serious and started crying because you were scared you couldn't stop yourself from asking and they'd really do it."

Bobbie and Wyatt laughed until tears were streaming down their cheeks. "Remember when we told Evan a few years later that Mom and Dad really tied me to the roof for asking and he was so freaked out he didn't speak a word on the entire trip to Yosemite."

"The poor kid almost peed his pants because he was too afraid to ask to stop for a bathroom. He didn't have a chance with the two of us as siblings," Wyatt said. "How's he doing?"

"He's good. I think he'll be back soon to work on the ranch. He's almost done with his program and wants to start applying the things he's learned as soon as possible."

"How do you feel about that?" Wyatt asked.

"I'm fine with it. We've talked quite a bit about it and he knows I have the final say, but it's his ranch too and the things he wants to do seem really cool."

"You going to stop riding the fence with that old horse and leave the watching to the drone?"

"Over my dead body. It's a pain, but there are just some things a drone can't replace. It wouldn't hurt to have the extra set of eyes though." Bobbie knew her intuition could never be replaced by a contraption, and there were more times than she could count when she knew something was wrong because things just didn't feel right.

"You're such an old-timer." Wyatt laughed. They sat in silence enjoying their beers for a few minutes before Bobbie finally spoke.

"I love her, Wyatt. I love her with everything I have, and I feel sometimes like I'm going to go crazy from missing her." Unwanted tears started to fall from Bobbie's eyes as she said the words she'd been holding in out loud.

Wyatt was silent, giving her the space she needed to speak to him at her own pace. After a few minutes he scooted his chair closer, wrapped his arm around her shoulders, and pulled her into him. Bobbie appreciated the comfort he was offering and knew despite their differences he would always be there for her.

"I love you, brother." She wiped the tears from her eyes with her sleeve, hoping he didn't notice her crying.

Wyatt gave her shoulders a squeeze. "I love you, too. Things will work out. You two kids were meant to be together. Give Grace the patience you promised her and she'll come around when she's ready."

"One serious girlfriend and you get all wise in the ways of love and relationships?"

They laughed and stood up to take their dinner stuff back into the kitchen. Patience, ugh. Bobbie knew Wyatt was right, but she hoped Grace would contact her soon. Living without her was getting harder and harder.

CHAPTER THIRTY-SEVEN

Grace pulled up to Lupe's bar at exactly nine at night. The bar had its typical Saturday night crowd, but Grace easily found Amy, Lena, and their vet tech Dani in their usual booth.

"Hooray," they all cheered as Grace walked up.

"Looks like you girls started the party without me," she said. The empty margarita pitcher on the table was her first clue.

"It was just a warm-up," Lena said.

"Well, I have some catching up to do. I'm going to go to the bathroom to change out of these scrubs and I'll be right back. The next pitcher is on me."

Grace laughed as they all cheered again at her offer to get the next round. The last few months had been particularly difficult. Grace was more than ready to relax with her friends and not think about anything other than having a good time.

Grace entered the bathroom and locked the door behind her. She'd brought a change of clothes to work with her that morning. She had to visit a farm at the other end of the county in the afternoon and knew she wouldn't have time to go home and change before going out.

As she rummaged through her backpack for clothes, she found Bobbie's shirt she wore the last morning they were together. She told herself she carried it around just in case she happened to run into its owner somewhere so she could return it, but she knew it was a lie. She would occasionally pull it out of her bag when she had time to herself and just hold it, breathing in the faint Bobbie smell that still lingered there. Clean with a hint of dust and leather. Steady. Comforting. Sexy.

Grace fell asleep holding the shirt more times than she liked to admit. It always centered her. She knew it wasn't the shirt that made her feel that way as much as the person it reminded her of.

She thought about Bobbie every single day and wondered where she was and what she was doing. The time apart had helped in many ways, but it had also been so much more difficult than she expected. Missing Bobbie was a given. She expected to miss her, but she hadn't realized how quickly she had become a part of her life.

Grace would think of her at the strangest times, like when she was looking for something to watch, wondering if Bobbie preferred action or romantic movies. If she was deciding what she wanted for dinner she would wonder what Bobbie was having. It was maddening.

Even though she hadn't made any definitive decisions about whether she would stay or move back to Seattle, she decided she would call Bobbie to set up a time for them to meet. Bobbie had been true to her word and hadn't pressured Grace to commit to more than she was ready for and she appreciated that. Grace would need to go back to Seattle soon to move out of her house, no matter what her future held, and she didn't want to leave without spending more time with Bobbie.

Grace was so distracted by her thoughts, she almost didn't hear someone knock on the bathroom door. "One sec." She stuffed her scrubs into her bag, checked herself in the mirror one last time, and headed back to the table with her friends.

As she approached the booth, she noticed Dani's older sister, Erica, sitting with her friends. The notoriously flirty older Castillo sister had a predatory look in her eyes. Grace couldn't imagine who her target was but figured they didn't stand a chance.

"Did you guys already order the pitcher?" She looked up as she scooted into the booth next to Lena, the breath was sucked from her lungs like a punch to the gut. Of course it would be Bobbie who had Erica in super hunt mode.

Grace could see her surprise reflected in Bobbie's blue-gray eyes. "Hey, Gracie," Bobbie said.

Just then, Amy came back to the table with a pitcher of margaritas. "I got tired of waiting for someone to come to us so I got all hunter-gatherer and procured another pitcher." She saw Bobbie sitting on the other side of the table. "Hey, Bobbie," Amy said weakly, as if she wasn't exactly sure what else to say.

"What have you been doing with yourself lately, Bobbie Del Ray?" Erica asked. Grace picked up on the flirtatious tone in Erica's voice. She couldn't deny the jealousy she felt but knew Erica was very likely completely oblivious to what was happening.

"You've sure grown into quite the sexy hunk of woman since high school," she added before leaning over to whisper something in Bobbie's ear.

"I'm going to put my bag in my car. Start without me." Grace turned and quickly walked toward the front of the bar.

When she finally wound her way through the crowd and out the door, Grace put her hand against the side of the building and sucked in big gasps of air. Seeing Bobbie again when she wasn't expecting it, and with another woman no less, was a jolt that left her in a full-blown panic attack. Maybe she wasn't as ready for this as she thought?

Even though she didn't think Erica had any idea what went on with her and Bobbie, she couldn't help but be upset when she saw them together. She took a deep breath and closed her eyes. She had no claim over Bobbie. She had no right to be upset that she would move on when Grace had made it very clear she wasn't sure she would even stay. *Had* Bobbie moved on? Erica was a stunningly beautiful woman who owned her own business and could offer Bobbie so much. What did she think would happen when she put on the brakes with Bobbie? Grace was sure Erica wasn't the only woman interested in her. It wasn't their fault or Bobbie's fault. Bobbie offered her love to Grace, and Grace told her she couldn't handle it.

Grace dropped her bag and leaned her back against the wall for support, still struggling to catch her breath. She heard Bobbie call her name as she jogged toward her. "Are you okay, Grace? I'm so sorry. I had no idea you were even here tonight." Bobbie was standing near her but kept a respectful distance. "Gracie? You don't look so good. Are you okay?"

Grace saw her reach out to comfort her but stop herself from actually making contact.

"I'm just having a hard time catching my breath," Grace said. "I'm sorry. I'm so embarrassed." This wasn't at all how Grace had hoped seeing Bobbie again would go. When she envisioned it there was much more coolness and less hyperventilating. "I'm sorry. You always seem to be coming to my rescue."

Bobbie laughed. "I'll always come to your rescue, Gracie. Any time, day or night."

"Is Erica going to be upset that you're out here with me? I'm sorry I interrupted your evening."

"Castillo?" Bobbie asked. "There's nothing between us. Holy shit, that's not what was going on."

"She was certainly into you. I feel bad I totally cock-blocked you." Grace felt completely demoralized. Why hadn't she just stayed at home tonight?

"Grace." Bobbie looked into her eyes. "Please believe me, there's nothing going on with me and Erica or any other woman. Castillo and I messed around a little right after high school, but that's it. She's a nice girl, but it was never more than that. I haven't seen her in years. I'm so sorry you walked up at the exact wrong time."

"I'm sorry I reacted that way when I saw you. I feel so stupid. I promise I'm not usually like that." Grace leaned back against the wall.

Bobbie sat next to her but still kept her distance. "How have you been?" Bobbie asked cautiously as if Grace was a wild animal.

Grace smiled. "You can scoot closer." She moved her bag to her other side and patted the ground inviting Bobbie to sit next to her. "I'm a bit chilly anyway and could use your natural furnace."

Bobbie looked hesitant but scooted closer, leaving a small space between them. "As for your question," Grace said, "I'm great. I rented the house we looked at and moved out of Amy and John's. It's been nice having my own space. I've been trying to cook more, but it's much harder than they make it look on Food TV."

"It seems easier when it's all done in half an hour." They laughed together and the tension in Grace's shoulders started to relax.

"Thanks for your patience with me lately." Grace was fidgeting with a leaf she found on the sidewalk next to her as she spoke. "I know it wasn't fair of me to allow things to get where they did before I was ready."

"And where are you now?" Bobbie tentatively asked.

Grace took a moment to gather her thoughts before answering. "I still haven't decided if I'm staying or not. Doc Randolph is coming back to the clinic in two weeks so I'll return to Seattle to get moved out of my house. I haven't decided if my stuff will be moved into another house in Seattle or a moving truck to come back here. I know that's completely lame and I owe you a better explanation, but I would rather do that somewhere other than on the sidewalk in front of a bar."

"I understand."

"I'm so embarrassed I acted that way about Erica. I have no right to question you about anything."

Bobbie finally broke the invisible barrier to touch Grace's hand. "You have every right to ask. I won't keep anything from you. The thing between Erica and me was a long time ago, and if she had known our history she wouldn't have openly flirted like that. It was unfortunate timing. Wyatt and I had dinner here earlier at the restaurant and I stayed for a beer when he left to drive back to San Francisco. Erica recognized me and asked if I wanted to sit at her table with Lena and Dani. Since the place was so full and seats were limited, I took her up on it. Nothing was going to happen. I'm not seeing anyone, Grace. I don't want anyone else. I've missed having my best friend to talk to."

Grace knew it was ridiculous to be as pleased as she was to hear her say it, but she couldn't deny the flutter in her heart when she did. Bobbie's hand still rested on hers, anchoring her in a way she had forgotten.

"Would you go on a date with me, Bobbie?"

Bobbie smiled and scooted a little closer, wrapping her arm around Grace's shoulders. "I would love to. How about next Saturday?"

"Saturday is perfect. Want to walk me to my car so I can put my bag in and then we can go back to hang out with our friends?"

Bobbie's face brightened as she stood, picked up Grace's bag, and held out a hand to help her to her feet. Grace didn't release her when she stood. "I missed you, Bobbie."

"I missed you, too, Gracie."

Grace snuggled Bobbie's arm and threaded their hands together as they walked toward the car feeling more content than she possibly ever had in her life.

CHAPTER THIRTY-EIGHT

Better?" Bobbie moved out of the way so Grace could test the new showerhead in her work bathroom. She knew she'd only be at the clinic another week, but the old one had been terrible and she wanted to do something special as a thank you to Doc Randolph for all he'd done for her. "Oh my God, I love it," she said excitedly. "Thank you so much." She wanted nothing more than to wrap her arms around Bobbie and give her a proper thank-you hug, but she was covered in dirt from work she did on the roof so a pat on the arm would have to do.

"This makes the bathroom faucet, the loose tile on the roof, I've replaced the door handle on the office door, and now the showerhead. I'm pretty sure you owe me lunch."

Grace rubbed her hand up and down Bobbie's arm and squeezed her biceps. "I thought you liked being all strong and fixing things for me? You're my own personal butch."

Bobbie moved like she was going to grab Grace with her soaking wet hands causing her to squeak and run out of the bathroom. "Can I use this fancy new shower to clean up?" she asked.

"You're awfully forward," Grace teased her.

"It would be forward of me to ask you to shower with me."

Grace felt her cheeks warm with blush and she swatted Bobbie's arm. "Get cleaned up, stinky. We're not going anywhere until your hair is free of cobwebs."

"You know, you seem like a very capable woman. I'm not convinced you couldn't have done all these repairs on your own."

Grace winked and handed Bobbie a clean towel. "Maybe, but I'm not convinced you didn't like showing off all your skills. Besides, I have to get the inventory done before I can officially hand the clinic back to Doc."

Bobbie lowered her head and started to unbutton the work shirt she'd worn. "Yeah."

The sad tone of her voice broke Grace's heart. "Hey, none of that." She brushed Bobbie's hands away and worked the rest of the buttons free. "I'm not falling off the edge of the earth. We'll still be in each other's lives. I promise to never disappear on you again, Bobbie."

Bobbie smiled weakly and pulled the shirt off, leaving her in only a bra and jeans. The sight of her tight body and smooth skin sent an immediate flood of wetness to Grace's center.

"I know, Grace. I won't let that happen again. I'll just miss you. I kinda got used to having you around."

Grace closed the distance between them and wrapped her arms around her. "I'll miss you, too." She pulled back and wiped a tear from her eyes. "I owe you an explanation, but you're going to have to put some clothes on or there's no way I'll be able to focus. Take a shower and I'll buy you dinner."

"Sounds good." Bobbie brushed a tear from her own cheek.

Not sure what else to say, Grace left Bobbie so she could take her shower. The urge to climb in and clean every inch of her body was a bit overwhelming so she restricted herself to the little deck attached to the back of the clinic. She sipped a glass of tea and watched the sky grow darker.

She wasn't sure why she was so sheepish about talking to Bobbie about the reasons she might stay in Seattle. Part of her worried Bobbie wouldn't understand and would be upset that Grace would even consider her career more important than being with her. Deep down she knew that wasn't likely. Bobbie would be supportive and understanding and everything Grace needed her to be because that was Bobbie. It was a trait she both loved about her and was frustrated by. It would almost be easier to leave if she wasn't so goddamn understanding. Grace blew out a frustrated breath.

"You okay?" Bobbie stepped onto the porch and sat next to Grace smelling more like raspberries than she normally did.

"I'm fine. You sure smell pretty." Grace laughed.

Bobbie growled a little and gave her a grumpy look. "It was my only soap option."

Grace wrapped her arms around Bobbie and took a deep breath. "You smell great, but I do miss that 'Bobbie' smell you usually have."

"'Bobbie' smell?"

"It's a combination of the clean smell of your soap and the very earthy smell of being outside and working in the sun. I have to admit, it's rather intoxicating."

"Really?" Bobbie asked with a pleased smile. She kissed Grace's neck and took a deep breath. "You smell like berries. It drives me a little bit wild."

Grace melted into Bobbie's touch. "If you keep this up, we're never going to make it to dinner."

"Is that such a terrible thing?" Bobbie asked.

She paused to think about the question and her stomach growled. "I guess that answers your question." Grace laughed and picked up her purse. "Ready?"

"Where are you taking me for dinner?" Bobbie waited while Grace locked up the clinic and then opened the truck door for her.

"How does the Wharf Steakhouse sound?" Grace asked.

"It's only my favorite." Bobbie's smile lit up her face and Grace couldn't help but reach out to hold her hand.

"I remember. I always wanted to take you but wasn't able to until now."

"I'm really glad we're able to go now," Bobbie said.

Grace squeezed her hand. "Me, too."

Once they arrived at the restaurant, they were shown to a table that overlooked the bay. Grace browsed through the menu and found a vegetarian mushroom ravioli that sounded good. When she looked at Bobbie she found her gazing longingly at the ocean just beyond their table. "You look like a woman who needs a boat."

Bobbie laughed. "I've always been fascinated by the ocean. I think in another life I would have been a ship captain. Maybe joined the Navy or the Coast Guard."

"Really? I never knew that about you. I could totally see you as a notorious pirate, stealing treasure and hearts in every port."

"Ahoy, wench."

Grace smiled and tossed a sugar packet at her from the glass bowl on the table. "I'm going to wench you."

"That sounds like it could be fun." She wiggled her eyebrows suggestively at her.

They both laughed and thanked the waitress as their meals arrived. "I should have asked this before but does it bother you that I ordered a steak since you're a vegetarian?" Bobbie asked.

"Nope." Grace took a bite of her ravioli. "You do you, my friend. It's a personal choice for me that I don't expect anyone else to follow."

"Good."

"How's Riley been?"

Bobbie smiled at the mention of her dog. "She's awesome. She's hanging out with Grandma today. I think my mom gets lonely sometimes so Riley hangs out with her when she's not with me. I've been thinking about getting my mom a dog of her own. Any suggestions?"

Grace loved the "what kind of dog should I get" game. "What kind of dog is she looking for? Does she want one that will curl on her lap or one that will get her out walking?"

"I think a little of both. She would want a rescue for sure but a breed suggestion would help me at least narrow down my search."

Grace thought about the question. "I'd suggest getting an older dog. Your mom's not going to want to deal with a puppy. As you know, they're a lot of work."

"You got that right. Riley has destroyed every stuffed animal I've given her. I think she's a good size though."

Grace nodded. "Okay, so medium sized older dog that is affectionate and devoted to their owner. I think you should look at poodle mixes, miniature schnauzer mixes and why don't you look for cattle dog mixes? You have plenty of land and if you get an older one they won't require too much work."

"That's a good idea. Thanks."

Grace smiled and dipped bread into the remaining sauce on her plate.

"Hey, is this a good time to talk about Seattle? I don't want to ruin your meal or anything."

Grace wiped her mouth with her napkin. "You won't ruin my meal. I think I'm done anyway." She smiled and took a drink of her wine. "I'm sorry I've been so cagey about it all. I wasn't trying to keep anything from you, but until fairly recently it wasn't a sure thing."

Bobbie nodded. "I understand. Does this have anything to do with the phone call you got at my house that time? I wasn't trying to listen, but I overheard you talking to someone and it sounded important. You sounded excited."

She took another drink of her wine and cleared her throat. "Yes. That's exactly what this is about. I have an opportunity to head a research team on a project I've been involved with for several years. We thought funding was a long shot, but it's come through and now they're waiting for me to get home so we can get started."

"Is the research in Seattle?"

"No, Peru, but there would be months of preparation in Seattle, the research in Peru and then possibly years back in Seattle sorting through our findings. It's something I've wanted my entire professional career. Not only is the research itself exciting, but it could lead to so much more."

Bobbie pushed her plate of food away and took a sip of her beer. She spun her glass in quarter turns, watching the bubbles float to the top. "Have you accepted the position?"

"I told them I needed time to think about it."

Bobbie took another drink of beer and set the glass on the table. She picked up Grace's hand in hers and kissed each of her fingers before pressing her lips to her palm. She was silent for so long Grace worried she'd upset her.

"Penny for your thoughts?" Grace asked.

"I'm so proud of you, Gracie."

Grace pushed back the tears that threatened to fall. "I haven't dec—"

"Hey," Bobbie interrupted. "I'm not going to ask you to give up your dream for me. I could never do that."

"You aren't. I know you wouldn't. There's so much more to consider. Doc offered to sell me the clinic."

"He did?" Bobbie sat up straight. "Not that I'm completely surprised since Carol's sick and all, but I guess I thought they'd have to wheel him out on a stretcher."

"The thought of losing your one true love makes you consider things you never imagined."

Bobbie seemed like she might say something but took another drink of her beer instead. "What did you tell him?" she asked.

"I asked him for time to think it over. He's coming back to the clinic next week so I can go to Seattle and get moved out of my house. Jake's buying me out so I'll just need to get my things out. I'm honestly giving him most of the furniture so it shouldn't be too big of a deal."

"How is Jake?"

Grace picked at the last ravioli on her plate with her fork. "He's fine, I think. We've talked a few times and he seems to be in a good space. He's dating a girl he works with and seems happy."

"I'm glad."

"Me, too." Grace and Jake had their problems throughout their marriage but their relationship started as friendship and she would have been heartbroken if they couldn't have ended it that way. "He's a good man and deserves to be happy."

"You ready to go?" Bobbie asked.

Grace handed the waitress her credit card and signed the receipt when she returned. The walk to Bobbie's truck was silent and she wasn't sure if she should say something or just give Bobbie space. She hated there was this distance between them now and she didn't know how to get them past it.

Bobbie opened the door for her when they reached the truck and she climbed into the passenger seat. Before she was able to close the door Grace reached out and tugged her closer. She turned in the seat and directed Bobbie between her knees. Bobbie wrapped her arms around her and buried her face in Grace's neck.

"I'm sorry this is all so complicated, sweetheart." Grace wished, not for the first time, the research offer hadn't even happened. The decision to leave Seattle wouldn't be simple, but there was no doubt at this point she'd choose Bobbie and the clinic over her old life if they hadn't gotten funding for the research. Now she was in an impossible situation and didn't know what to do.

When Bobbie pulled back, Grace wiped the tears from her cheeks and leaned forward for a kiss. Bobbie slid her hands down Grace's body to rest on her ass. She jerked Grace forward, practically pulling her off the seat. "Bobbie, please take me home. I need you."

Bobbie pushed Grace back into the seat, shut her door, and jogged around to the driver's side of the truck. She knew they had more to discuss but it could wait. She needed Bobbie like she needed the air she was breathing.

As they drove through the darkness, Grace took Bobbie's hand from where it rested on her lap and cradled it to her chest. Tomorrow could wait. Decisions, responsibilities, and heartache could wait. She wanted Bobbie wrapped around her, inside her, the rest would have to wait.

CHAPTER THIRTY-NINE

Bobbie gasped as Grace pulled a painfully rigid nipple into her mouth and gently sucked. "Grace—"

"Shhhhh…"

The drive home from the restaurant had been eerily quiet. There were so many conflicting emotions swimming around in Bobbie's head she wasn't sure if she was going to cry from sadness or scream from frustration. Grace said she hadn't decided what to do, but Bobbie knew there was only one clear choice. She didn't want to be the reason Grace passed up the opportunity of a lifetime to play rancher's wife with her. It wasn't right and Bobbie knew she had to let her go. The right thing to do would be to encourage her to stay in Seattle even though the mere thought of saying it made her sick to her stomach.

"Are you still with me, Del Ray?" Grace took Bobbie's hand and placed it on her breast, encouraging her to squeeze.

"I'm with you. God, you feel so good."

Bobbie needed to take control. There were so many things she couldn't control where Grace was concerned, but in that moment she could control this one thing. She turned Grace around and pushed her against the wall. She held Grace's arms behind her back and whispered in her ear. "I want you, Grace Hammond. If you need me to go slow and be gentle, you have to tell me now."

Grace gasped and tugged at Bobbie's grip on her wrists. "I want you to take what you need from me."

Without another word, Bobbie tugged the zipper down the back of Grace's dress and let it fall to the ground. The sight of her delicate shoulders, the curve of her back, her gorgeous ass, sent Bobbie's brain into overload. She pressed her body against Grace from behind and slid her hand down the front of her panties. The wetness she found when she slipped a finger into her folds was a welcome discovery.

"You're already so fucking wet for me, baby. Such a good girl."

"Yes." Grace pressed her head against the wall and gasped for breath. "Please, Bobbie."

"Please, what? Please fuck you? Please make your pussy feel good?"

"Please make me yours."

With a single digit, she played around the edge of her entrance before slipping inside. Nothing compared to the closeness she felt when she was inside her. With a gentle rhythm, she pushed her finger in and out, wrapping an arm around Grace's body to keep her from collapsing to the floor.

"I've dreamt about this so many times." Bobbie added another finger and drove deeper into Grace's pussy. "Fuck, you're so wet."

Grace started to slide down the wall, but Bobbie pulled her back up and held her in place. "I'm going to take you fast so get ready."

"Yes, fuck yes."

Bobbie curled her fingers forward and found the spot deep inside Grace that sent a gush of wetness onto her hands. "That's it. Come for me, baby." Grace screamed Bobbie's name when she bit down on her shoulder enough to leave a small mark.

"Bobbie, yes, don't stop."

"I'm not going to stop until you tell me, baby."

She struggled to keep holding Grace up when her body completely relaxed and became limp.

"Please, stop, I can't…"

Bobbie carefully pulled her fingers free and picked Grace up so she could carry her to the bed. She gently set her down before guiding her to turn onto her stomach. "Stay just like that, sweetheart. Let me look at you."

Grace's body was pure perfection. Bobbie pulled off the rest of her own clothes and straddled her narrow hips. She brushed the long strands of strawberry blond hair to one side and leaned down to place kisses on the back of her neck, along her shoulder, and down her spine.

She could feel her own wetness paint Grace's skin as she ground her sex against her perfect ass. "You're so beautiful. I missed you so much, Gracie."

"I missed you, too. I need you, baby."

The confession pulled the thread on the last of Bobbie's ability to restrain herself. She slid down Grace's legs and with a hand on each hip, pulled her lower body up onto her knees. In this position, Bobbie had a clear view of Grace's pussy. "Beautiful."

Bobbie leaned forward and pushed her tongue into the wet folds on display. She heard Grace moan which only encouraged her to take more. She never wanted that moment to end. Grace tasted so sweet and the thought of Bobbie being able to give her such pleasure was like a dream come true.

She used her thumbs to pull the folds apart to make it easier to slip her tongue inside her core. Grace was delirious, repeating Bobbie's name over and over. "Lay flat for me, sweetheart." Bobbie guided her to lay flat on her stomach again and straddled her thigh once more.

"Can you rub your clit for me, baby?" Grace slipped a hand down to rub her clit while Bobbie rocked back and forth on her thigh. "I'm going to go inside you again. I'll be gentler this time." She slipped her fingers back into Grace and used the rhythm of her own body to guide them in and out, rubbing herself against Grace with every thrust.

"Fuck, I'm close." Bobbie knew she couldn't last much longer but hoped Grace would be close enough to come at the same time. "Are you close?"

"Yes, don't stop."

Bobbie pushed her fingers deep into Grace once more as her entire body went ridged and she coated Grace's thigh with her own release. When she knew Grace's orgasm had subsided, she pulled her fingers free and collapsed next to her on the bed.

"Jesus, I'm not sure I'll ever be able to move again. You're fucking amazing at that, Del Ray."

Bobbie chuckled and gave Grace a playful smack on the ass. "You're not too shabby yourself, Hammond. Wanna go again?"

Grace laughed and rolled onto her side. "Maybe later. Would you just hold me for a bit? I want to be close to you."

Bobbie pulled the covers over both of them and Grace snuggled in next to her. "Can we talk about us for a minute?"

Grace held her a little tighter. "Sure."

"I don't want to lose you, but I can't let you give up your dreams for me."

"It's not—"

"Hold on." Bobbie knew she had to get this out before she lost all her nerve. She'd just have to hope Grace would hear her out. "I can't let you give up your dreams for me, but I also don't want to be without you. I know it would be incredibly difficult, but would you consider a long distance relationship?"

Grace's brow did the wrinkled thing it always did when she was deep in thought. Bobbie had always thought it was adorable, but this time it only left her in knots. "Grace?"

"I can't ask you to do that, Bobbie. It could literally be years. I just don't know at this point. I can't ask you to put your life on hold so I can run off to Peru."

"What if that's what I want? I don't want to be without you, Grace, but I'm willing to do whatever it takes to make things work."

Bobbie worried she'd pushed her too far, but after a few minutes, Grace reached up and kissed Bobbie on the lips. "Okay, let's try. If it becomes too much for you, please let me know. We have to communicate and be as open as possible. That's the only way this is going to work."

"Promise." Bobbie kissed Grace's head. She was scared of what the future would hold, but she was also very hopeful. She told herself to focus on the hopeful.

"Want to watch something on TV?"

"Something funny."

"Roger." Bobbie found the remote and turned on a comedy.

A few hours later, the sound of a gunshot woke Bobbie from sleep. She sat up to find a cop drama on the TV and a sleeping Grace tucked into her side. The sight of her lying naked in her bed had Bobbie ready for another round, but she knew she should give Grace's poor body time to recover from the night before.

"Hey, baby, are you awake?" Bobbie placed gentle kisses around Grace's temple and the corner of her eyes.

"Mmm...five more minutes."

Bobbie laughed and brushed her hair back from her face. "You can sleep as long as you want, sweetie. Unfortunately, I have to take a shower and head out to do my chores. You take your time and sleep as long as you want. Make yourself at home if you get up before I'm back."

"I'm sorry, so sleepy." Grace reached out and squeezed Bobbie's arm.

"No problem at all, sweetheart. I like the thought of you lying here in my bed, naked as a jaybird."

Grace smiled. "You crack me up."

Bobbie kissed Grace's cheek and reluctantly slipped from the bed. She knew a long distance relationship wouldn't be easy, but they'd make it work. They had to. Bobbie couldn't bear the thought of a life without Grace in it.

CHAPTER FORTY

Grace reluctantly left Bobbie's house to go home and get ready for the day. Her time in Preston was almost at an end, and she had one more thing she needed to do before she left for Seattle. She knew she would never be able to move past the issues with her mom until she at least attempted to make peace with the woman who had caused her so much pain. The vindictive part of her wanted to charge her mom for the years of therapy Grace had needed after a loveless childhood. Between that therapy and the maturity she now had under her belt, she decided to take the high road and move forward.

They hadn't spoken to each other since the day Grace walked out after their argument and the thought of voluntarily putting herself in her mother's crosshairs once more made her stomach turn over.

With a sigh, Grace pulled her phone from her pocket to send her mother a text.

Grace: *Hey, Mom*

Phyllis: *Grace*

Grace: *Are you around this morning?*

Phyllis: *I'm at home if that's what you're asking*

Grace: *That's what I'm asking. Would you mind if I drop by?*

Phyllis: *If you must. If this is about money, contact our accountant Barry, although I don't think you'll be able to squeeze more from your inheritance than you've already been given.*

Grace: *It's not about money, Mom. I'm fine. I'll be there in 10 minutes.*

Grace could already tell this wasn't going to be any fun. She locked up her house and drove toward her family home. She had so many memories of that house, but it was never really a home. She'd always been more comfortable at friends' houses or her grandparents' than she ever was in her own home. Everything about the cold place sent shivers up Grace's spine.

When she arrived she was greeted at the door by her mother's housekeeper. "Hey, Susan, is Mother around?"

"She's on the back patio. She asked that I tell you to be quiet because you'll scare the birds if you're too loud." Susan rolled her eyes as she relayed the message. She'd been with her parents since Grace was a girl and had always done what she could to make Grace's life as easy as possible.

"Thanks." Grace gave Susan a quick hug. "When this talk with my mom blows up in my face and I storm out, please know how much I appreciate all you've done for me over the years. Let's not be strangers. I would love to see you occasionally if the old bat gives you time off." Susan and Grace laughed as they shared one last hug before Grace walked to the back patio.

As she stepped into the covered area, she found her mom sitting on a plush couch reading a book. Without lifting her eyes from the pages, she said, "Hello, Grace, what is it that you want?"

"Hello to you, Mother. I don't want anything. I didn't want the last communication we ever had with each other to be the day I left Jake and moved out of your house." Grace sat on a matching couch across from her mother. "Would you mind putting the book down and talking to me for a minute?"

Grace rolled her eyes when she dramatically closed her book, set it on the table in front of her, and folded her arms over her chest like an irritated teenager. "It's too late to apologize, Grace. The damage has been done. I am the laughing stock of the country club."

Even though Grace expected everything her mother was saying, the lack of surprise didn't remove the sting of her words. She was used to being a great disappointment to her mother's high social expectations but it still hurt. With a deep breath, she closed her eyes and reminded herself to stay calm. If she wanted this visit to be worth her time she needed to bite her tongue and let the little stuff go. She was going to deserve an award after this performance.

"I'm sorry my divorce has affected you and your status at the country club, Mom. I did what I had to do for my own happiness and I regret that I had to hurt others to do it. I came here because I don't want there to be this wall between us. I expect distance because there has always been distance, but I don't want our last words to each other to be angry ones."

She relaxed her arms a little, and Grace could see the ice queen she called Mother was beginning to thaw just a bit.

Her mother straightened the creases in her skirt and sat a little straighter in her seat. Grace braced for whatever mean comment she knew was about to be lobbed back over the net.

"It appears Jake has moved on and found someone more suited to him. His mother called to let me know he would be just fine without you."

She never disappointed. Grace took another deep breath and slowly exhaled. "Look, Mom, you don't know how much I regret trying to please you by marrying him. I should have known I'm not the daughter you had hoped for and could have never pleased you, so it was all for naught." Easy, Grace, she coached herself as she felt her blood pressure rise. "I should go. I won't keep you any longer. I wanted to say that I'm sorry for any grief I caused you and that even though we haven't ever gotten along, you're my mother and I love you."

Grace stood to leave, but her mother reached out and took her hand to stop her progress. "Please sit, Grace." Grace wasn't sure if it was a trap or if she was being punked, but she was a little freaked out and not sure how to react other than to sit back down.

They were both silent for a minute. She wasn't sure where to go from there. They'd never been in this position before, and she was cautiously hopeful they may have turned some kind of corner. She decided to start by talking about something her mother was interested in. That seemed the safest path. "How many birds do you have now, Mother?"

Grace looked around at the cages lining the covered outdoor space and counted at least twenty. She never understood why such an uptight person like her mother would love birds of all things. Birds were messy and noisy and wouldn't follow commands unless they felt like it. Everything her mother should have hated in a creature, but she had always loved them.

She seemed to light up when Grace asked about her birds. "I have twenty-four out here and more on the balcony upstairs. I recently added a breeding pair of rose-breasted cockatoos. They are very sweet."

"I would love to see them if you have time to show me." Grace was actually enjoying herself. She didn't want to jinx things by acknowledging it, but she wasn't even miserable.

She smiled and stood to walk Grace over to where the newest birds were kept in a huge enclosure with several cockatoos. "As you know, I have an ornithologist on staff who cares for the birds. She studies them and has written articles in various publications about her findings. My Victoria crowned pigeon was featured on the cover of *Birding* magazine."

Grace could see the pride her mother had for her birds and wished she had been the recipient of that pride even once. She knew she would just have to take what she could from a relationship with her and let the rest go.

"That's amazing. You have quite the collection and they all seem very happy and healthy." Grace enjoyed seeing her mother actually smiling but was afraid of pushing her luck and staying long enough to get into another argument with her. "Well, Mom, it was lovely to see your birds. Maybe sometime I can come back and see them again?"

She stared at Grace for a moment. "That would be fine. Please call Susan for an appointment with more than one day notice. I have a busy schedule and won't always be available."

Grace smiled. There she was. There's the mother she remembered. "I will. Thank you for making time for me today." She wasn't sure if she should shake her hand or hug her or what. She couldn't remember ever hugging her in the past so she didn't think their budding relationship was ready for that just yet. Settling on an awkward half-ass bow, she said good-bye, and quickly left before her mother could say something to ruin the moment.

CHAPTER FORTY-ONE

The noise from the tractor drowned out the sound of Bobbie's phone. She'd been out in the back pasture all day putting the finishing touches on a project she'd been working on. The time alone had given her a chance to think about her future and what mattered most.

She checked her watch and calculated how much time she had left before she needed to get home and get ready for Grace's call. They'd fallen into a routine over the last month since she'd returned to Seattle, and Bobbie looked forward to their nightly video calls more than anything else during her day.

At six on the dot, Bobbie pulled the tractor into the barn and she and Riley jumped down and hurried into the house. She knew it was silly to shower and put on clean clothes before each call, but she wanted to look her best. The invention of video calls were both a blessing and a curse.

Once she was clean and dressed, she sat at her desk and booted up her computer. She used the extra few minutes before the call to make a whiskey sour and check herself in the mirror one last time. "Good Lord, Del Ray, stop fussing over how you look," she said to herself.

She let the call ring a couple of times before connecting hoping it wouldn't make her look as desperate to talk to her as she was. "Hey, baby. How was your meeting with the team?" Grace had told her the night before that she was nervous about a big team meeting with representatives from National Geographic. The project was still in the early stages, but from what Bobbie gathered, things were happening quickly.

"Good. Great." Grace glanced away from the camera as if she was uncomfortable before focusing back on Bobbie with what seemed like a forced smile. "How was your day? Did you get your mom's raised garden beds built?"

Bobbie wasn't sure if she should press or not, but she decided to give Grace a chance to talk to her about what was bothering her on her own. "It was good. I built the garden beds and helped mom plant all kinds of things. I hope having them raised like that will save her back from all that stooping over."

"Me, too. You should get her one of those scoot carts that allows you to sit and will also carry her stuff."

"That's a good idea." Bobbie took a sip of her drink, and watched Grace pick at a thread on her sweater. "How's Seattle? Was the weather any better today?"

"It was fine." Grace slid onto her side and stretched out next to her laptop. "I miss you, baby."

Bobbie smiled. She never got tired of hearing Grace call her "baby." "I miss you, too. If you were here right now I would snuggle up behind you and kiss that little spot on your neck that always makes you giggle."

"I hate it when you make me giggle."

Bobbie was happy to finally see a smile on her face. "No, you don't. Especially when kisses are involved."

"I am a sucker for your kisses." Grace's smile faded as she wiped a tear from her cheek. "I really miss you, baby."

"I miss you, too. What's going on, sweetheart? Did something happen to upset you?"

Grace sighed and covered her eyes with her hands. Their time apart had been emotional at times, but this seemed different. She suspected it was more than just missing Bobbie that had her upset.

"You know you can talk to me about anything, right?"

"I know. I love you."

The time they'd spent just talking on the phone had taught Bobbie many lessons. The most important was to allow Grace the space to work things out without having someone pressuring her. It went against all of Bobbie's instincts, but she'd learned it was worth the wait.

"I love you, too. Have you talked to Jake lately?"

"Not since I picked up the last of my stuff from the house. Carla was supposed to move in last weekend so I'm sure they're pretty busy."

Bobbie thought Grace was honestly glad to see Jake move on after they split. She'd been really hard on herself after leaving him and the thought that Jake might have found happiness beyond his relationship with her, seemed to relieve some of the guilt she had.

"Have you talked to her?"

"Who?"

"Carla."

Grace shook her head. "No. I think that ship has sailed, unfortunately." They'd been friends before Grace and Jake broke up, and Bobbie thought that seemed like the one regret she had about Carla and Jake being together. She'd told Bobbie before that it was just too awkward between them now to ever really be friends again.

"Sorry."

"It's okay." Grace smiled. "Is it going to drive you insane if I mention again that I miss you?"

Bobbie laughed. "I'll never get tired of hearing it so, no. Hey, why don't I come out and visit? Would that be okay with you?"

The light seemed to return to Grace's eyes as she sat up a little and smiled. "Really? Do you think you could make that work?"

"I'm sure I can. Evan's been back for a couple of weeks, and I think he can handle stuff just fine. He and I do things a little differently since he has all that learnin' and I just have my instincts, but he seems to be settling in." Bobbie winked at Grace and she laughed.

"You have more than just instincts going for you, sweetheart."

Bobbie took another sip of her drink and pulled out her calendar from her drawer.

"Is that a paper calendar?" Grace sounded shocked which made Bobbie roll her eyes.

"I won't lose this because my computer crashed."

"No, you'll just lose it because you spilled your coffee on it or the dog ate it or any number of reasons why it's insane to still have a paper calendar."

Bobbie looked down at Riley suspiciously. "Riley, don't eat my calendar, okay?" Riley tilted her head as if she was wondering why Bobbie would ever think she would do that. "Okay, I hardly ever drink coffee and Riley agrees to leave it alone so we're all good."

Grace laughed. "Evan and I are going to pull you into this century if it kills us."

"Yeah, yeah. When do you want me there? I don't want to cause issues when you need to be working with your team."

She watched as Grace scrolled through the calendar on her phone. "Okay...gosh...I want it to be yesterday, but the next two weeks are really busy. Want to see what tickets look like for three weekends from now? If it's too much trouble I'll see what I can do to get down there."

"No, no, no, that'll be just fine. It'll give me a little more time to get Evan situated."

Grace grabbed a pillow and held it close to her body. Bobbie could see how lonely she was and wished more than anything that she could be there to comfort her. "I can't wait to kiss you, Gracie."

Grace smiled and touched her finger to the laptop screen. "Oh, yeah? What else are you going to do?"

"One sec." Bobbie picked up her laptop and carried it over to the recliner she had in the corner of her office. She sat in the chair with the laptop in her lap and pushed up the feet so she could recline back. "Okay, now I'm more comfortable."

"Good. Now, what else are you going to do to me when I see you?"

"Will we be alone or is this going to be in front of other people?"

"Alone. In my hotel room."

"Well then, first I would suggest we take a hot bath together. Do you have a decent bath tub in that room?"

"Yep, nice and big."

"Perfect. I love taking baths and have had a fantasy or two where we were taking one together."

"Oh, really? In the bath at your house?"

"Yes, the tub in my master bath."

"Then what?"

"I would sit in the back and you would lean back against me so I could play with your breasts and make sure they're super clean and cared for."

Grace laughed. "You're obsessed with boobs."

Bobbie winked at her. "Maybe, but in my defense, yours are amazing so it's not my fault."

"Okay, so my boobs are clean, now what?"

"Next I would kiss your neck and your shoulders and run my hand down beneath the water to slide my fingers through your folds."

"Mmm...I like the sound of that." Grace lifted the hem of her shirt and lazily traced circles on her stomach. The move sent shivers down Bobbie's spine. "You know what I would do?"

"What?" Bobbie croaked out.

"I would sit up on the side of the tub and spread myself open for you."

Bobbie popped open the buttons on her jeans and slipped her hand inside. "Oh really? That's awfully bold of you, Dr. Hammond." She ran her fingers through the neatly trimmed hairs and slid a finger over her engorged clit. "Are you wet, baby?"

She watched Grace unbutton her pants and drag her zipper down, exposing pink lace panties.

"Mmmm...those are nice." Bobbie loved how feminine Grace was. She'd never felt comfortable being feminine herself, but nothing turned her on more than a confident femme woman.

"They were in my things that were left here. I thought about you this morning when I put them on and wondered if you would like them. I guess that answers my question." She watched Grace slip her hand into her panties and close her eyes when her fingers found their target.

"Are you wet, baby?"

"I'm so wet, Bobbie."

"That's my good girl. Get nice and wet for me. I bet you feel so nice." Bobbie's own pussy was soaking her underwear as she rubbed herself faster. "I don't know if I'm going to last very long, sweetheart. I've had dirty thoughts about you all day."

"Tell me what you'd do if I was sitting on the side of the tub, open and ready for you."

"Fuck." Bobbie slowed her fingers, doing her best to stave off her impending release. "I would take my fingers and spread you open so I could look at you. You have the most beautiful pussy, baby."

"God, Bobbie, I'm so close."

"Make yourself feel good for me, baby. Close your eyes and pretend it's me."

"Yes." Grace did as she was told and closed her eyes. Bobbie watched her lean her head back and open her mouth as if holding back a scream.

"When I couldn't take just looking anymore, I'd lean forward and take your folds into my mouth and suck. Just the way you like it. I'd suck one labia into my mouth and then the other, giving them each a gentle tug until you were writhing on the edge of the tub and begging me to suck your clit."

"Bobbie, fuck." Grace wiped sweat from her brow as it threatened to drip into her eyes. "Don't stop, baby, tell me more."

"Your clit would be so hard and I'd take my time, gently running my tongue over it. You'd be bucking your pussy into my face, trying to force me to go faster so I'd wrap my arms around you to force you to be still."

"I'm going to come, Bobbie."

Bobbie felt her own orgasm quickly bubbling to the surface. "That's my good girl. Come in my mouth, Gracie. Give it to me. I want all of you, my love. I want everything you can give."

She felt herself tip over the edge as she listened to Grace quietly scream her name in a hotel seven hundred and eighty-nine miles away. Bobbie closed her eyes and pushed back the tears that threatened to fall. She wasn't sure how long she could handle the distance between them. The life that seemed so important only a year ago suddenly didn't make much sense.

"Baby? Are you okay?"

Bobbie opened her eyes to find Grace watching her with a concerned look.

"I am. I'm just a little overwhelmed with emotions at the moment. Don't mind me."

Grace smiled but still seemed concerned. "You're such a softy. A big strong, tough, softy."

"Yeah, yeah, don't tell anyone else. I have a reputation to uphold." Bobbie lowered the footrest on her chair and walked back over to her desk. "It's getting late, I can't believe we've been on here this long."

Grace looked at the watch on her wrist. "Holy shit. I have to get to bed. We have some people coming in tomorrow to talk to us about the tents we'll be taking to Peru. They're using some new material that's supposed to be lighter but still be waterproof. We'll see. They all like to make promises they're very seldom able to keep."

"I wish I could fall asleep with you in my arms."

"I want that, too, baby. Soon. You'll be here before we know it and I'm not letting you out of my sight. I hope you aren't one of those people who has to close the bathroom door when you're on the toilet. I'm not letting you out of my sight."

Bobbie drained the last of her drink. "You're a complete weirdo, Grace Hammond, but I think you're incredibly cute so I'll pee with the door open, you freak."

"That's my girl."

They both laughed but there was a hint of sadness to it. "Night, night, my love. I love you."

"I love you, too, baby." Grace kissed her fingers and then blew the kiss toward the camera on her laptop. Bobbie pretended to be blown over by the kiss which made Grace laugh. "Go to bed, you goofball."

Bobbie waived once more before closing the connection on their call. She knew she couldn't continue to live like this, but wasn't exactly sure what to do about it yet. It seemed like they were in an impossible position, but maybe that was only because she was thinking of their lives as if they were in these cages with no way out. What if she simply opened the door and walked through?

Riley whimpered and walked to the office door. Bobbie knew she had a lot to think about, but for now she needed to sleep. She was too exhausted, and too sad, to solve any problems that night.

"Come on, Riley, we need to get some beauty sleep so we can figure out what we're going to do."

A week later, Bobbie and Riley drove to her mother's house in the ATV for dinner. She'd been so busy getting Evan up to speed on the ranch, she worried her mother might feel neglected. Unfortunately, there was more to her request to get together than just dinner and a visit. She hoped her mother would listen to what she had to say and understand. There was no doubt in her mind what she had to do so it was happening with or without her mother's blessing.

"Hey, Mama." Bobbie kissed her mother's cheek when she found her in the kitchen. "I brought cake, just like you asked."

"Oh, bless your heart. I've been craving cake something fierce and it looks like you picked up my favorite. Chocolate cake with chocolate frosting is a gift from the angels."

Bobbie laughed and placed the cake in the stand her mom kept on the counter. "You're a chocoholic, lady."

"This is true. Take this to the table and I'll be right behind you with the rest."

Bobbie took the casserole dish from her mom and set it on the table. "This looks incredible, new recipe?"

"I hope you like it. It's creamed spinach layered with butternut squash. I saw the recipe on that Pintrest thing you showed me and it looked so good I just had to try it." Her mom placed pork chops and a bowl of salad on the table and sat down with Bobbie. "How's my grandpuppy? I feel like I haven't seen her in forever."

As if she knew they were talking about her, Riley lifted her head and gave a quiet bark. "No bark, Riley," Bobbie said. "You spoil her."

"Well, none of my children have given me human grandchildren so I have to make do with the four legged kind for now."

Her mom liked to tease them about the fact that none of them had settled down and had a family of their own. It had always annoyed her and her siblings, but this time it might be the perfect way to bring up the real reason she was there.

"Speaking of grandchildren—"

"How is Evan doing?"

Bobbie didn't miss the fact that her mother had cut her off and changed the subject. She wondered if what she wanted to talk to her about wasn't going to be the surprise she thought it was.

"He's good. In fact, I wanted to talk to you about something that has to do with him."

She cleared her throat and took a big drink of her water in an attempt to wash down the lump that had set up residence in her throat. "Mom…I—"

"I know, Bobbie."

Bobbie was speechless. She'd been worried about what to say for days and now her mother seemed to have relieved her of the most stressful part of the entire thing. Hopefully, it wasn't because she didn't actually know what Bobbie wanted to talk to her about.

"So, you know that I'm leaving the ranch to live with Grace in Seattle, if she'll have me."

"I've known this was coming for quite some time now. Your old mom knows more than you think. Does Grace know that's your plan?"

Bobbie absently moved the food on her plate around with her fork. She hadn't exactly talked to Grace about her decision, and part of her worried she wouldn't be as happy about it as she hoped she would be. "No, I'm going to talk to her when I go out there. I've been working with Evan to get him ready to take over the ranch. He knows my plan and has agreed to allow me to co-manage remotely. I can take over the paperwork portion of things and he'll handle the day-to-day stuff here."

"You love this ranch, Bobbie. Are you sure you want to give up your life's work to move to another state with a girl you've only dated for a couple of months."

Bobbie sat up straight in her chair. "I love Grace more than the ranch. I love her more than anything, and to be honest, this seems like a small price to pay for a lifetime of happiness."

Her mom smiled and kissed her cheek. "That's all I needed to hear, sweetheart."

"That's it?" Bobbie had been gearing up for much more resistance, and this sudden acceptance by her mother was a little unnerving.

"That's it." Her mom reached out and placed her hand over Bobbie's and squeezed. "I've only ever wanted you to be happy, Peanut. If you say being with Grace is the only thing that will do that, I support you one hundred percent. Evan and I can hold down the fort. Who knows, maybe after this thing she has going on in Seattle is done, you'll come home. If that day comes, we'll be here to take you both in with open arms. I love you, Bobbie. You are my heart, and if you say Grace is the one, you have to go out there and get her."

Bobbie wiped a tear from her cheek and wrapped her arms around her mother. She'd never been away from her or the ranch for more than a couple of weeks at a time. The thought of moving hundreds of miles away both excited and scared her to death, but she knew it was the only choice she had. She couldn't go on living her life without doing everything she could to be with Grace.

"So, what's the plan? Isn't she going to be going to Peru soon?"

Bobbie nodded her head and began eating her dinner again. "Yeah, I'll talk to her about it when I'm out there and if she doesn't mind, I'll stay until she has to leave. While she's in Peru I'll probably come back here and then officially move to Seattle when she's done. That will give me more time to get Evan ready to take over."

Her mom silently placed her napkin on the table and stood. Bobbie closed her eyes and soaked up the love as frail hands cradled her face and a gentle kiss was placed on her forehead. "I love you so much, Roberta Del Ray. I've wanted nothing short of a perfect life for you since the moment I knew you were in my belly, and if Grace Hammond is the one to give you that life, I couldn't be prouder of you for going after what you want."

Bobbie stood and held her mom in her arms as they both cried. She wasn't sure how many of those tears were the happy sort and how many were sad, but she'd never forget the gift her mother had given her. She knew this conversation could have gone so much worse and she'd be forever grateful for her mother's love.

CHAPTER FORTY-TWO

B obbie surveyed the piles of clothes laid out on her bed. She was only packing a week's worth of stuff, even though she hoped she'd be there longer. If things went as planned, she could always buy more things in Seattle.

Riley grumbled from her bed in the corner. Bobbie sat on the floor and called her over. "I'm sorry I have to go, sweet girl. It'll only be a week and if it turns out we're staying in Seattle, Uncle Evan agreed to send you to me on an airplane." Riley covered her face with her paw as if she understood what she was saying and didn't like the idea of flying. Bobbie chuckled, and kissed her nose. "I know. I don't like it either, but it's what we need to do to be with Grace." At the mention of her name, Riley licked Bobbie's hand. "I feel the same way. If all goes well we're going to be a happy family. I think you'll like Seattle. I've never been, but the pictures I've seen look beautiful. We'll go for walks in forests, and I think they even get snow sometimes. That'll be a new experience for us." Riley rolled over so Bobbie could rub her belly. "We'll get through this together, buddy."

Bobbie and Riley both sat up at the knock on the door. After a second knock, Riley barked while Bobbie quickly pulled on a pair of jeans. They weren't used to having people knock on their door since the only people that came to the ranch were usually delivering packages, and those were sent to the big house where her mother lived. Her family had their own keys, and weren't known to give any warning before barging in like they owned the place.

Riley excitedly danced around in circles as Bobbie followed her to the door. "Who is it, girl?" When she looked through the peephole she almost wept at what she saw.

She threw open the door and picked Grace up in her arms. Grace wrapped her legs around Bobbie's waist, and they kissed. They kissed as if it was a matter of life and death. Bobbie had been privileged enough to experience many good kisses in her life, most of which involved the beautiful woman in her arms, but this kiss... There was something altogether magical about this kiss that she didn't quite understand, but wasn't about to question. It was perfection.

When they finally came up for air, Bobbie eased her to the ground. "Why are you here, Gracie? Is everything okay?" Riley excitedly jumped up and nipped at the hem of Grace's shirt to get her attention.

"There's my baby girl," Grace said. She knelt down and took the scruffy dog into her arms. They both laughed as she allowed her to shower her with kisses all over her face. "I missed you so much, you little monster."

Bobbie sat next to them on the ground. "What's going on, sweetie? I was just getting packed for Seattle."

"Would you mind if we go inside and talk?"

Fear coursed through Bobbie. Grace leaned forward to plant a kiss on her cheek and wipe what she was sure were worried wrinkles from her forehead. "Everything is wonderful, baby. There's nothing to be worried about so no scowling."

Bobbie stood and held out a hand to help her to her feet. "Do you have a bag?"

Grace pointed toward the mid-sized sedan parked in front of the house. "It's in the car, but let's talk first. We can deal with that later."

Bobbie led Grace into the house and onto the couch. She wanted to be as close to her as possible and knew this would be the easiest place to sit where they could still touch. When they were seated facing each other Bobbie picked up her hand and kissed each knuckle. She couldn't believe they were together and wanted to relish every second.

"I want to start by asking you to just hear me out before you say anything. I know you can be all noble and stuff, and I really need you to let me explain first. I'm also asking you to trust that I know what I want."

Bobbie nodded and threaded their fingers together. "Shoot. I'll be a good listener, I promise."

Grace smiled, and rubbed her thumb across Bobbie's jaw. "I love you, Bobbie. I always have, and even though I've said I always will, I didn't realize until I was in Seattle how true that was. I don't want to spend another night tossing and turning because you aren't next to me. I don't want to spend another day not sharing my life with you. If you'll have me, that is."

"What about Seattle and your research?"

The look on Grace's face reminded her of the promise she'd just made about listening. "Sorry."

Grace winked, and kissed her. "I'm getting to that part. I'm not going to Peru—"

"But—"

"Good Lord, Bobbie," Grace laughed.

"Sorry."

"It's okay." Grace leaned forward and wrapped Bobbie's arm around her shoulder as she rested her head on her chest. "I have a good team. They can do Peru without me, and once they have all the data I may need to make a few trips back and forth occasionally, but much of what I need to do I think I can do from here. It won't be easy, but we'll make it work. Besides," Grace sat up so she could look at Bobbie, "I have a clinic to run."

"Wait, you bought it?" Bobbie's smile was so big it made her cheeks hurt.

"I did. I called Doc this morning. I'll need to finish the paperwork, but his last day is in two weeks, and then it's all mine."

"I...how...holy shit." Bobbie was sure she would wake up at any moment and realize this was all a dream. "I'm so confused."

"I know, baby, and I'm sorry I didn't talk to you about all this first, but it was a decision I had to make on my own, for myself. I love you and want to be with you, but you aren't the only reason I've decided to move back to Preston. I'm happy here. This is where I want to spend the rest of my life. I want that life to be with you, but if it's not, that doesn't change the way I feel. I love the clinic. I love my friends. I may have actually figured out a way to have a tolerable relationship with my mother. I have so much here that makes me happy in addition to you, and that's enough to adjust what I thought I wanted my life to be. This is the life I want, and I'm hoping you want that, too."

Bobbie was so overwhelmed she didn't know how to react. Part of her oddly wanted to tear all her clothes off and run around the yard, but she'd keep that urge bottled up for now. "It's all I want. I'm so shocked I know I'm not going to adequately express my feelings right now, but fuck yes, I want to share my life with you, Grace Hammond. This one and every one after this if there's any truth to that reincarnation stuff. I've been yours from the moment I saw you, and I'll be yours until the day I die."

Riley put her paws on Bobbie's leg and looked up at her excitedly. "I think she knows something amazing is going on."

"I think you're right." Grace laughed. They both scratched Riley behind her ears and showered her with kisses.

"So, where do we go from here?" Bobbie asked.

"Well, I only have a weekend bag packed in the car in case I needed to stay, but I also have a ticket on the same flight you have to Seattle tonight. I thought if all went well, we could use this week to pack up my belongings and bring them home."

"Home as in the ranch?" Bobbie didn't want to make any assumptions, but she was hopeful that's what she meant.

"Oh, I guess I just assumed, I—"

"Yes, yes, yes. Of course, this is your home. Everything I have is yours without hesitation. Holy shit."

Grace laughed nervously. "Is that a good, holy shit or a bad holy shit?"

Bobbie smiled and pulled Grace onto her lap. "Oh, it's the best, holy shit you could ever imagine, sweetheart."

EPILOGUE

Grace patiently waited for the other passengers to pull their bags from the overhead storage. Her trips back and forth to Seattle had been more frequent over the last few months, and after two years of commuting, she was ready for this project to wrap up so she could focus on her family and the life she and Bobbie built together.

Once she debarked and was clear of the crowd, she headed straight toward the luggage pickup area where she knew Bobbie would be waiting. It was amazing how much they had become a part of each other's lives. Grace knew her marriage and feelings for Jake weren't what they should have been, but she had no idea how wonderful it was to love someone and be loved back as deeply as she did now.

As the escalator down to baggage claim descended, she saw Bobbie waiting at the bottom. Bobbie never failed to send the butterflies in her stomach into a frenzy. When she finally reached her, she fell into her big strong arms. Bobbie took Grace's backpack and led them to the side so they wouldn't block other passengers as she kissed her a week's worth of kisses.

"I missed you so much, baby. How was your flight?" Bobbie held Grace's hand and walked her over to wait for her bag.

"I missed you, too. It was okay. I'm so glad to be home. I'm ready to take a shower and wash the travel off. Airplanes have become a breeding ground for ickiness." Grace was dirty from head to toe even though she'd showered that morning before she left.

As they drove home Grace noticed Bobbie was quiet. She was occasionally quiet but it was usually when she had something weighing on her mind. "Everything okay, sweetheart? Did something happen while I was gone?"

Bobbie turned to her and smiled. "Nope. I'm sorry, I'm just thinking." She reached out and took Grace's hand in hers and squeezed. "I'm so glad you're home, Gracie. Riley and I missed you terribly. It's never the same when you're gone."

"Well, it's almost over. We have one more round of reviews and then we'll be ready to publish our findings. I suspect there will be more work done related to this project, but Jan will take the lead on that. I told them once this is published it's time that I settled down with my sexy rancher."

Bobbie looked at Grace and smiled. "Did you really say that?"

Grace winked. "I might have left out the sexy part since that's just for me to know, but the rest of it is true."

When they arrived at the ranch, Bobbie led Grace straight upstairs and ran her a bubble bath. Once it was ready, Grace settled into the tub with a book for a much needed soak.

"I'm going to make lunch while you relax. Can I get you anything?"

"No thanks, baby. This is perfect."

Grace tried to focus on her book but struggled to keep her mind off of what she needed to discuss with Bobbie. They'd dreamed about their future so many times, but she wasn't sure how Bobbie would react to what she had in mind. She wasn't known for embracing change, and Grace did her best to have reasonable expectations about how she would react.

Once she was done with her bath, she put on a robe and walked downstairs to find Bobbie setting the table for their lunch. "It smells wonderful. What did you make?"

Bobbie pulled out the chair for Grace and poured her a glass of wine. "Vegetarian tortellini minestrone soup and garlic toast. I hope you're hungry."

"You are the girl of my dreams, Bobbie Del Ray." She moaned as she hungrily dug into the amazing meal before her. "This is heaven."

"Once you're finished, I want to show you something outside."

"Should I get dressed?" Grace looked down at her robe.

"Nope. You'll be fine. We'll just be out back. Did you learn lots of stuff in Seattle?"

"Besides the fact that I missed being home with you?" Grace laughed. "I learned some stuff. I'm really proud of the work we've done. I think it's going to go a long way toward getting the short-eared dog on the protected species list."

"That's amazing, sweetheart. I'm so proud of you."

Grace's cheeks warmed as she blushed. "Thanks. How were things here at the ranch while I was gone?" Grace finished her soup and pushed her chair back from the table.

"Good," Bobbie said. She kissed the top of Grace's head before taking their bowls to the kitchen and placing them in the sink. On her way back to the table, Grace saw her pick something up from the counter. "Ready for your surprise?"

"This thing you're showing me is a surprise? That's exciting."

Bobbie stood behind Grace and held out a piece of cloth where she could see it. "I'm going to put this blindfold on you and help you out to the backyard. Okay?"

"Okay... Is this a dirty surprise? I'm all for dirty surprises, but I'm not sure I want one in the backyard where any number of ranch hands or your mother can get a peek at my goods."

Bobbie laughed and kissed Grace before placing the blindfold over her eyes. "This isn't a dirty surprise, but maybe we can use this blindfold for a dirty surprise later. Your goods are for my eyes only." Bobbie pushed the robe to the side exposing Grace's breast. She leaned down and ran her tongue around a puckered nipple as Grace let out a satisfied moan. After only a few seconds, Bobbie pulled back, closed the robe, and stood.

"Are you ready?"

Grace pouted but let Bobbie help her to her feet.

"You're a tease, woman," Grace said in mock frustration.

Bobbie laughed and led her out the back door, down the stairs of the deck, and through the yard. Grace could feel the unevenness of the lawn under her feet. "Don't let me fall, sweetie."

Bobbie lifted Grace into her arms and carried her the rest of the way, gently setting her down on what felt like a flat stone. Bobbie hadn't removed the blindfold yet, and the suspense was making Grace fidget. She felt Bobbie's soft lips against hers and returned the kiss until she was breathless.

Grace was a little dizzy as Bobbie stood behind her to remove the blindfold from her eyes. It took a moment for her to register what she was seeing, but when she did, she couldn't stop the tears from coming. "Oh, Bobbie." Grace looked up at the beautiful tree house Bobbie had built in an old oak they'd always loved behind their house. A large wooden staircase led from a flagstone patio up to a railed-in porch complete with two large rocking chairs. The door looked like it was hand carved and was tucked between two windows with boxes of daisies in front.

She turned to Bobbie and found her kneeling on one knee, holding out a tiny box with a ring.

"I love you, Grace Hammond. The last two years with you have been the best of my life and I'm humbly asking you to do me the honor of becoming my wife. I can't promise you—"

"Shut up, Bobbie." Grace dropped to her knees and kissed her. "The only promise I want is that you'll love me forever."

"I thought I might love you at least forever, and maybe more." Tears were streaming down Bobbie's face. They'd talked about marriage many times, but it had always been something that would happen someday. Grace wasn't surprised that she had asked, but that lack of surprise didn't lessen the overwhelming feelings of love and happiness that she felt.

Grace collapsed into Bobbie and they tumbled to the ground laughing. She placed her hands around Bobbie's face and kissed her all over until they were both giggling like girls. "I can't believe you did this, Bobbie. How in the world did you build this tree house without me noticing?"

Bobbie picked a piece of grass out of Grace's hair and brushed a lock behind her ear. "Well, you aren't the most observant person in the world sometimes, sweetheart." Bobbie tried to dodge her hand as Grace smacked her. "It's true. I think being up in the tree helped to hide it, too. Amy, John, Evan, Wyatt, everyone came over this week to help me put the finishing touches on it and get the stairs and deck finished. Do you like it?"

Grace stared up at a tree house version of what she had told Bobbie her dream house would look like so long ago when they'd had that picnic in the park. All the way down to the rocking chairs and window boxes full of daisies. "It's amazing. You might be the most romantic person in the entire world. I can't believe you're actually going to be my wife."

Bobbie smiled and helped Grace stand. "And you're going to be my wife. What do you think our teenage selves would think if they knew this was the life we would share one day?"

The thought of being this happy would have been impossible for Grace to comprehend only a few years ago, let alone when she was a teenager. "I think they would imagine it was worth whatever the world threw at us if this was our reward in the end."

Bobbie pulled Grace toward the stairs. "Let's go check it out."

"What made you build a tree house?"

"A couple of reasons, really. First, I've always wanted a tree house."

"No surprise there." Grace winked at her.

"Second, I know I can be a bit of a big, loud puppy sometimes, and I'm a lot for you to deal with."

Grace laughed. "More like a big, loud gorilla, but I totally get what you're saying."

Bobbie smiled and continued. "I wanted to give you a space where you could go to escape the hustle and bustle of me and ranch life. A place for you to relax and be closer to nature. I decided on a tree house mostly because I thought about Josh."

Grace stepped inside and looked around. She noticed bookcases on the back wall and a skylight in the vaulted ceiling. A couch sat at one end with a desk at the other.

"Josh who?"

Bobbie pulled her over to the couch so they could both sit down. "Your mom's bird that you accidentally released when we were kids."

"Oh my God, I'd totally forgotten about that bird."

"I remember how upset you were at school the next day. It made me so sad to see you like that, and even then I just wanted to fix it and take away your pain. It's always stuck with me. You told me that day that you just wanted to take him out so he could stretch his wings and feel free. I know you never got that from your parents or Jake and I wanted to give you a space here where you felt the freedom to stretch your wings. What better place than up in a tree with the birds." Bobbie pointed and Grace noticed there were birdhouses attached to limbs all over the tree. "I know birds can make their own nests, but I thought if I gave them little houses, too, they might be even more willing to live up where you can watch them."

"Jesus, Bobbie. You're…I don't even know what to say."

Bobbie smiled and kissed her on the lips. "I'm glad you like it. There's something to show you up there, too."

Grace looked up and noticed a ladder that led to what appeared to be a loft. "Oh…I see lots of tree house naps in my future." She climbed the ladder and found an overstuffed mattress with big comfy looking blankets. She slipped off her shoes and jumped on top, patting the spot next to her to invite Bobbie to snuggle with her.

Bobbie stretched out next to her and slipped her hand inside Grace's robe. It was warm and slightly rough from hard work. She loved that Bobbie worked with her hands and lived up to so many of the romantic ideals of the cowboys she'd read about in novels. "You're the whole package, my little rancher."

Bobbie slid her hand up to rest on the inside of her thigh, only inches from her center.

"I'm happy to show you my whole package if you'd like," Bobbie said.

"Oh, really?" Grace unbuttoned her flannel shirt, placing kisses on her chest as the skin beneath was exposed.

Bobbie kissed Grace's neck and eased her hand toward her pussy, delicately grazing the edge of her slit with her fingers.

Grace rolled them over and straddled Bobbie's lap letting her robe drape open around her. Bobbie took advantage of the new position by reaching up and playing with Grace's warm folds. "You're so wet. I missed you terribly when you were gone. I missed this. I hate being away from you." She captured Grace's gasp with a kiss as she slipped a thick finger into her greedy hole.

"God, Bobbie, you feel so good inside me. I missed you so much. I thought about you to distraction. I'm never going to get any work done if this constant, desperate need to have you inside me doesn't stop." Grace rocked back and forth on Bobbie's hand as a second then third finger was added. "You're so deep, baby. Fuck me. I'm close."

Bobbie used her thumb to rub circles over Grace's clit as she fucked her faster, pulling the robe completely open and sucking a nipple into her mouth. "Come all over my fingers. I love you so much." Grace's pussy contracted as she came. She buried her face in Bobbie's shoulder and screamed her orgasm in a muffled cry. Bobbie continued her rhythm until she begged her to stop.

Grace gasped for breath as she lay on top of her. Without warning, Bobbie flipped Grace onto her back and crawled between her slick thighs. "Hold yourself open for me. Let me see how wet your beautiful pussy is."

Grace's fingers shook with excitement and exhaustion as she held herself open. She could feel Bobbie's warm breath against her delicate folds. She would never get tired of this. No one had ever made her feel so beautiful, so special, so loved. "I love you, Bobbie."

"I love you, too. I love how beautiful your pussy is, and it's all mine, isn't it?" Bobbie brushed her labia with her soft tongue. "Tell me your pussy is mine, baby. Only mine."

Grace gladly told Bobbie what she wanted to hear. "It's yours, my love. Only yours. Forever." Bobbie leaned closer and began cleaning the wetness that had collected there with her tongue. She swirled the muscle all around except where Grace wanted it most. "Please, I need you. Please." Grace knew she was begging but didn't care. She thought she might come apart if Bobbie didn't touch her clit.

"It's my pussy, remember? I will make it come when I'm ready. I'm not done playing with it yet. You're so sweet and wet. I dreamed about doing this while you were gone. I would lie in our bed at night and close my eyes imagining I was licking your pussy while I made myself come. Don't you think I deserve to take my time and appreciate the gift you have given me?" Bobbie smiled up at Grace when she grabbed her hair and tried to push her face harder into her center.

"I'm going to lick your clit and stick two fingers into your sore pussy. I won't be as rough as I was a minute ago, but I'm going to touch you in just the right spot that will make you explode. I want you to try to hold off as long as you can, okay? Can you make it last as long as possible?" Bobbie was getting Grace so hot she knew it would be impossible to hold back very long.

"Yes. Please fuck me. I want to feel you inside me. Now, Bobbie."

Grace heard Bobbie chuckle at her desperation as she latched on to her clit and slid two thick fingers into her eager depths. Grace felt the stretch of the intrusion in her tender pussy, but the pain only helped to heighten her need. "Fuck me, Bobbie. Make me yours. Take my pussy." Grace sounded almost crazed as she rode the fingers inside her.

Bobbie curled the digits until they were bumping against her most delicate spot. She licked and fucked as Grace bucked and tried to hold off her release. "I can't hold it anymore. I can't. I'm going to come."

"Come for me. Come in my mouth, sweet girl." Bobbie sounded as desperate as Grace was, and it only heightened her need. With a guttural scream Grace didn't realize she could utter, she came in wave after wave, coating Bobbie's mouth and fingers with her release.

Grace thought for a moment she might have blacked out. When she opened her eyes she felt Bobbie still licking her clit and reached down to gently push her away. "No, no more. I'll die."

She clamped her legs shut to restrict access before closing her robe and collapsing into a sated puddle on the bed. "Come up here, stud. Come and hold me now that you've completely broken me."

Bobbie laughed and scooted up the bed to wrap her arms around her. "You okay? That was a big one."

"Holy fuck. I thought I might die there for a minute, but what a way to go."

"Don't do that. I'm going to need you to take care of me and make me pudding and stuff when we get old." Bobbie laughed.

Grace kissed Bobbie's lips and breathed a sigh of contentment. "Speaking of getting old, you're going to have to build our kids another tree house. This one is mine."

"Our kids?" Bobbie leaned up on one elbow and smiled down at Grace. "What kids?"

"The grandchildren I promised your mother. What other kids would I be talking about?"

"Seriously? I mean we've talked about it a little, but I just wasn't sure if…"

Grace pulled Bobbie back down and snuggled into her side. "Of course I want to have babies with you, Bobbie. I'd actually been planning to talk to you about it today but wasn't sure how you would feel since we weren't married yet. But you took care of that little issue. I'm not getting any younger and Sabrina brought her five-year-old daughter with her to work this week because school was out. There was something about her that reminded me of you and it made me think what a wonderful mom you would be."

Bobbie fidgeted a little. "Grace, I don't know if I would want to be the one to actually have the baby."

Grace smiled and placed Bobbie's hand on her bare stomach. "Nope, I'm going to do all the baking of those little buns. Sabrina's pregnant with their second child and I'm not exactly sure how it's all done, but she said she's carrying a baby that is from her wife's fertilized egg."

"Neat. Well, we have some time to figure all that out."

"I agree." Grace was struggling to keep her eyes open after the travel and excitement of the day. "Baby, should we test the bed out to ensure its nap worthiness? I'm sleepy."

Bobbie kissed Grace's lips and squeezed her tight. "Sweet dreams, future Mrs. Del Ray."

"Umm…we'll have to discuss that name change thing after our nap." Grace smiled and drifted off to sleep in the arms of her one true love.

The End

About the Author

Angie Williams, winner of a third grade essay competition on fire safety, grew up in the dusty desert of West Texas. Always interested in writing, as a child she would lose interest before the end, killing the characters off in a tragic accident so she could move on to the next story. Thankfully, as an adult she decided it was time to write things where everyone survives.

Angie lives in Northern California with her beautiful wife and son, and a menagerie of dogs, cats, snakes, and tarantulas. She's a proud geek and lover of all things she was teased about in school.

Books Available from Bold Strokes Books

Face the Music by Ali Vali. Sweet music is the last thing that happens when Nashville music producer Mason Liner, and daughter of country royalty Victoria Roddy are thrown together in an effort to save country star Sophie Roddy's career. (978-1-63555-532-5)

Flavor of the Month by Georgia Beers. What happens when baker Charlie and chef Emma realize their differing paths have led them right back to each other? (978-1-63555-616-2)

Mending Fences by Angie Williams. Rancher Bobbie Del Rey and veterinarian Grace Hammond are about to discover if heartbreaks of the past can ever truly be mended. (978-1-63555-708-4)

Silk and Leather: Lesbian Erotica with an Edge edited by Victoria Villasenor. This collection of stories by award winning authors offers fantasies as soft as silk and tough as leather. The only question is: How far will you go to make your deepest desires come true? (978-1-63555-587-5)

The Last Place You Look by Aurora Rey. Dumped by her wife and looking for anything but love, Julia Pierce retreats to her hometown, only to rediscover high school friend Taylor Winslow, who's secretly crushed on her for years. (978-1-63555-574-5)

The Mortician's Daughter by Nan Higgins. A singer on the verge of stardom discovers she must give up her dreams to live a life in service to ghosts. (978-1-63555-594-3)

The Real Thing by Laney Webber. When passion flares between actress Virginia Green and masseuse Allison McDonald, can they be sure it's the real thing? (978-1-63555-478-6)

What the Heart Remembers Most by M. Ullrich. For college sweethearts Jax Levine and Gretchen Mills could an accident be the second chance neither knew they wanted? (978-1-63555-401-4)

White Horse Point by Andrews & Austin. Mystery writer Taylor James finds herself falling for the mysterious woman on White Horse Point who lives alone, protecting a secret she can't share about a murderer who walks among them. (978-1-63555-695-7)

Femme Tales by Anne Shade. Six women find themselves in their own real-life fairy tales when true love finds them in the most unexpected ways. (978-1-63555-657-5)

Jellicle Girl by Stevie Mikayne. One dark summer night, Beth and Jackie go out to the canoe dock. Two years later, Beth is still carrying the weight of what happened to Jackie. (978-1-63555-691-9)

Le Berceau by Julius Eks. If only Ben could tear his heart in two, then he wouldn't have to choose between the love of his life and the most beautiful boy he has ever seen. (978-1-63555-688-9)

My Date with a Wendigo by Genevieve McCluer. Elizabeth Rosseau finds her long lost love and the secret community of fiends she's now a part of. (978-1-63555-679-7)

On the Run by Charlotte Greene. Even when they're cute blondes, it's stupid to pick up hitchhikers, especially when they've just broken out of prison, but doing so is about to change Gwen's life forever. (978-1-63555-682-7)

Perfect Timing by Dena Blake. The choice between love and family has never been so difficult, and Lynn's and Maggie's different visions of the future may end their romance before it's begun. (978-1-63555-466-3)

The Mail Order Bride by R Kent. When a mail order bride is thrust on Austin, he must choose between the bride he never wanted or the dream he lives for. (978-1-63555-678-0)

Through Love's Eyes by C.A. Popovich. When fate reunites Brittany Yardin and Amy Jansons, can they move beyond the pain of their past to find love? (978-1-63555-629-2)

To the Moon and Back by Melissa Brayden. Film actress Carly Daniel thinks that stage work is boring and unexciting, but when she accepts a lead role in a new play, stage manager Lauren Prescott tests both her heart and her ability to share the limelight. (978-1-63555-618-6)

Tokyo Love by Diana Jean. When Kathleen Schmitt is given the opportunity to be on the cutting edge of AI technology, she never thought a failed robotic love companion would bring her closer to her neighbor, Yuriko Velucci, and finding love in unexpected places. (978-1-63555-681-0)

Brooklyn Summer by Maggie Cummings. When opposites attract, can a summer of passion and adventure lead to a lifetime of love? (978-1-63555-578-3)

City Kitty and Country Mouse by Alyssa Linn Palmer. Pulled in two different directions, can a city kitty and country mouse fall in love and make it work? (978-1-63555-553-0)

Elimination by Jackie D. When a dangerous homegrown terrorist seeks refuge with the Russian mafia, the team will be put to the ultimate test. (978-1-63555-570-7)

In the Shadow of Darkness by Nicole Stiling. Angeline Vallencourt is a reluctant vampire who must decide what she wants more—obscurity, revenge, or the woman who makes her feel alive. (978-1-63555-624-7)

On Second Thought by C. Spencer. Madisen is falling hard for Rae. Even single life and co-parenting are beginning to click. At least, that is, until her ex-wife begins to have second thoughts. (978-1-63555-415-1)

Out of Practice by Carsen Taite. When attorney Abby Keane discovers the wedding blogger tormenting her client is the woman she had a passionate, anonymous vacation fling with, sparks and subpoenas fly. Legal Affairs: one law firm, three best friends, three chances to fall in love. (978-1-63555-359-8)

Providence by Leigh Hays. With every click of the shutter, photographer Rebekiah Kearns finds it harder and harder to keep Lindsey Blackwell in focus without getting too close. (978-1-63555-620-9)

Taking a Shot at Love by KC Richardson. When academic and athletic worlds collide, will English professor Celeste Bouchard and basketball coach Lisa Tobias ignore their attraction to achieve their professional goals? (978-1-63555-549-3)

Flight to the Horizon by Julie Tizard. Airline captain Kerri Sullivan and flight attendant Janine Case struggle to survive an emergency water landing and overcome dark secrets to give love a chance to fly. (978-1-63555-331-4)

In Helen's Hands by Nanisi Barrett D'Arnuk. As her mistress, Helen pushes Mickey to her sensual limits, delivering the pleasure only a BDSM lifestyle can provide her. (978-1-63555-639-1)

Jamis Bachman, Ghost Hunter by Jen Jensen. In Sage Creek, Utah, a poltergeist stirs to life and past secrets emerge. (978-1-63555-605-6)

Moon Shadow by Suzie Clarke. Add betrayal, season with survival, then serve revenge smokin' hot with a sharp knife. (978-1-63555-584-4)

Spellbound by Jean Copeland and Jackie D. When the supernatural worlds of good and evil face off, love might be what saves them all. (978-1-63555-564-6)

Temptation by Kris Bryant. Can experienced nanny Cassie Miller deny her growing attraction and keep her relationship with her boss professional? Or will they sidestep propriety and give in to temptation? (978-1-63555-508-0)

The Inheritance by Ali Vali. Family ties bring Tucker Delacroix and Willow Vernon together, but they could also tear them, and any chance they have at love, apart. (978-1-63555-303-1)

Thief of the Heart by MJ Williamz. Kit Hanson makes a living seducing rich women in casinos and relieving them of the expensive jewelry most won't even miss. But her streak ends when she meets beautiful FBI agent Savannah Brown. (978-1-63555-572-1)

Date Night by Raven Sky. Quinn and Riley are celebrating their one-year anniversary. Such an important milestone is bound to result in some extraordinary sexual adventures, but precisely how extraordinary is up to you, dear reader. (978-1-63555-655-1)

Face Off by PJ Trebelhorn. Hockey player Savannah Wells rarely spends more than a night with any one woman, but when photographer Madison Scott buys the house next door, she's forced to rethink what she expects out of life. (978-1-63555-480-9)

Hot Ice by Aurora Rey, Elle Spencer, Erin Zak. Can falling in love melt the hearts of the iciest ice queens? Join Aurora Rey, Elle Spencer, and Erin Zak to find out! (978-1-63555-513-4)

Line of Duty by VK Powell. Dr. Dylan Carlyle's professional and personal life is turned upside down when a tragic event at Fairview Station pits her against ambitious, handsome police officer Finley Masters. (978-1-63555-486-1)

London Undone by Nan Higgins. London Craft reinvents her life after reading a childhood letter to her future self and in doing so finds the love she truly wants. (978-1-63555-562-2)

Lunar Eclipse by Gun Brooke. Moon De Cruz lives alone on an uninhabited planet after being shipwrecked in space. Her life changes forever when Captain Beaux Lestarion's arrival threatens the planet and Moon's freedom. (978-1-63555-460-1)

One Small Step by Michelle Binfield. Iris and Cam discover the meaning of taking chances and following your heart, even if it means getting hurt. (978-1-63555-596-7)

Shadows of a Dream by Nicole Disney. Rainn has the talent to take her rock band all the way, but falling in love is a powerful distraction, and her new girlfriend's meth addiction might just take them both down. (978-1-63555-598-1)

Someone to Love by Jenny Frame. When Davina Trent is given an unexpected family, can she let nanny Wendy Darling teach her to open her heart to the children and to Wendy? (978-1-63555-468-7)

Tinsel by Kris Bryant. Did a sweet kitten show up to help Jessica Raymond and Taylor Mitchell find each other? Or is the holiday spirit to blame for their special connection? (978-1-63555-641-4)

Uncharted by Robyn Nyx. As Rayne Marcellus and Chase Stinsen track the legendary Golden Trinity, they must learn to put their differences aside and depend on one another to survive. (978-1-63555-325-3)

Where We Are by Annie McDonald. Can two women discover a way to walk on the same path together and discover the gift of staying in one spot, in time, in space, and in love? (978-1-63555-581-3)

A Moment in Time by Lisa Moreau. A longstanding family feud separates two women who unexpectedly fall in love at an antique clock shop in a small Louisiana town. (978-1-63555-419-9)